SKIP
SHOT

SKIP
SHOT

A NOVEL

By
Kyle C. Fitzharris

Story by
Harry Stedman

 L.O.R.E. Media
www.kylefitzharris.com

SKIP SHOT
A NOVEL

iUniverse books may be ordered through booksellers or by contacting:

iUniverse
1663 Liberty Drive
Bloomington, IN 47403
www.iuniverse.com
1-800-Authors (1-800-288-4677)

L.O.R.E. MEDIA

Because of the dynamic nature of the Internet, any web addresses or links contained in this book may have changed since publication and may no longer be valid. The views expressed in this work are solely those of the author and do not necessarily reflect the views of the publisher, and the publisher hereby disclaims any responsibility for them.

Editors: Tracy Marcynzsyn, Colleen Reid
Cover Graphics: Lisa Pujals
Photography: Dan Herron & Boaz Milgalter

ISBN: 978-1-4917-9110-3 (sc)
ISBN: 978-1-4917-9109-7 (hc)
ISBN: 978-1-4917-9111-0 (e)

Library of Congress Control Number: 2016904043

Print information available on the last page.

iUniverse rev. date: 4/26/2016

For More Information About Best-Selling Author Kyle C. Fitzharris, SKIP SHOT, his other novels, or his Ghostwriting Services, please visit WWW.KYLEFITZHARRIS.COM

DEDICATION

This miraculous book is dedicated to the many people with whom I have interacted during my almost 75 years. I can only hope the readers get the same satisfaction from reading it as I got from getting it down on paper. What is amazing about this novel is that Kyle was able to create this much story out of what little information he could extract from my brain. To my son and his two sons—I take great pride in them and hope they never give up on a thought or idea and that they put their ideas down on paper much sooner than I have managed to do.

FOREWORD

"**F**ITZHARRIS' NEW THRILLER, *Skip Shot* will keep you on the edge of your seat with your head down safely away from a sniper's clean shot! Once again Fitzharris brings real world experience to life with his latest work. Lee Child's *Jack Reacher* may have met his match as Will Pierce chases the world's deadliest sniper bent on settling old scores and drastically changing the global landscape through murder-for-hire assassination. Hang on tight for this thrill ride."

- Bob Hamer, veteran FBI undercover agent &
co-author with Lt. Col. Oliver North (retired)
of the best-selling, *American Heroes on the
Homefront* & *Counterfeit Lies*

CHAPTER 1

SOMEONE HAD REALLY WANTED it to stand out. Unsatisfied with its already extraordinary size that dwarfed every vehicle around it, they had buffed the black limousine convertible to a high gloss from its elongated hood to its customized extended rear.

The deep coats of enameled black paint reflected the early afternoon sun so strongly, many onlookers lining the streets had to squint and shade their eyes from the glare. There wasn't much out there more extraordinary than this pristine vehicle, except for perhaps the occupants who were riding inside.

The limo driver was well trained and experienced, closely observing the throngs of people: admirers, curious, and especially the rabid and uncontrollable fans, careful to keep his advance slow as they wound through the streets. He was aware that someone could be so overcome by the excitement that they might rush into the street.

The screams of excitement, cheers, and shouts for attention were nearly deafening coming from the crowd that had swelled from a few dozen earlier that morning to the thousands that now packed every square inch of curbside, risking everything just to catch a view.

Yet the limo still limped slowly onward to ensure everyone could get a look, perhaps even a wave, or please God, a handshake from one of the famous occupants inside. The transport never sped up, not even once as it headed toward its seemingly endless destination. It glided along like a prized show pony conspicuously exposing everything it had to offer to all whom were willing to view it.

It would crawl down Main Street, hook a right at Houston, then a slow dogleg left hook at Elm. It was constant, methodical, calculating, and purposeful. It meandered for a reason, but was by no means aimless in its travels.

A Hoppy's Transmissions sign rose high above the crowd and was hard to miss by the driver, the occupants, or any of the thousands of well-wishers. As it cornered to parallel Republic Savings, half a dozen teenagers suddenly began clapping in anticipation of the arrival.

The teens had argued over the best spot to see and hopefully be seen, finally agreeing to make their way to a favorite Saturday evening hangout. Clambering up the rigid 15-foot rooftop perch above the office building, they pulled the still cold cola bottles out of a pack and passed them around. With a mock toast to each other, they took a long swig of the cola, settling themselves as best they could on their precarious perch.

Now as they heard the cheering crowds announcing the approach below the cavalcade, they stretched their necks, jostling to see who managed the first glimpse of their objective. One pointed, shouting in his excitement and the others craned forward, careless of his balance.

From the higher vantage point, the handsome man's thick, youthful brown hair was visible inside the limousine. The teens weren't old enough to know that his suit was of a conservative cut, and they were too far away to appreciate the niceties of his dress.

Those who were fortunate enough to be up close could more clearly see the grayish, almost mauve, two-piece wool suit complete with a lightly striped white dress shirt, blue-checkered tie, mother-of-pearl cufflinks, and just the tip of a handkerchief peeking out from his vest pocket—the result of his careful care to detail, all carried off with apparent ease, that so-difficult-to-attain marriage of dignity AND style.

His arm had already settled into a heavy ache from waving to the endless stream of people, so the object of their veneration rested his right elbow on the car door above the lowered window. He had perfected a technique that allowed him to merely lift his forearm and hand to wave in a sort of loose figure eight. It enabled him to maintain his contact with the crowds and still at the end of the day pick up a fork to eat dinner.

The crowd hardly took notice of this minor detail, as it was clear that anything this man did was remarkable. It was, to all appearances, as though they believed that, truly, a deity was now among them.

Next to him sat his bride: a young, innocent-appearing brunette. Dark eyes, seemingly as big as a doe, reflected her pleasure in the reception they were receiving. She was one of those highly unusual people who could be truly happy for her husband, rather than being aware of or caring about the equal amount of attention and affection she herself was receiving from the fans that had flocked to see her as well. She didn't see herself as they did. In their eyes, she was *the* queen of everything fashionable, and her dress, paired with a matching cropped jacket and hat, shouted New York super model.

Although she was model material, she truly didn't think of herself that way. In her mind it was enough for now to simply be the perfect wife to the perfect husband for their perfect fans. It was a role she had been raised to play, and she played it perfectly. It was one she had lived with for so long she could no longer consciously feel an awareness of it. She played the role perfectly and lived for nothing less than adoring her beloved husband. Leaning slightly forward to see around her husband's broad frame, she joined him in cheerfully acknowledging the cheering onlookers.

What made the priceless limousine so unique, besides its obvious celebrity occupants, was more than just that it was extremely long, longer than most vehicles of its type. In fact, the bumper was extended more than a foot on either side of the enormous, polished metal spare tire cover. But it had, in addition to all of its other amenities, two raised handgrips welded to the top of the trunk. These handholds made it possible for anyone to literally jump onto the running board and hold on for dear life, should the need arise.

The ruby red hazard lights below the headlamps would flash almost the same as a police car, complete with siren might, and since it was an official mode of transportation for dignitaries and celebrities that came to town, the driver felt justified in keeping them pulsing. He heaved out a deep breath as he reviewed their route in his head, surreptitiously shrugging some of the tension from his shoulders.

It was an exhausting day for the driver, as he had to stay alert constantly to avoid that one crazed fan that would be willing to sacrifice an arm and a leg jumping into the path of the limo prior to it passing.

Four policemen zigzagged and traversed the hot pavement on state-issued Harley Davidson's in order to control the vibrant, yet surprisingly disciplined crowd, as they would take up a post on one or the other side of the limo prior to it passing. They could be seen hopscotching past each other so as to always have someone leading as well as someone bringing up the rear.

Another pair of patrolman would temporarily ride tandem, pull up side-by-side, then would break rank and circle around to one side of the limo in order to be prepared to protect its occupants, should it become necessary, from the heavy barrage of well-wishers.

It was a glorious day for the people of this burgeoning city and they felt truly blessed and humbled to be as close as they would ever come to something approaching royalty. The cheers were heartfelt. The tears flowed like Georgia rain.

The elation was palpable. It was, for many, the perfect day... until a single gunshot cracked sharply through the cheers and an almost bewildered hush settled over the crowd like a dark storm cloud.

CHAPTER 2

"IT'S NOT FLAT ENOUGH! You gotta find a flatter stone or it won't skip right! It'll just sink!" shouted Timmy Callahan.

The breakwater from the Mediterranean Sea was far enough from the inlet that the three boys could make a game of trying to skip the right stone from one side of the narrows clear across to the other. The small cove pooled like a lazy pond and yet the saltwater was relatively still compared to the often-rougher seas just beyond the rocks and crags past the beachhead.

This was the boys' favorite spot: in sight of the tumultuous seas, far enough from the city center that few people bothered them, yet wild enough for them to just be the youngsters they were.

"I want to go swimming at Ouzai soon!" yelled Nassar, wiping his nose with his sleeve. The runny nose stemmed from a cold he'd been trying to shake for several days.

"Nah, let's hit the Rivoli. I think there's a new movie playing," Robert retorted.

He reached down immediately though, picking up a good-sized rock that was partially buried in the beach and brushing off the sand to inspect it. It was a little big, but not too large. It had some pocks on the bottom side from millions of years of wear and tear as it laid on the ocean floor with the strong undercurrent tossing it over and over again, eroding it with pressure, smashing it into the sand, and trying to melt it away with the high salt content of the water. Yet all in all, he thought it a perfect projectile for his needs.

Robert bounced the stone off his palm a number of times trying to gauge its weight and balance, wrapped his index finger around the edges, bent slightly at the hip, took aim, and then threw the stone sidearm for maximum skipping or Skip Shots, as the boys called them. All three of the boys followed it closely with their eyes as the rock made its first contact with the water.

It hit rather hard, then recovered, bouncing back up, then skipping once, twice, three times, even squeezing in a fourth bounce to the sound of Robert's encouraging shouts, before the energy that had launched it was spent and it sank to the bottom of the tide pool.

"Come on, *Habibi!* Let's get going. I'm hungry!"

Timmy tried his best to draw the other two boys away from the beach.

"Not yet! I want to beat that!" Nassar hollered back. He scoured the beach to find the perfect stone.

"*Insha' Allah!*"

Nassar prayed to himself as he found exactly the stone he had been looking for and examined it closely before readying it for his dynamic launch. He ran his left hand over the stone to ensure the smoothness of the stone, and then rolled it over to his opposite hand to double-check the symmetry.

"I'm hungry!" Timmy wailed, but flopped down into the sand, knowing his protest was in vain. They loved each other more than brothers, but the competition within their band was still fierce.

Nassar mumbled something in Arabic about Timmy ALWAYS being hungry, but he was grinning as he did so, so he never truly violated the friendship. Habibi was an Arab term of endearment, more Egyptian than Lebanese perhaps, but a term the boys often used to describe each other, their tight friendship and the incredible bond as boys tended to do in Lebanon in the those days.

As pre-teenage males, their entire lives revolved around their friendship and they were thick as thieves in every aspect of their lives.

They were blood brothers, and they'd even made a blood pact after seeing a western at a Saturday afternoon matinee, so taken were they by the ritual that they determined to solidify their friendship in exactly the same fashion.

Their determination led to the bright idea of rummaging around Robert's house until they found one of his father's old Eagle lock blades. After watching the Sioux, Kiowa, Cherokee and every other member of the Indian Nation popularized in the movies, they came up with their own private version of a rite of passage.

They took the borrowed knife out, and after making a large fire on the beach, they heated it up with a Zippo lighter they'd also borrowed from his father, and then sliced each of their thumbs to produce just the right amount of claret.

Pressing their bloody thumbs hard to the others, they swore a blood oath to always stay loyal friends, just as the Comanche and Sioux had done on the silver screen.

The three were inseparable and made a promise to always stay close and never, ever let anyone come between them. One nearly indistinguishable from the other, except for the narrowest of margins, they were beginning even at a young age to hatch their plans for the future in earnest.

Back then, it was not uncommon to see light-skinned Europeans, even Americans, touring, sunbathing, and residing in Lebanon, as it was, after all, considered the Paris of the Middle East. Beirut was gorgeous, modern, moderate, even progressive, but under its skin, tensions simmered between the Maronite Christians and the Muslim population.

Beirut, or *Beyrouth* as the French called it, had just settled down from years of unrest after President Camille Chamoun, a pro-western Christian, had requested and received the help of the United States when religious issues began to flare up in the midst of political power sharing. This, of course, did not sit well with the Lebanese Sunni Prime Minister Rashid Karami, who had endorsed the threatening of the newly formed Egyptian and Syrian United Arab Republic.

All three boys had fathers who worked in either government or for the embassy and had the luxury of living in this thriving modern city. Timmy Callahan's father, Brendan Callahan, had brought his family to Lebanon during Operation Blue Bat, which just happened to be the first purposing of the Eisenhower Doctrine to support U.S. allies abroad against foreign or other types of aggression.

It didn't matter that Russia's Soviet Premier Nikita Krushchev rattled his sabers and threatened to use nuclear weapons if the U.S. intervened, that was just standard operating procedure for the Russians and Ike would call his bluff on many occasions. Although Brendan Callahan's classification was that of a diplomat, that term was rather loosely applied, as he was really part of Robert Murphy's, or more specifically, Ike's personal representative's team sent to Beirut to *calm the lions*, as it were and attempt to keep the peace by supporting the incoming Christian President Fuad Chehab.

Young Robert Miller's father, Thaddeus Miller, was Chief of Security, or what is now known as (RSO) Regional Security Officer, at the embassy, tasked with keeping Timmy's father, and all the fathers and mothers that worked on foreign soil, safe. Thaddeus was a large man, a hard-boiled U.S. Marine who preferred to dress in civilian clothes to blend in with his surroundings and stay below the radar, but standing nearly a head taller than most Arabs, it proved challenging to remain anonymous.

He seemingly had eyes in the back of his head as he was constantly on high alert both at the embassy and in the streets walking with his wife and children. He would check every pane of glass, every mirror hanging from a bazaar line, or shone parabolic object for a reflection or bank shot to make sure no one was following them or attempting to ghost his patterns.

He knew everyone in Beirut was a potential enemy, but since it was then, in effect, a resort town, his blood pressure never rose above normal, and Robert was content that his stern and disciplined father was satisfied with his posting and issued no complaint about their situation within the boy's hearing.

"Insha' Allah!" Nassar prayed to himself as he found another stone and readied it for launch.

Rocking back slightly, he twisted his slight form in the same side arm throwing posture his friend had adopted and shot his stone out over the water. He fell to his knees in mock despair amidst the shouts of laughter from his friends as the flat stone defied all appearances of being perfectly formed and perfectly thrown and simply fell flat and disappeared.

"Now can we eat?" Timmy grabbed at Nassar's arm, dragging him up as Robert joined them, still laughing.

"Fine!"

"Fine, what?"

Nassar groaned dismally, before lunging and grabbing his still laughing friends and driving them to the sand in mock fury.

Anyone observing them wrestling and laughing on that beach could have thought them related, with their sun-bleached hair and tanned slim bodies. As the three staggered up to the road, sand-covered and happily still half engaged in their mock wrestling, they would have been thoroughly surprised that anyone could consider them anything but brothers.

Nassar Khumari was truly a rare breed. He was Assyrian or Chaldean. He was forever being mistaken for an American, or a Brit, German, or even a Scandinavian. A towhead blond with big blue eyes and just slightly olive skin. Still, this could be attributed to the warm sun and natural tan that everyone enjoyed in Lebanon, so it was understandable that the locals occasionally treated him like a tourist.

People were certainly fooled by his appearance, but he considered himself every bit an Arab: he read, wrote, and spoke fluent Arabic, yet he was a Christian, unlike over half of the Lebanese population. His family had immigrated to Lebanon after the Ottoman Empire's genocide of their Assyrian people during World War I. And now, into their third generation, the Khumaris were part of the unique fabric that made up Beirut.

Nassar's father, Ibrahim, like Timmy's father, also wore the moniker of Diplomat, although in his case, it was more factual than fictional. He had been involved in his embassy's affairs considerably longer than the other two boys' fathers. Ibrahim had the uncanny ability to live in both Lebanese worlds: Muslim and Christian. He was often called upon to adjudicate disagreements or fly to other countries to confab with other like-minded, as well as hard-minded, diplomats.

He was well liked, well meaning, and above all, and most important in this region, well respected. He had a knack for being able to straddle the fence and appease both sides during fierce arguments, but could also become tough and coercive when the parties would come to a stalemate or become unreasonably aggressive.

All three boys had come with their families to this tiny, mountainous nation to help build upon its positive growth in this buffer region of Western Asia. It was the jewel in the crown of the Middle East with all the modern comforts of the West as well as ethnic diversity, yet it possessed the tradition and disciplines of thousands of years of religious practice.

Unfortunately, in the volatile years that would follow, the boys would be tested, as Beirut became a simmering pot about to boil over.

CHAPTER 3

TINY WAFTS OF RED clay dust circulated upward into the shard of sunlight penetrating the old wooden door of the county sheriff's station. Will Pierce lie back in his reclining desk chair, his sweat-stained Stetson hung over his eyes and nose as he dreamt. As tall and lean as he was, he never snored. In fact, his breathing was nearly stealthy, unlike most men his age; you'd never even know he was in the room when he was asleep and the light was dim.

His chest didn't heave as most men's did either; it was more like a bird's: a barely perceptible rise and an even subtler fall. He could've easily been mistaken for a statue or one of Madame Tussaud's wax sculptures if one was caught staring. Whether by design or luck, Will had the ability to be almost invisible when he wanted to.

At a particularly tense part of an action-packed dream sequence, Will twitched from the cerebral message and his deerskin Corral cowboy boots shifted against the old metal military desk. This caused even more dust to come off his boot. The heavier dirty dust fell to the floor as the lighter, more pollinated dust rose like a cloud. His dogging heels had been worn down from his days of riding young horses in bullpens to break in green horses.

It was hard enough to walk in those cowboy boots without practice, but Will had practically ridden out of the womb wearing them.

He dreamt of the challenges of breaking a wild horse, as it was pure pleasure for Will. It took a level of patience beyond most people's and the ability to try and connect, if that was the applicable term, to the horse in a sort of telepathic way. Horses weren't stupid, not to Will; he thought them every bit as cunning as a man, every bit as devious, but with the natural sense to survive and be free. It was because of his understanding of equine that Will could tame the wild spirit in a horse nearly every time. And he often dreamt about it as it permeated his mind.

Ever since his father had homesteaded their land and built the ranch, everything equine-related had become his hobby. Barrel racing, trotting, hunting, jumping—you name it—Will did it on a horse. He loved that type of activity more than just about anything. He once even told a friend, *"I've never had nightmares about horses… only of men."*

The sheriff's station was small and looked like something out of a low-budget western. The exterior was constructed of wooden planks, like many of the older buildings that straddled the Rocky Mountains. The thick-cut pine planks had been lightly stained decades before and were now darkened by weather and age. The state of Wyoming employed maintenance workers that would travel, year round to power wash, repaint, and make general upgrades on the facades of the older "classic" government buildings.

Will's station was no different. State and county funds wouldn't allow for a new, modernized building and there were no local billionaires to pick up the tab for a hefty "write off," so it was up to Will and his crew to do their best with what they had.

The inside of the sheriff's station was pretty bland, as most sheriffs' stations are, but it did have new hardware. At its nerve center, the station had both outdated and cutting-edge technology. Primarily, it had several types of radio communication equipment needed in this part of the country. Many of the systems were older, but still used by farmers, ranchers, and truckers, so Will thought it prudent to keep as much variation at the station as possible.

The entire eastern-facing wall housed HAM, shortwave, EMS, Mountain Emergency, CB, broadband, repeater for the walkie-talkies, trunked and digital, encrypted, analog, scanners, cell, and a landline that looked like it had been built around the station long before.

The offices were partitioned by glass but were so ancient that they were still wood-framed, rather than the metal or alloy that modern stations have. And although the state of Wyoming had plenty of resources from Homeland Security, FEMA, and other federally funded government agencies, as well as the numerous military bases and installations that dotted the landscape, it refused to upgrade outdated stations merely on the basis of cosmetics.

But the sheriff and the other employees couldn't have cared less. Will was from another time. He had spent his hard years in the big cities and nearly every day he spent away from Wyoming was a day he felt was lost. Only a few pictures remained on the wall behind his desk, and most of the framed accolades and citations filled the large drawer to the lower right of Will's boots.

It was Martha Day, his dispatcher, who would wait until Will was out of the office, then rehang the pictures Will had taken down and thrown into his desk drawer. It was like a game with those two; Will knew she was doing it, but Martha figured Will would just forget he took them down the older he got. Every so often when Will would take a picture down, Martha would wait until evening when she heard the engine on his county-issued SUV roar to life, drop into gear, and finally drive off into the sunset. She'd sneak into his unlocked office, retrieve the frames from the bottom drawer, and rehang them in the very spot they'd been taken from.

Martha loved Will like a son and was so proud he had made something of himself, unlike most in those parts. She wasn't gonna let any damn country humility stop people from knowing how important Will was, or at least had been.

She'd grab the photo of him next to the Bureau's director, shaking his hand when he graduated from the academy at Quantico. Then she'd retrieve Will's photo a fellow Special Agent had taken of him while on a manhunt high in the Catskills with his weapon drawn, just before they released the bloodhounds. That one was exciting, she thought.

She'd carefully remove the photo of when he and Sara were married, then rifle through the seemingly endless citations for Meritorious Service, Bull's Eye Sniper Training, Special Weapons and Tactics *SWAT* graduations, commendations, you name it, Will Pierce had done it, won it, beat it, and earned it.

The problem was Will Pierce didn't want anyone else to know about it. Will was a straight shooter in every sense of the word and since Sara had lost her courageous fight against breast cancer, all he wanted now was to live a quiet life.

Will seemed to nap more and more these days, not due to depression or sadness, quite the contrary. It was because the phone rang less and less for the sheriff's services. When it did ring, Martha would relay the dispatch to Will if he was at Cora's Diner having his daily coffee and bran muffin for breakfast or if he was taking an executive lunch of 90 minutes or more rather than the state-mandated 60.

She'd even buzz him in his office when all she'd merely needed to do was lean back in her chair and call out to him in a normal voice.

Martha followed what she deemed proper protocol, but most of the calls of late were for nothing more than lost pets or runaway stud bulls causing commotion on the newly paved two-lane highway. Occasionally there'd be a "Critter Call," as Will liked to call them: a meandering rattler looking for a nice fat rat in Jacob Marr's barn, an antelope that got its antlers tangled in a downed barbed-wire fence, or perhaps a buffalo that got too close to the elementary school, causing the daydreamers to run out of their classes and head toward the peaceful animal.

Yet these days, problems had seemingly been righting themselves with no help from either the sheriff or his staff and that didn't sit well with Will Pierce. But what could he do?

Will never trusted easy; he was naturally suspicious, which got him through Quantico and made him one of the best FBI agents the Bureau was ever honored to have. Even though he felt he'd been put out to pasture prematurely, after a series of particularly hard and gruesome cases, when his temper was short and suspects were turning up beaten and bloodied due to his frustrations and lack of "anger management" as the Bureau's appointed psychiatrists called it.

He was actually proud of the fact that the ACLU had *him* on its "Top 10 List"—that was a picture he'd like to frame and put on his wall. It was getting to the point then where he and the Bureau felt it was time to part ways. Ironically, he would never bat an eye or shed a tear over the move.

Secretly, it was what he'd always wanted. He had a nice federal pension, his ranch was paid off, and the county paid him well, maybe too well, he thought, for a job he felt a monkey could do in his sleep. He equally knew he was that monkey.

Rusty Jenkins, Will's deputy, was a high-strung, kiss-ass of a young man with a heart of gold and a serious case of intimidation by the man he revered. He was told from an early age that he was hyperactive, had ADHD, ADD, or some such malady, when really it was just a matter of him finding something worth focusing his tremendous attention on.

When he failed to become a firefighter up in Laramie, he applied to the Sheriff's Academy, and to the surprise of many, especially his parents and his girlfriend, he made top honors and became the envy of all state and local law enforcement.

Nonetheless, Rusty was happy to live in Will's shadow and would do absolutely anything the sheriff asked of him. The mere fact that his mentor and boss had been to exotic places like Chicago, New York, and Kansas City was nearly overwhelming. And that case that took Will to Western Europe, well, he could sit around the saloon and talk about that for a week, if anyone would listen.

Rusty was more like a kindhearted Barney Fife, yet looks were certainly deceiving as he also possessed real detective skills, which he did not even know he had until the time came to use them. That is one thing that Will Pierce did see in his deputy and come hell or high water, he was going to bring out the best of Rusty Jenkins' percolating God-given talents.

Will began to chuckle in his sleep. He smacked his tongue against the roof of his dry mouth as though he were eating barbecue spare ribs. He opened his eyes slightly, half-consciously, to investigate whether his room or the outer offices or perhaps the station had changed in the past few hours.

A quick check to see if Martha had come back from her granddaughter's graduation or if Rusty had tracked down Mrs. Novacek's Jack Russell terrier who loved to tear ass around the neighborhood in pursuit of smaller, quicker vermin. He'd take one more look, and then slowly slip back into dreamland.

As he moved in his chair, his Colt model 1911 shifted slightly in the worn rubbed leather of his hip holster. His appearance as well as his dress combined with his stature was ironic, a detail not lost on him.

He realized how cliché he looked, like a lawman from the Old West frontier, but after all, this was the sticks of Wyoming and if you needed to fire more than six shots at a man, you're gonna need a bigger gun. He knew things like that all too well. Besides, he always carried a "Baby" Browning .25 ACP in his boot, in a small slip he had hand-stitched by his tanner, and, of course, there was a whole arsenal of weapons buried in his SUV and under lock and key in the station's weapon closet.

Will kept strict count of all the shells, not just the ones in the belt around his waist, but in his weapon rack that held his Remington 30.6 Woodmaster and his Benelli 828U *up & down* nickel-plated 12 gauge with satin walnut stock. The station housed various other rifles, along with a confiscated M249 from a drunken soldier off base and two high-powered crossbows that the teenagers were using to illegally hunt coyotes for their hides, since the county paid $25 a pelt to line service jackets. The latter weapons had yet to be retrieved for fear the boys would actually have to face Will to get them back.

The weapon lock-up was no further than a few steps away from Will. He always kept a sharp eye on it, even though it was completely installed with a state-of-the-art security alarm system. He also made sure no one could ever get into his ammo lockbox, the locked left lower desk drawer, or the concealed stash he had under and above the spare tire in his truck.

He was fastidious about weaponry, as it was known to him to be a killer of children and fools… but not in Wyoming; those mistakes were reserved for the big city folks. In these parts, from an early age children are taught to respect firearms and to understand the responsibility they had, especially when taking the life of fellow creature.

Something tickled his nose as Will's hand automatically brushed a fly off his face as he slept. It danced gingerly across his cheek, careful to avoid the minefield of facial hair, but Will's brain alerted his hand to the presence of a threat or annoyance and sent the signal to kill, or at least swat it away. Will, who had normally ascribed to the face and hair high and tight, went unshaven more often these days.

His graying beard was still peppered with dark patches, perfectly symmetrical to where they should be, so those that looked directly at him couldn't quite tell if he was a fit older man or a younger man looking well beyond his years. Even though he sported a beard these days, he always kept it close-cropped. Either out of laziness, convenience, or sheer orneriness, Will felt comfortable looking his age and didn't give a rat's ass who thought different or would be brave enough to say it.

His face was wrinkled, the kind of wrinkled that lonely housewives yearned for. He had deep crow's feet around his eyes, just deep enough to question whether he was friend or foe, but not deep enough to conceal his striking blue eyes. His grooved dimples were more fearsome than cute and told the tale of a man who had seen it all and probably wrestled with a lot of it along the way. His hands were large and knotty like those of a farmer's and he knew the osteoarthritis would be creeping in in the years to come.

He too had worked his father's land as a young man, but he learned from his Norwegian mother the importance of moisturizing his skin throughout his life. Because of that, Will had strong, but gentle features, solid, veiny, and youthful. He was altogether an attractive man, and, although his demeanor could confuse and perplex someone to the point of never being able to read or understand him, he was truly a kind and generous human being.

When Will was at the Bureau, he kept his hair short and cropped, military-style, and was always clean-shaven. He wore the proverbial blue suit, concealed clear plastic-coated earpiece when required, and covered his Glock 19 with a double-stacked magazine easily under the back flap of his jacket. He was lean enough to pull it off and somehow that backroom government tailor seemed to make him look like he stepped off a runway with every suit he was issued.

Will had a special talent of being quick on the draw. It wasn't from the hours of training at the Academy or the years of practice to re-qualify or stay sharp, but more from the drought days of his childhood. Back then when rain fell rarely, the snakes would infest his father's barn and attempt to fill their bellies with delicious chicken eggs, or if lucky enough, the chicken itself. Reaching into a chicken coop or pile of wood became a risky proposition if it weren't for his fast-on-the-draw technique.

A man could get pretty good with a gun when his life was threatened on a daily basis. Thankfully, this part of Wyoming had been blessed with above-average rainfall for the past few decades, so battling his old nemesis seemed like a problem that had been resolved.

The dark vinyl top on his old desk covered the rusted metal underneath and had faded to a dull gray from years under direct sunlight from the single-paned window in the back wall of Will's office. Will always loved to have the sun over his shoulder, perhaps it was to ensure the person opposite him had the sun in their eyes, and that way he'd always have the high ground and be in a better position.

He always had the advantage, always, and if he didn't, he'd maneuver to make sure he did. The large mug half-filled with coffee had long since cooled and only the fly bothered to pay it any attention. Will was too busy battling demons in his dreams and attempting to right the wrongs of others upon the innocent in his fractured second chance scenarios to bring back the dead and reunite them with their loved ones.

Will's body jerked and convulsed again slightly, like a dog's paw flickering as it napped on a throw rug near the fireplace. He was deep into rapid eye movement sleep now and his theta waves were firing off the chart. He was at war with something or someone from his past and he was determined to win at whatever cost. His nostrils flared and his breathing deepened. His dream was just about to climax when… the phone on his desk suddenly rang.

CHAPTER 4

CUMULONIMBUS CLOUDS FLOATED HIGH and down in the vast Wyoming sky like angry anvils about to be hammered by Thor's blacksmith. The cool air aloft colliding with the hot air below caused a beautiful but monstrous dance as far as the eyes could see. Boomers and Thunderheads were just some of the nicknames the plainsmen would give these lumbering giants. Those enormous clouds that looked like great cotton balls on steroids growing ever larger as the hot air rose high from the valley floor.

Those in the Mountain states had an uncanny relationship with nature, especially the Indians whose generations could read a sky for danger like a blind man reading a Braille bible. Every sight, every smell would be a clue to what impending tumult would soon be upon them.

If the air tasted sweet, it was going to rain. If the static electricity in the air made your hair stand on end, you're looking at thunder and lightning. If the skies turned from clear blue, to orange, to green, to brown, to black, you better haul ass to a shelter, because wind, rain, and hail were coming. And all that foreplay led to the strongest and deadliest weather events of all—tornadoes.

The old man repositioned the strap of his old M40 bolt-action rifle over his shoulder for better comfort as they hiked since it had been digging an annoyance into his trapezius muscle. He was an old-schooler who liked to dress for the occasion: he wore expensive, durable hiking boots, extra-thick denim jeans, a thick flannel shirt, and a well-worn khaki-colored hunting vest with so many pockets to hold things, even he couldn't fill them.

His Aviator sunglasses, usually reserved for pilots, were top-of-the-line with a polarized amber tint and titanium rims that wrapped around the backs of his ears. His ball cap had a Celtic knot design for a logo and words that advertised his company: Callahan Security. Little Timmy Callahan from Lebanon was now Mister Timothy Callahan, CEO of Callahan Security, one of the finest security corporations in the world.

But even CEOs can be physically and mentally taxed after a hard day of hiking, and Callahan's legs were beginning to feel like jelly. He thought of himself like one of those COPD commercial actors having trouble breathing and complaining about how hard it was to move around, let alone climb a mountain.

But he was older and stubborn and used to be a hard young man, so if a young boy could take it, so could he! Besides, he was responsible for his ward, so he wasn't about to show signs of fatigue and get shown up by a child decades his junior.

Michael, Callahan's grandson, led the way as he had been allowed to since he was six years old on any outing that involved a skilled hunter or explorer, as that was what he was being groomed to be. Michael Callahan and his grandfather had set out early that morning and drove the 85-plus miles from their luxury hotel in Cheyenne through the early daytime toward their remote destination.

Callahan had found the perfect spot and decided to pull over his expensive rental car, complete with LoJak, voice-control navigation, audio system, and moon roof. Michael really enjoyed the moon roof and thought it was the next best thing to having a convertible.

Callahan chose a spot in a remote area off the long stretch of desolate road, as it seemed to be public property; no private property or BLM warning signs were posted, and it looked like the perfect place to park. The hotel concierge had warned him that he should be doubly careful because Wyoming land was precious to those who owned, farmed, ranched, or lived on it.

Callahan looked around and didn't see any signs for half a mile in either direction, nothing that would indicate any problems. It wasn't Arapaho, Bannock, Comanche, Crow, Kiowa, Apache, Cheyenne, Dakota, or any other Native American reservation land, and he knew well that if it were, it would've been posted miles before with redundant posts from there all the way to Cheyenne.

He flipped down the driver's side visor, exposing a copy of his hunting permit, to ward off any interested or nosy parties who may come across the rental and feel it was an easy target. This way at least, they would know the car belonged to hunters, and hunters carried rifles. So, Callahan presumed, the permit alone would be a fantastic deterrent for any ne'er-do-well.

Callahan and Michael had already bagged up the food and water, secured their packs and made all the preparations for the long hike and expedition. They felt totally prepared. Although in this part of remote Wyoming, no one is ever truly prepared for what may come upon him or her.

He and Michael had set out and hoofed it in brand new mountain boots and thick winter socks toward their destination. As they started out, it first seemed as far as the horizon, but it became closer and closer with each step they took together.

Callahan had already crumpled up the original hunting license, stuffed it deep into the front pocket of Michael's jacket and patted his chest as they walked. He wanted Michael to hang onto it in case they happened upon anyone or if any inquiries were made about their legitimacy of being there on that land.

Callahan and his grandson had left their vehicle miles back in the flats and strode across the barren plains toward the distant plateau. It was easy going for the first two hours, but became a strenuous hike, even for a young man, as they began their ascent up the long, high hill. He braced himself for the challenge ahead.

Callahan was unfamiliar with this part of the country and wasn't used to its strange weather and drastic changes in both temperature as well as humidity per atmosphere as they climbed. He was just beginning to realize that these trips with his grandson might have a level of difficulty his body was no longer willing to accept.

"Hey, look at that off to your 9 o'clock," Callahan said to his grandson.

He pointed to a lower ridge on an adjacent rocky outcropping. "Bighorn sheep. See how they balance their hooves on the rocky crags? It's amazing how they can cling onto the tiniest outcropping in order to secure their footing, don't you think?"

Michael nodded.

"It looks impossible for any creature to keep from falling to their death, but somehow they've adapted over thousands of years to their environment and are now thriving in it."

Callahan found the exposed gun next to the canvas bag he was carrying, then pushed the butt of his second, back-up rifle upward from behind him, swinging the rifle from up and behind his shoulder to a ready position. He peered into the eyepiece of the scope and followed the crosshairs until they landed square onto a ram. He tightened his sight up in his target and found his center directly into the face of the bighorn. This was no ready, aim, fire; he was merely ranging his quarry, although he could've easily taken the shot and zeroed a bull's eye directly into its skull. But that's not what Callahan was into.

"Come on, I don't like the look of those clouds. Let's get to the top and find your target," Callahan said as his lungs puffed a little from the strain of the altitude.

"Okay, Grandpa, we're almost to the top. I think we'll get something big today!" Michael beamed as he surefooted himself double time up the rocky embankment to the top of the cliff, leaving his grandfather in a cloud of dust as he scampered upward.

Callahan could only smile as he dutifully followed his young protégé like an old hunting dog. *This kid's gonna be the death of me*, he thought.

CHAPTER 5

THE HASHEMITE KINGDOM OF Jordan was as beautiful to the eye as it was to its sovereign people. The city itself, like old Lebanon, was primarily Arabic, but these days it was modern, tolerant, and considered a thriving rare jewel of the Middle East.

It was a pristine city and could've been compared with any modern Western city and yet it stood on its own. A boulevard café along the East Bank could've easily been mistaken for any along the Champs-Élysées, except that palm trees lined the streets, minarets lay in the foreground, and it was bordered by other less-tolerant Arab nations, such as Saudi Arabia, Syria, Iraq, Palestine, and Israel.

Abdullah II bin Al-Hussein, or King Abdullah as he was known and affectionately referred to, had raised his tiny kingdom up while other Arab nations had kept their people ignorant and impoverished. His father preceded him and taught him the value of human life as well as the value of his people and he was greatly loved because of that.

The king's father wanted his son to rule with experience and knowledge of the world, so as a boy, he was educated in the West and taught about countries that were socially and culturally moderate, to say the least. He learned nuances of diplomacy and the desperate need to try and find middle ground within disputes, especially when dealing with the religious variables that his and other Middle Eastern countries would find growing discontent in the near future of his kingdom.

King Abdullah was an impeccable dresser: suits from London and tailored by the finest craftsmen and women. He knew his appearance meant everything in the West and in his own region and he grew into the knowledge that the value of meeting with, trading with, and creating great diplomacy with other leaders from around the world could quite possibly secure his tiny country's future.

He was much beloved by his people and respected around the world as one of the truly great leaders among a group of not always so great ones: Saddam Hussein, Ayatollah Khomeini, and Muammar Gaddafi, to name a few. He had panache, was engaging, and even had a sense of humor, something that was in short supply in this volatile age in the desert landscape.

What with Daesh and competing splinter factions running around the Middle East decapitating women and children and tossing suspected homosexuals from high towers to be witnessed in the public square, Jihadists murdering whilst shouting "God is Great!" perverting the word of Islam, and the endless killings in the name of Allah, the king knew he needed more help to keep his utopia from floundering.

It was because of this he relied heavily on technology and tight security to keep his country neutral, like Switzerland of the Middle East. And as a moderate, he did his best to keep his country and his people out of the constant warring and fighting and disagreements of the other Arab nations. And by all past, present, and future accounts, it was working.

Security in the region was an enormous undertaking, so much so that the kingdom looked to a favorite son to help secure the interior and exterior of Jordan. And it was Nassar Khumari, now Chief Executive Officer, and his burgeoning agency, Falcon Securities that ran much of the operations of the country as well as kept safe the king's queen and the entirety of his royal family.

Falcon Securities was housed in the older part of downtown Amman amidst the bustling city center. And like almost any other city in the world, pedestrians walked to their local grocery stores, to the lush green parks, to their offices, and often had to fight just to manage to cross the busy streets.

Roads here, unlike in most of the West, were without painted lanes and offered a racing course-type challenge, even to the likes of well-seasoned Monaco or even California drivers.

Because of the open road set up, any driver would not only have to gauge his or her skills, but perhaps his life, by the flow, speed, and temperament of the traffic.

One lane, two lanes, three lanes, all the vehicles converged and congealed, nearly bouncing off each other as the average Jordanian went about his daily life. Amman, too, had traffic jams like Los Angeles and Chicago, taxis for the youth and aged, and FedEx trucks moving along these streets as in Manhattan and Johannesburg.

Al-Balad was Amman's oldest section, and it was because of this that Nassar felt he could pay tribute to his father's legacy and to the city of his birth. Even though he spent a great deal of his youth in Lebanon, playing carefree with his two best friends, he decided to build his empire within sight of Jabal al-Qal'a (Amman Citadel) and the Temple of Hercules to remind him of his Arab heritage and the great history of this land.

After all, the city had risen from the desert to become one of the oldest continuously inhabited cities in the world. And although Falcon Securities was located in the crumbling and questionably designed area of such ancient structures, Nassar was determined to reinforce his legacy with steel, concrete, and a promise.

An enormous tower rose high above Amman like a phoenix. It was surrounded by shiny polished metal and reflective dark glass and had a crane on the roof for what seemed like years of construction that never waned. Falcon Securities had been growing ever larger, ever higher, and appeared to be competing with other Middle Eastern oddities like Dubai's Burj Khalifa or Mecca's Makkah Royal Clock Tower Hotel.

Nassar wanted his company to be seen, not only by every Jordanian or tourist alike, but also by the world. It wasn't enough to have a very public and eccentric presence, he wanted a presence that no one would forget. Standing over 600 meters high, Falcon Securities was like a point of a scimitar rising skyward toward the Arab nation's prosperous future. He knew if he brought his vision to life correctly, someone in the world would be talking about it on any given day, and this made him very proud.

Nassar had always remembered what his father had taught him and used his father's vision for his future to create one of the tightest, most respected security agencies in the world. Nassar was in his late 30s when the tech bubble began to rise, and since he was always a tinkerer and lover of all things tech and futuristic, he put his heart, mind, and his father's millions all in. Lasers, motion detection, artificial intelligent computers, Kevlar—you name it—if it had to do with security of any kind, Nassar found it, bought it, developed it, and loved it all!

Falcon Securities would become the Middle East's premiere security agency and would extend into paramilitary, munitions, weapons, and beyond, but attempted to not only supply those various friendly armies throughout the world, but also the Dairat al-Mukhabarat al-Ammah, the General Intelligence Directorate of Jordan. He also worked very hard to ensure that the enemies of his country and those that refused to promote peace were not able to get their hands on his products in order to perpetuate war.

Nassar was happy to even do a great deal of his business in Israel, and surprisingly, as an Arab he had no compunction whatsoever, as the color of money had no ethical or religious barriers and since he was raised to cherish life and respect all mankind, his decisions, although perhaps frowned upon by many of his peers, were always the right ones.

And now with Israel becoming the next Silicon Valley, as well as the hub of high tech, Falcon Securities would rely on its close ties to them and the United States and their weaponry, software, and future tech. In fact, Falcon Securities had so much clout with colleagues, Falcon was often given unfettered access, the kind of access that only favored nations or American contractors might be given by the Pentagon.

Nassar worked hard at being as good and fair a businessman as he was a dedicated family man. It was only those few proclivities, those habits, hobbies, the aching that Nassar possessed that would separate him from a normal man.

CHAPTER 6

I N EARLY 1995, DENVER International Airport replaced the obsolete and outdated Stapleton as a preeminent air transportation hub in the United States.

This new and modernized airport was some 34,000 acres large and had state-of-the-art technology: automated baggage handling, a 10-megawatt solar photovoltaic array spanning dozens of acres, and the artistic design on the scale of the world-renowned Sydney Opera House.

But, like so much folly of men, DIA didn't open until more than a year and a half after the scheduled date, running $2 billion over its $4.8-billion budget. Ironically, that automated baggage-handling machine ended up wreaking so much havoc on the passengers' luggage, clothes, and personal belongings that the airport administrators ended up replacing the monstrosities with humans!

Even so, Denver and DIA had a number of things going for it— location for one. Denver's new airport was practically smack dab in the middle of the United States. It would end up being easy, convenient, and capable of handling more flights in a single day than most other airports around the world could handle in a month.

At its height, DIA would be in the top 5 busiest airports in the U.S.

and 18th in the world. Hundreds, thousands, millions of passengers would pass though its halls, by the McDonald's, the magazine kiosks, and the duty-free shops merely to grab the last snack item or the first one if they'd just come in.

So many people came to Denver to experience all its beautiful land had to offer: skiing, mountain climbing, hiking, rafting, whatever, making it the perfect destination for everyone. Denver was also perfect for dinners, events, conventions, and parties… and not just any party, a very unique type of party.

Robert Miller had the distinct pleasure of following his family around the world as his father was assigned the extremely choice position of Regional Security Officer at American embassies. Also with being an RSO, Thaddeus Miller ended up being a consultant to the United States and also foreign governments.

Because of his father's influence and clout around the world, Robert Miller had been to nearly every country on Earth, learning untold customs and languages, seeing what few people would ever see, and experiencing more than a year's worth of episodes on the National Geographic Channel.

At the end of the day, though, Robert Miller preferred the Rocky Mountains and the people of Colorado proper and would gladly stack them up against any other culture as the finest, kindest, and most deserving. That's why Miller, as his friends called him, decided to settle and put down roots here.

Miller had opted to join the U.S. Marines after growing up around the world and being educated at the finest schools. He went to college, but it was his experiences in the field and abroad that gave him an advantage that rivaled those heading the U.S. military.

Miller would end up rising to the ranks of officer quickly, get promoted, get bored, then challenge himself by applying, being accepted and transferring to Special Forces for the training of his life. He would embark on the most challenging and dangerous missions just to prove he could. He was always challenging himself and felt it was his duty to challenge others, too.

Miller was that unique individual who had a higher than average IQ, was the perfect 6-foot, 3-inches tall with a 200-pound physique, and combined the types of training reserved for the most elite fighters on Earth, including Brazilian Ju Jitsu, hand-to-hand combat, weapons and tactics, strategic warfare—you name it, he learned it.

He brushed up on his language skills, not that he really ever needed to, but since the U.S. government was paying for it and it allowed him to take a few weeks of rest every time he was accepted to a new program and heal whatever bullet wound, broken bone, or combat-related injury he had sustained, he'd do so.

Miller had married his high school sweetheart, Stephanie, and they raised four beautiful children. They had since grown up and, by no small coincidence, had succeeded in their own respective rights in becoming accomplished, outstanding, and productive members of society.

After all the wars and battles Miller had fought in, or as he felt, had been allowed to participate in, the United States Marines decided to force him out since his pay grade was too high. If he wasn't going to take a high-ranking position in Washington, D.C., then he'd better just take the Thanks of a Grateful Nation pat on the shoulder, a pathetic soldier's pension, and not let the door hit him in the ass on the way out as he left.

Miller, though, as tough as he was, still felt pretty dejected when he was first RIFF'ed. The military always claimed reduction in force as the perfect reason to throw out the old and bring in the new, but Miller knew he had done his country proud, and maybe it was time for him to explore new things. He quickly recovered as the private sector came calling almost immediately after his forced retirement, looking for his unique brand of services.

He would spend the next few years being paid handsomely to speak at various VFW meetings, fundraisers, and World Affair Councils, to name a few. Yet all the while, Miller was being asked—more like begged—by other groups and individuals if he might be interested in training men and women for the new and crucial role global security was beginning to play.

Miller quite happily took the small fortunes that were bestowed upon him by corporations and tiny nations but soon began to bore of the tedium of working for someone else's uncle. Then he read about a new breed of security company called Blackwater and the lengths they were willing to go to, to create an entire security compound that would change the face and concept of worldwide security.

This new type of company came complete with dozens of acres of wilderness in which to train soldiers, complete with RIFF'ed soldiers, RIFF'ed heavy machinery, and RIFF'ed trainers. Miller saw that he could build his own private army and, together with an almost endless series of government contracts, could secure his place in the world as one of the leading security companies.

What better way to build a security force than to customize, and more importantly, privatize professional and executive security services? Intelligence, counter-intelligence, terrorism and counter-terrorism training and services, roadside bomb detection and removal, IED search and demolitions dismantle missions, specialized liberation and crowd control, and the one that every frustrated soldier and civilian wanted most: sniper training.

Miller had another bright idea. An idea he knew would not be boring and would allow him to use his incredible talents and call upon the highest-ranking officials in the world to help him.

If a country needed to create and establish an army? Miller was your man! Need a private security team to infiltrate Al Qaeda without the U.S. or another allied country to be on the books? Miller had your six! Need to guard an embassy, protect an ambassador during crucial talks, or resupply heavy equipment to one of our "friendly" nations? Miller was the first call anyone would make. He could see it all before him and he became hungry for more.

Miller immediately set out utilizing his lifetime of contacts, both military and civilian. He flew around the world and procured man and machine and began to build his dream of a private security firm comprising contractors, mostly former Special Forces soldiers from various armies, including those overseas, and rose to fame and notoriety in an incredibly short period of time.

And since the bottom line was what governments really looked at with more scrutiny than compassion, Miller knew he could go in front of any subcommittee or delegation and undercut a bid to provide anything and everything to those powers. It was all a matter of experience, skill, and dollars—millions and millions of dollars. He knew he could do it and he knew how to do it.

So Miller thought, where better to build Miller Strategic Management than in Colorado? The mountainous terrain was perfect for MSM as it could double as the backdrop to nearly any country on Earth. The hills of Afghanistan, no problem; Iraq, certainly; Korea, no comparison; you name it, if it had a mountainous or hilly terrain, it could all be doubled by Miller.

There may be a few exceptions, such as jungles and perhaps deserts, but that was no problem as Miller would be able to solve those issues by building a facility in Belize or any black site in Central America and do tag-alongs with the SAS and other British Forces, under the banner of jungle training.

Miller also decided to build other secret locations within the primary rain forests and heavily dense and humid mountains of Central America and around the world to satisfy any requirements to train soldiers for Vietnam-like combat. But to him, the Rocky Mountains were perfect, no matter where he'd send his trainers and trainees; he always planned to stay in Colorado.

Miller knew that his contacts alone at nearby Cheyenne Mountain would prove invaluable, as even those desk jockeys tasked with satellite, cyber, crypto, and space warfare at NORAD and STRATCOM from time to time needed a weekend junket of shooting targets and running live-fire scenarios like the boys in the field they were jealous of and secretly wanted to join in combat.

Miller found himself often trading luxurious tours and mini-staycations for all the top brass and those grunts who would simply ask, for a little consideration and the occasional heads up on some new tech or contract coming down the pipe. Miller had spent decades currying favor with the U.S. military elite as he'd proved himself in battle; now he was proving himself in corporate America.

MSM became a shooting star and as administrations changed over the years from conservative to liberal and back again, Miller's agency began to take on larger and larger roles worldwide. It didn't matter the politics du jour, MSM would position itself as the dominant force for both public and private conflicts.

He knew this is where he wanted to set up shop and this is where he made plans for his and his family's future. He had spent too many years away from his wife and his children, as a Special Forces Operator would take him to undisclosed countries on secret missions, for varying lengths of time.

He had put his family through enough strife and vowed that he would be a better father and husband since now his company was flourishing in the same area where he had settled down with his family after his retirement from the Armed Forces. He knew his wife, Stephanie, was a saint, but she was also a woman and a human being; if he tried to take a single day extra from traveling or training or take a business trip to present a scenario to Congress, she might pack her bags and leave him.

That was one scenario he definitely worried about. She had put his feet to the fire many times, but he had always taken his service to his country as his first mistress. Now that he was in the real world, he would have to deal with real-world issues, and divorce wasn't something he ever wanted.

But now he had something real, something tangible to offer the world and his family. A future, Miller might have added, that included his two lifelong friends, Callahan and Khumari, and the idea of making the world a better and safer place for all of mankind.

After a time, Miller began to formulate an idea that, once he passed it by his other unofficial partners, might just create a program for other like-minded individuals who agreed with their outlook on life and the idea of doing something that was rewarding, and he might add, challenging without the confines of federal, state, county, city, or even international laws. Something he, his partners, and their families could be proud of and pass on to their children.

CHAPTER 7

"**O**KAY GRANDPA, I'M GETTING into position," Michael said in a direct and even tone.

Since they were so high up and far from their target, even the boy knew he wouldn't spook his prey. He stopped at the edge of the precipice and knelt down, careful not to drop his pack suddenly and hard to the ground for fear of crushing the water bottles or whatever gear his grandfather had packed.

Michael slowly took the padded rifle case off his shoulder and gently placed it on the rocky ground on the high plateau. He moved the long zipper down and around the edges and opened the flap to expose a newly oiled and pristine-looking rifle. The kind of rifle a young boy would rarely see, let alone get to fire.

It was a M1C .30-06 caliber and although it may have been considered ancient by some, Callahan had kept it polished and cleaned all these years and was proud to hand it down to his grandson, whom in turn, cared for it with kid gloves.

The M84 telescope was conspicuously absent from the old sniper rifle, so Michael reached in, grabbed it, and slid it into place. He maneuvered it into position, and then locked it down with a snap. The M84 scope was long and purposeful, yet it also appeared to have some type of modifications.

It was tightly mounted with a low forward profile-mounting platform, which was bolted on easy and could be separated at the touch of a button, yet somehow it cleared the metal so as not to interfere with the bolt-action slide. It also had a quick detach button that would allow the shooter to break down the rifle stock easier, if need be, perhaps for a clean getaway or for repacking quickly.

But what made this refined relic so state-of-the-art and interesting was that it had the technology that was more like a tiny computer than an eyepiece. It was a scope of Callahan's own personal design and he was up there with the greats.

The scope was sleek, dark, and sharp looking. It could range your target digitally and easily and its on-board ballistics calculation could sight-in the distance and drop value instantly, like a Burris Eliminator III. It could account for wind direction and velocity and easily factor in the light 10 mph wind blowing so high above the valley floor at this time of day.

Callahan had already plugged in the ammo specs for his grandson, as they were also of his own make and design, so Michael could at any time engage the 1,200-yard laser range finder and wait for the dot to appear in the center of the crosshairs. Even at such a young age, Michael was already a proficient shot.

Only the best for his grandson, Callahan thought. After all, this young boy would be inheriting a good deal of his interests when he was no longer on this Earth. Yet what Michael didn't know, at least that day, was that the special sniper scope had a few more tricks that would make it extremely rare and sought after.

And although the gun was from another era, solid in its manufacturing and sturdy for its reliability, Michael was still strong enough to handle it, albeit with the slight unsteadiness of a maturing boy's growing muscles.

The stock was stained brown and the wood ran smooth to the touch. The black metal was polished to a shine and it smelled of gun oil and lubricants. It hadn't been shot for a while and Michael was so excited to be the first to fire this legend in dozens of years, he'd hardly slept at all the night before.

He made sure he put himself through the paces, weighing the relic first in his hands, holding it for long periods so as not to tire, and making sure every square inch, inside and out of the rifle, was oiled, cleaned, and ready for action.

Michael suddenly noticed that the wind had picked up on top of the plateau, so he was careful to grab a big rock and place it on top of the padded rifle carrier. He didn't want it to blow off the top of the mountain, so he got everything into place, just the way his grandfather would want it. He was becoming just as fastidious as Callahan.

After securing everything, he decided to inch his way to the edge of the plateau where it was almost like crawling over the cliff. It was a forward drop-off with sheer cliffs on either side; so one wrong move would mean disaster.

He knew he'd have to be *very* careful, because where they were was very dangerous and he could not take nature for granted, at least that's what his grandfather had hammered into him the night before in the hotel.

"Okay, Grandpa, I'm in position," Michael said, this time turning his head to look at Callahan as a burst of wind kicked up and nearly drowned out his voice.

"Right!" Callahan shouted back as he too knelt down, swung his rifle case off his shoulder, caught it in one stroke, and quickly unzipped it.

"Let me find it first."

He fumbled around the bag momentarily, then retrieved a small ammunition clip. It looked like a clip from an old WWII-era carbine, but it also seemed to have slight technical modifications. Callahan reached deeper into the bag and retrieved a small box of shells with blue tape around them covering any sign of manufacturer or product identification.

He sliced the box open with his fingernail and retrieved three long, missile-tipped bullets.

"Phhh." Callahan blew any potential dust off the shells before loading them one by one into the clip, sliding them in smoothly as though he'd been doing this his entire life.

He double-checked whether the shells were tightly packed into the nest, tapping it hard against his hand three times. When he was sure the bullets were ready, he slowly and carefully stood and walked over to Michael.

"Okay, let's try a new position this time," he said with a wide grin across his face.

"Can I?!" Michael replied.

Michael's dark wavy hair began to blow into his eyes as he stood atop the plateau. His dark complexion was something the Callahan family had not seen in their bloodline, making him all the more special to his grandfather.

He always seemed to get special treatment as well, but he never quite knew why he was his grandfather's favorite or why he would be more privileged than his cousins, but it was okay with him. The lavish attention was all Michael knew and he enjoyed every moment of love and teaching his grandfather gave him.

"Sure, I think it's about time you try a new, harder position when you're going for a long shot," Callahan beamed.

Callahan lowered his knees and brought his arms down as he slowly sat down next to Michael.

"Okay, sit down with me and carefully hand me your rifle, stock forward." Michael complied and slowly sat as Callahan was still maneuvering to get into position. He took a few moments, nudged himself around on his ass, then crossed his legs as best he could for a man his age, bringing his arms together as though he were cradling the rifle.

Callahan brought the scope up and carefully placed it to his right eye. He aimed the rifle outward at no particular target, merely to illustrate to the boy how to hold the weapon one last time before giving him carte blanche.

"This is probably the toughest way to shoot. The slightest twitch of your body can cause you to miss your target and shoot God knows where the bullet might end up," Callahan instructed.

"Your breathing is key, like with any shot you ever take, controlling your breathing will determine if you hit your target or just be another weekend warrior with a gun."

"Yes, Grandpa," Michael nodded as he hung on every word from this old sage.

"I like to call this the *cradle* position, because you're cradling your rifle like a baby." Michael wrapped his arms together, the same way his grandfather was doing, emulating his every move with exact precision.

"This position is for those times when you don't have enough area to spread out or your targets at an odd position or there are obstacles in your way. The key to being a great sniper is the ability to adapt to your environment. So what you need to do is triangulate your body."

Michael's eyebrow rose as he obviously didn't understand and was attempting to figure out what was just said in his head.

"What's that mean, Grandpa?"

Callahan had been sitting in a pike position when he brought his knees up. He leaned forward a little, placing his elbows on the tops of his knees. He took the rifle and pulled the butt to his right shoulder, then used the top of his left forearm and the beginning of his bicep to rest the barrel on and steady it.

His left hand opened, and he wrapped his fingers around his right forearm, gripping it. He leaned in, cocked his head, and keeping both eyes open, he placed his right eye on the eyepiece of the scope until he was sure he was aligned.

"Now, once you get this position down, I'll show you how you can do it without even using your legs to prop up the gun. You'll look like swami doing yoga with your legs crossed."

The image his grandfather had just described made Michael chuckle.

"Do you see what I'm doing here?"

Michael nodded.

"I'm cradling the rifle like a child, keeping it tight and balanced, but my body is comfortable and at ease. Now watch my breathing. I'm breathing normally, slowly, because every time my chest expands from inhaling, it moves the rifle, so once you sight-in your target, you take a small breath and hold it." Michael nodded again.

"Then as your fingertip is steady on the trigger, you slowly exhale *as* you're pulling the trigger. It should be natural, a natural feel like you're just sitting and breathing."

Callahan watched his young grandson mimic his every move and knew the boy wanted nothing more than to please him. Even if he didn't the first few times, he knew Michael would nearly kill himself until he got it right. That was one trait everyone in his family seemed to possess—that was the Callahan way.

Callahan handed Michael the rifle as though an Indian elder were passing down his most prized pony to the heir.

"Get into position first," Callahan said as he helped the boy turn toward the edge of the cliff.

He pushed his shoulders and rotated Michael as the boy followed the instructions to a T. When Michael was in position, he peered into the scope's eyepiece and followed the magnification toward an unspecific target.

He searched the valley floor, rocky outcroppings, behind brush and trees, of which there were few, and followed a sightline until he saw the biggest ram he could find.

"Grandpa!" Michael whispered loudly, "I've got a huge bighorn in my sights!"

Callahan beamed with pride.

"Make sure the crosshairs are just behind the elbow; that's a kill shot because it explodes the lung and heart… it has to be a kill shot because you would never want an animal to suffer."

Callahan, who had been carrying a pair of binoculars, brought them up to his eyes to find the ram his grandson had targeted. He zeroed in on it quickly like a sniper's personal range finder and waited for his grandson to make him proud.

Callahan sensed that Michael may have been getting buck fever, so he whispered again to his grandson.

"But Michael, remember we're not here to kill him!"

Michael steadied his weapon, took in a breath, held it as he stroked his finger on the trigger lightly, then slightly exhaled. *Blam.* Michael pulled the trigger and the report from the rifle shook the top of the plateau. It resonated down and across the desert floor like thunder after a moment.

"The farther away the target, the longer it will take for the noise to reach us," Callahan whispered.

Callahan peered through the eyepieces of his binoculars only to see the bighorn sheep's front knees drop to the ground. He couldn't have been a prouder grandfather. It was then Callahan sensed something was amiss.

Suddenly, a scream rang out that curdled Callahan's blood. As he dropped the binoculars and looked down, he saw Michael falling off the edge of the cliff. He lunged to grab his grandson, but it was too late, he was tumbling downward.

"Michael!" Callahan screamed.

CHAPTER 8

OF COURSE, GAIUS WASN'T the sniper's real name; he just fancied the moniker after reading Greek and Roman literature about the betrayal and ultimate murder of Gaius Julius Caesar by his trusted Roman Senate.

He was deeply touched by Caesar's power and authority as well as his reach, but equally as impressed by how quickly someone so powerful could be knocked off his perch and betrayed by even his best friend—*Et tu, Brute?*

Gaius had used, reused, used again, and recycled various identities, from driver's licenses to passports and visas, you name it, Gaius had used it. He could easily pass through the highest levels of security without so much as a blink, yet he was constantly leery of unattractive female TSA or security agents as he had a penchant for making them blush and swooning over him. It was just another of his narcissistic tendencies that kept him living on the edge. And, like any true sociopath, Gaius knew how to manipulate people, especially women.

Gaius had olive skin and a swarthy complexion with thick dark hair, giving him an Italian or slightly Portuguese appearance. The color of his eyes were amber, striking enough, but the whites of his eyes were a deep-set blue and had the thinnest dark line under them as though he were wearing mascara like some Johnny Depp character in one of those pirate films.

He loved wearing dark blue or black shirts and jackets that accentuated his exotic look, and although he was attractive, he had learned to keep a low profile while cruising through an airport or crossing a public plaza.

He was well educated, had a great deal of money, and was always employed, even if those employers tended to be the unscrupulous organized crime syndicates and Mafioso types.

Arguably one of the world's greatest snipers, Gaius never seemed to use his talents for good. After all, he was a contract killer without equal, so why not go with the highest bidder? That's just good common sense.

He had grown up, like so many of his counterparts, in a rural area in the countryside. And, like so many farmers and ranchers and people of the Earth, he hunted daily. He spent his mornings shooting game with his father, then went off to school like the other children, and eventually he would join his country's armed services in order to take him away from what he perceived to be a boring existence.

Yet, unlike his peers, Gaius was more bored of people and places because of his grandiose narcissism, as he was a unique sociopath with barely an equal. How else could one explain his dispassion for taking lives at the pulling of a trigger from a distance of nearly a mile away from his quarry?

And the best part was Gaius never had to get his hands dirty, and as such, never had to come to terms with what he was really doing or how it might affect anyone else that might be involved. As delusional as Gaius was, he still slept very soundly at night.

Ironically, Gaius was also very well known to every law enforcement agency on Earth. The FBI, INTERPOL, the IPA, HKP, MI5; all local and federal departments and bureaus, as well clandestine agencies like the CIA, MI6, and FSB knew all too well about his infamous reputation.

Gaius had a lengthy jacket: a dossier of his killings, his murders, the lives he'd taken and mayhem that it provoked, and every agent, detective, or flatfoot worth his salt kept the thought of him in the back of his mind, if not the front. The only reason Gaius hadn't yet been caught was because no one had ever seen a photo of him. No one had any idea who he was, what he looked like, or when he'd strike again.

Not a single picture, not a single frame worth inspecting on a security camera. He had been upgraded on Homeland Security's website and now had a reputation as a terrorist, like Carlos the Jackal, and yet no one had been able to capture his image; nobody really knew who he was, at least no one alive did.

Gaius loved his anonymity; he reveled in it, but he seemed to love his bad reputation more. He'd often pass law enforcement, smile at a young child, or go grocery shopping like any other person, and no one would have an inkling of who or what he really was.

He loved to play different roles. He had postal uniforms, courier uniforms, police and fire uniforms; any uniform you could imagine, Gaius was prepared to get in, and more importantly, get out of, as well as get out of any situation.

The only time he was ever even remotely vulnerable was when he travelled with his rifle. It was the one piece of office equipment—if you could call it that—that kept him in business. Being mobile was imperative to Gaius.

Yet, as vulnerable as he was, he always enjoyed coming up with new and better ways to conceal his gun. He liked to challenge himself and perhaps wrap it in a long flower delivery box or maybe in fishing tackle, or he might try hiding it in a triangle-shaped cardboard container that letter carriers and Federal Express deliverymen use, or some sort of case meant for a long musical instrument.

But today, Gaius was assuming a new role, by playing the character of a hipster architect. He carried a long black rounded tube and would happily pull out a long set of blueprints to some fictitious project he claimed to be working on, if asked to do so, when all the while his rifle lay dormant inside, ready to use.

Gaius took great pride in playing the part, at least for a while, that is, this month it might be that of a Northwest coastal trendy professional. He had carefully grown a bougie beard that was dark and healthy and was paired with a neatly groomed handlebar mustache.

He had been watching late night designer beer ads and realized he needed to keep up with fashion, whether or not he was in one of the oldest and deadliest professions. Other professionals take great pride in their looks, why not a contract killer?

He had gone so far as to use beard oil on his face to soften the bristles and give it a luxurious sheen. He really took his characters seriously. It was the cornerstone of his profession and never to be underestimated.

The flight Gaius had taken to Wyoming arrived 20 minutes early due to a strong tailwind. He collected his belongings quickly and quietly, and with his pack and rifle swung over his back, he jumped from the airport shuttle bus, hit the step-down, and landed squarely on the red carpet of the car rental agency.

He had already pre-checked in and a rental car attendant was waiting for him at the three-digit stall where an anonymous dark American sedan sat. He smiled at the attendant, who was already printing his receipt from a remote hand-held computer.

A long thin receipt quickly popped out of the top of the portable machine and as soon as it stopped, the attendant ripped it off and handed it to Gaius.

Gaius snapped up the keys to the rental car and the long paper receipt and offered only a slight smile. A smile just enough to acknowledge the parking lot attendant, but not enough for him to be remembered.

"Thank you, Sir!" the attendant shouted as Gaius was already ignoring him.

Gaius felt the key fob for the raised buttons that would control the trunk and unlock the car at the same time. *Chirp.* The trunk to the dark sedan popped open and he could hear the locks tumbling to the open position. He swung the long black tube and a small duffle that carried his clean clothes into the trunk in one motion.

He stopped momentarily to take in the warm Wyoming sun and thought about stopping at a tourist destination and picking up a tri-fold of local attractions. But alas, Gaius was on the job and never mixed business with pleasure.

He jumped into the front seat and tapped the touch screen display to find his way to the navigation and began to plug in his coordinates. Gaius was fastidious about latitude and longitude and made sure he had the precise coordinates and vectors down before ever making a move on his subjects.

He dug his large hands into the padded leather steering wheel. He had surprisingly soft hands for a man in such a profession, but a light touch

SKIP SHOT | 43

and sensitive fingertips actually made him a better marksman as he could *feel* the trip of the trigger of any gun and know where and when the bullet would hit its mark.

Vroom. Gaius gunned the engine once, twice, then once again. Passersby and tourists just arriving at the rental car lot would look at him oddly, as though they would when scolding a child, but the rental car valet just smiled and nodded.

"Yeah, Dude!" The valet shouted as Gaius gunned the engine once again before dropping it into gear.

"See what it's got!"

Gaius had very few true pleasures in life, but driving fast on the open prairie in an American muscle car, well, now that was truly a dream come true for him. He pulled the shift back, put one foot on the brake and one on the gas pedal, and punched it.

The torque of such a powerful engine, the low profile and low center of gravity, combined with the grip of the wide rubber tires on the heated asphalt made for Indianapolis 500-type conditions. Such conditions seemed to be just right for a hit man to get his rocks off just before taking a life and, once again, getting his rocks off.

The tires screeched as Gaius peeled out of the rental car parking lot as the heavy front-end power caused the car to fishtail back and forth. He couldn't resist himself and began to do donuts in the lot in front of the entrance as he had seen in old movies from the 1980s, causing an incoming airport shuttle bus to pull hard to the right to avoid crashing into him.

Gaius could only laugh hysterically as he saw the terrified faces of tourists and holidaymakers as he jetted out onto the deserted two-lane highway. The navigation began to speak.

"Your destination has been calculated!"

CHAPTER 9

"PROCEED 1800 METERS," THE robotic navigational voice directed. "Your destination is on the right."

Gaius slowed the car for the first time in hours as he had redlined the engine for most of the trip, almost to the point of blowing it. Since most of Wyoming had no speed limit in the rural and remote areas, Gaius decided he liked Wyoming, perhaps even more than Germany with its pretentious Autobahn.

Who would've known that puritanical America could have such wonderfully lawless places like this with blatant disregard for other drivers' safety? This was exactly the kind of reasoning Gaius believed in, so maybe the "Home of the Brave" and "Land of the Free" wasn't such a bad place after all.

Well, at several points during his drive he thought he had certainly endangered a few lives, as he passed into oncoming traffic without the slightest elevation of his heart rate. He couldn't help but chuckle at the looks on the faces of men, women, and children as he passed recreational vehicles, campers, truckers, and family vans at speeds exceeding 140 mph with blatant disregard for common sense or safety.

But alas, Gaius had barely seen anyone in the past hour even at those speeds and he was getting bored of listening to talk radio and the "Super Sounds of The 70s." His trigger finger was getting itchy and he began to process the hit ahead.

As he bounded over a high hill, he saw an outcropping of trees and brush with a sandy swale just inside the grove. He had seen this spot on the Google Earth map when he was researching this job and it pleased him to see that it was as he expected. It was less than a mile ahead and as he peered, he saw another sedan parked on the near side of the road.

He checked his GPS on his navigation system, and then checked his Smartphone with its duplicate app against his position that also showed the coordinates of another car dead in front of him. People didn't think about the fact that LoJak can be used to track any car or any person driving it, as well as a stolen car. He had used this little tool several times to find his way to a kill. It tickled him that this supposed safety tool actually led to his mark's death.

He decided to pull his dark-colored vehicle off to the opposite side of the road in order for it to be cloaked by the small grove of trees. He chose a spot in between two large trees that practically buried his car in a mini forest of low-hanging willows and hundred-year-old oaks.

Anyone would be hard-pressed to see his car from the highway, if they were even looking for a car like his in particular. Gaius knew this type of camouflage would keep nosy drivers and locals from curiously wondering why a late-model sports car had stopped here, of all places. There were no watering or fishing holes, no caves to explore, no large amounts of indigenous creatures to gaze upon, so why would someone park here, if not for car trouble?

But then they might also ask why would there be another late-model sedan parked just a mile or so up the road from the coupe? And upon closer inspection, they might also surmise that both vehicles had license plate holders from different car rental companies. Perhaps they had a new local attraction that hadn't been discussed at the last town meeting?

Gaius cut the engine and stayed very still for a few moments. He didn't move inside the car, he didn't have the radio blaring, or the engine gunning. He never worried too much when a kill was out in the open like this. He knew, even in Europe, there would be no CCTV cameras poking their prying eyes into his business, and since he'd done all the requisite planning himself, not trusting an ounce of it to those who'd hired him, running scenario after scenario through his mind to diminish any chance of failure, he was, as usual, supremely confident.

He always knew, of course, that there was the *X factor*, the human factor. This was the eventuality that at some point, somehow, somewhere, someone would do something, come upon him or otherwise put a hitch in his well-thought out and executed plan. He would always account for the X factor, or red herrings, as he liked to call them after his favorite director, Alfred Hitchcock.

Gaius spent a few more minutes scanning the horizon for any movement. Nope, just the warm wind blowing through the tops of the trees. Turning, he slid his body until he lay halfway between the front seats and back compartment.

Since he was a consummate planner, Gaius always rented cars that had access to the trunk from the compartment behind the front seat. This way he could collect his work tool without anyone watching him pull it out or getting out of the car and head to the back of the vehicle and wonder at the long package that he would pull out of the trunk. Even out here in the middle of nowhere, he maintained his tradecraft. It just wouldn't do to get careless.

Though, he thought, at the end of the day, if anyone got too close or too nosy, or if he decided they looked like they were taking too much interest in either his vehicle or himself, they too might meet the same fate as the target he was tracking. If that, in fact, ended up being the case, well then that would just be a bonus for Gaius. He considered it spillage.

CHAPTER 10

"**9**11, WHAT'S YOUR EMERGENCY?" the operator asked in a calm voice answering the urgent call.

"Michael? Michael?" Callahan could be heard shouting with the receiver near him, but not up to his ear.

He had only one bar on his cell phone and had been trying to get a signal, WiFi, cellular, anything to try and get help to save his beloved grandson.

"Sir, are you there? Sir?" the operator interrupted.

Callahan realized the tinny sound that was impinging itself on his consciousness was in fact the phone. "It's my grandson! He fell over the cliff!"

Pinning the phone to his ear in an effort to bring the operator a little closer, Callahan crawled out a bit and over the point where Michael had fallen and looked down in a panic. It wasn't late, but the heavy clouds and shadows cast by the plateau itself combined to obscure anything below, yet Callahan was just able to see Michael about 30 feet below him, lying lifeless on a rocky outcropping.

"Oh thank God!" he whispered to himself.

"Sir, can you see him from where you are? Can you tell what kind of condition he is in?" the operator was pushing for information.

Callahan bit his lip hard to fight back tears. He wanted to scream in agony, but simultaneously he also knew he needed to compose himself in order to save the boy.

"He's about 25 or 30 feet below me. He fell off the cliff and landed hard, I think, but I didn't see how he landed. He's not moving, oh God!" he finally cried out.

"Sir, I need you to remain calm; he needs you right now, so call down to him and see if he responds, but before that, give me your location," the operator said in a soothing voice.

"We're way out on the top of some plateau about 85 miles north, northeast of Cheyenne between Wheatland and Fort Laramie off I-25," Callahan barked, retracing the map in his head.

Lying flat on the rough surface, he pushed his head further over the edge and called down as loudly as he could. "Michael? Michael?"

The operator broke in, but was careful not to upset Callahan any more than he was. She was typing in the information, correlating the location with the local districts that would need to be notified.

"That's good, Sir. Keep talking to him; let him know you're there."

Suddenly Callahan saw movement, the faintest of movements, but movement nonetheless.

"Michael! Michael! Can you hear me? It's Grandpa! Michael, don't move." Callahan called down, repeating himself, trying to convey a calm he certainly wasn't feeling. Tipping his head to try and hear more, Callahan could hear a groan turn into a whimper, then a scream.

"Ah, Ah!" Michael screamed from below.

This scream was even more terrifying to Callahan now than the fall, because it was the kind of sound he remembered making as a boy when he was truly hurt.

"Grandpa!" Michael cried.

"I'm here Michael! I'm just above you. Don't move! I'm calling for help; just don't move!" Callahan yelled, panicky.

"I think I broke my arm, Grandpa. It really hurts." Callahan let out a gasp of temporary relief as he prayed that was the only injury his young grandson had sustained.

"We'll get it all fixed up, Michael, I promise. Just don't move! You're close to the edge and I don't want you to fall any further."

He saw Michael raise his head slightly and look at his surroundings. That's when the screams and tears really came out.

"Grandpa! Help me!"

Once again the operator grabbed for his attention. "Sir, I've alerted local authorities and they will be coming to you soon. Please stay on the line with me. Can you do that for me?"

"Yes, yes, of course, I'll stay on the line!" Callahan barked impatiently. He needed to be dealing with his grandson right now.

"What is your name, Sir?"

Biting back a snarl and a sarcastic comment, Callahan realized this was not only informational, but a trick to keep him from any heroics.

"Tim Callahan. My grandson's name is Michael... please, is anyone coming yet?"

The operator knew how desperate the situation was, but what Callahan didn't know was that there were thunderstorms in the area and night was fast approaching. No one knew the extent the boy was injured and every second at this point counted, but that was the last thing she wanted Callahan to think about.

"Hang on, Michael! Help is on the way. I am here and I am talking to the 911 operator now. Try to breathe calmly; you know how to do that. I know it hurts right now, but the calmer you are, the less it will hurt. Can you do that for me?"

"What do you do, Sir? In case I need to call your office if we get disconnected," the operator said, attempting to take Callahan out of his own head.

Callahan looked at the phone incredulously. "Do? What do I do? I own a security company."

"Oh, my brother works as a security guard for a mall in Jackson Hole."

"Not that type of security. I'm the CEO of Callahan Security."

He began to explain the difference between a security guard company and a multibillion-dollar global security company when he caught himself and decided to stay on point.

"Listen, I have got to keep talking to my grandson. I won't hang up, but I really don't have time for chitchat right now. I know you are doing your job, but you need to know I won't do anything stupid. Also, if the rescue units are coming in from the road, I left my car on the side of the road with my visor down. They'll be able to spot it—it's a rental, a 2015 dark sedan… damn it! I can't remember what model it is, but it's a four-door for sure!"

Callahan could hear static, but not from any loss of cellular signal, but from the different radios the operator had at her end interfering with the call. He tried to think of anything else that could help.

"Wait! Wait! It has LoJak!" Callahan remembered he'd decided to pay extra for the LoJak since they would be in remote areas.

"You could *ping* my location. Call Buffalo Rentals in Cheyenne and give them my name. You'll be able to trilaterate the signal within 10 meters of the car."

"Yes, Sir, thank you. We will do that. Keep the line open if you can. I will let you alone. Try and keep Michael talking."

"Yes, yes, of course, I apologize for barking at you. Thank you for your help. Please let me know as soon as you know anything."

"Don't worry, Sir, help will be there soon." Down below, Michael moved his good arm and felt around the rocks and dirt becoming soft from the intermittent drops of rain. Not looking for anything in particular, but simply restless from the pain and anxiety, he almost flinched in surprise when his hand bumped something solid.

He slowly moved his fingers, then his hand over it, feeling along its cool length. It was his grandfather's rifle. Michael suddenly felt an overwhelming sense of pride. Pride that he hadn't lost his precious gift. Pride that he was able to save something that his grandfather valued so much.

He didn't really understand omens, but in a way, his boy's heart took the fact that the old rifle had survived this fall and so, it meant, that he too would survive. He would be okay.

Michael ran his fingers up and down the barrel of the gun, over the scope and down along the stock. The rifle had been damaged; Michael could feel that, maybe bashed by a rock or deeply gashed when it landed next to him. But all in all, it was intact, and that was all Michael needed to know. He closed his eyes and relaxed for the first time since waking up in pain.

CHAPTER 11

"SANDY LITTLE BEAR, GIT your ass moving… wheels up in 5!" Will Pierce barked over his walkie-talkie as he watched the color of the sky changing over his head.

The 911 Emergency Operator had patched her call to the sheriff's office and Will had already grabbed his pack, was out the door, and in his vehicle in seconds flat. He loved his down time, but he loved the action even more.

"Sandy Little Bear, do you copy?" Will sung out again. "You better not be sleep'n on the job again."

"Dang it, Will Pierce, I can hear ya, and I was copied by dispatch when the 911 came in! I've already started doing my flight plan and weather check and I'll be done in 30 seconds if you'd get off the line." The stern female voice came over his radio.

Will snickered hearing this. No one out here in Wyoming paid much attention to things that the State and County Human Resources Departments would cringe at: sexual harassment, using profanities when talking to coworkers or on broadcast frequencies or to other government employees, downright rudeness, just to name a few.

This was still the Wild West and not Will Pierce, or just about anyone else over the age of 40 in the remote areas of the plains, would ever be caught being politically correct. Everyone had their role to play and everyone seemed comfortable in playing their part, no matter what that part entailed.

It was a short drive to the airport. Will had already parked his vehicle and was heading to the hangar when he saw Sandy getting up from her desk and reattaching her walkie-talkie to the Velcro strap on her shoulder epaulet. She had just turned around and could see Will carrying his emergency pack and heading straight toward her office. She decided she'd jump up to intercept him.

"You know Sheriff, you're gonna have HR back in your office for more sensitivity training again if they hear the way you were talking over the radio."

Will just shrugged as he tugged his pack up over his shoulder.

"You know you can't say things like 'ass' over the airways, don't you?"

Will was no longer the easygoing Podunk lawman he played most of his days of late; he was in work mode now. He was all business during business hours, and an injured boy that had fallen off a cliff in these parts is serious business.

"Why don't I hear those props spinning, Sandy?" Will barked.

Sandy shot him a look while she quickly ran through her preflight checklist one last time to ensure she hadn't missed or forgotten to account for something.

"Aren't you Lakota Sioux supposed to have the ability to see these kinds of things coming? Hell, all you have to do is just look up at the sky and see it."

Will marched into the hangar and looked around with a hard expression on his face for something. Whatever it was, it was supposed to be there, but it wasn't.

"Sandy?!" Will called out hard in an angry tone as he continued to search.

Sandy stopped what she was doing and put up her hands in front of Will as if to deflect something. She knew he wasn't going to be happy.

"I was gonna tell you, Sheriff. Richey had to take the Life flight chopper out to Medicine Bow for the scheduled repairs. I could almost predict we would get a call like this; we always have an emergency when one of the machines is off for maintenance."

Will began to squint.

She beat him to it. "I sent your office an email about it last week and made sure I copied you on it."

She knew the situation was critical and every moment could mean life or death. She wasn't about to make any excuses, because none of that would matter if the young injured boy on that mountain wasn't able to be rescued.

"Come on, let's roll. We're gonna have to fly out to them in the Rotorway."

Will had turned to follow Sandy back to the other side of the hangar, but his long stride stuttered when he looked across the tarmac at the small helicopter the young pilot was climbing into.

Sandy had clambered into the chopper from the left side door and pulled her headset on before Will could finish shoving his pack in the narrow space behind the seat. Will pushed his way into the seat, though not as quickly, as his frame was long and his shoulders wide, not the perfect occupant for a small helicopter.

"Radio check," Sandy spoke into the microphone.

Sandy began to flip switches and tap onboard dials as all the lights in the cab lit up like Christmas in Boston Harbor. The propellers began to spin slowly, then eventually started *whomping* with ferocity and downdraft that would give it the perfect lift.

"You're clear for takeoff," said a voice in her headset. "No traffic from here to your vector."

"Copy that, tower!"

Sandy turned toward the light in the observation control tower off her left shoulder and gave a thumbs up.

Will was still fumbling with his cross seat belt as it had been tangled by the last passenger. Will was becoming frustrated.

"How do you work this dang thing?"

"Just flatten the belt on your chest first, then you see where the tangle is. Worst case, just buckle it up tangled, it's not really gonna matter that much if we have to ditch." Sandy smirked.

"That's reassuring," Will mumbled.

"Okay tower, we're taking off," Sandy said as she pulled the large joystick toward her and the helicopter lifted quickly into the air that would soon become turbulent.

Managing to subdue the straps that seemed to have taken on a life of their own, Will adjusted the mic at his mouth. "Little Bear, this is a damn two-seater! We got an injured boy and an old man! How in the hell are we gonna be able to transport them in this tiny piece of…?"

"Well, I've been thinking about that, Sheriff," Sandy said sheepishly, as she piloted the light craft forward to their destination. "I've got an idea how we can save that boy, but I am pretty sure you are not going to like it. Not one little bit."

CHAPTER 12

THANKFULLY, CALLAHAN HAD COME prepared.

He always carried more than his fair share of penlights and Xenon flashlights with keychain clips and necklace ties, as he'd accumulated dozens of them over the years. He had also brought water and food to last at least one night, but he needed a way to somehow get them down to Michael, a problem he had yet to solve.

Continuing to carry on his mostly one-sided conversation with Michael, he pummeled his brain for ideas. Pulling his and Michael's backpacks over closer, he simply dumped them out in front of him.

"I am trying to find something to tie onto the water bottles so I can send them down to you!" he called as his fingers scrambled through what had been a neatly packed pile. "You know how important it is to stay hydrated when you are injured. Remember that course we took out in California?"

He dug through the miscellaneous gear bag, hard and furiously, and suddenly his fingers felt the braided cord. Grinning, he pulled it out. Must be losing his mind; he should have remembered he had that in there.

"Yeah, I remember," Michael answered, his voice just barely making it up over the edge.

Callahan had insisted the boy make an effort to answer him as much as he could. He knew it would not only give the youngster's mind something to focus on, it would also give Callahan a handle on how Michael was doing.

Boom. A deafening crack of thunder erupted in the distance. Callahan raced to untangle the rope, realizing the situation was becoming direr. The clouds above them had already begun to thicken and congeal and were beginning to pound each other as the darkness closed in around the mesa.

Boom. The second clap echoed across the valley. This time, it was so loud and forceful it aroused Michael, who had lapsed into silence.

"Grandpa? Grandpa, help me!" Michael shouted at the sudden terror he was feeling. He was getting restless from the pain and the awkwardness of his position. He shifted slightly to try and gain some small measure of relief and only jarred his damaged body into louder protest.

Callahan could hear his shouts, and it broke his heart, but he knew he had to concentrate and finish what he was doing if there would be any chance of saving him.

"It's okay, Michael. It's only thunder making all that noise," Callahan said loudly as he was almost finished tying the rope to a water bottle. "It looks like a storm is coming and we might get a little rain, but we're gonna be okay."

"Grandpa, I'm scared!" Michael shouted up this time a little weaker than he'd sounded before. This worried Callahan as he still didn't know the extent of Michael's injuries.

"Just hang on buddy, and don't move! I'm gonna lower some water down to you!" Callahan called down to the boy, keeping aware that his voice could easily reveal his fear, which was the last thing his grandson needed to hear.

"Sit tight and don't be scared! I'm not going anywhere. We're in this together and someone will be here soon to help," Callahan continued.

He listened hard as the wind began to blow and he wasn't quite sure if he'd be able to hear Michael as easily now, but he wasn't going to waste a single second worrying about that as he had bigger problems at hand. He began to slowly, carefully finalize the small pack he would send down.

After a moment, Michael called back to his grandfather. "Okay, Grandpa!"

Michael was whimpering now and Callahan knew he was in great pain, but was trying to be brave and not show any cowardice in the presence of his hero. This was eating away at him, as he knew he could probably never have been as strong as his own young grandson.

He quickly untangled the last bit of rope and realized it was too thin to lower himself down or to pull him up. He quickly emptied the pack and found a small waterproof pouch. He scooped up two plastic bottles of water and some protein bars, shoved them into the satchel, and tied it closed.

He made a fast knot by tying one end of the rope to the top and making sure it was secure. He then lifted the sack up and bounced it a bit to check the weight, just like he used to do in Lebanon to check the weight of rocks with his two best friends before skipping them across the water.

It felt perfect, not so light that the wind would knock it against the rocky cliff and not too heavy that Michael would get hurt if it hit him.

"Don't move, Michael. I'm going to lower the pack down to you and you're gonna feel it on the back of your legs in a minute when it comes down. Just let the pack land gently on your legs, then slowly, carefully reach behind you with your good arm and slowly pull it over the backside of your back."

With that, Callahan slowly dropped the pack at the end of the length of rope and just before he got to Michael's legs, he swung the satchel ever so slightly like a pendulum so it would land perfectly on his butt cheek or in the small space between his legs.

He knew a boy Michael's age was still limber enough to reach behind and grab something with barely moving and he could only hope Michael's back wasn't broken or some other injury that would prevent him from getting the much-needed and life-saving water.

Michael's leg twitched when he felt the pack land on the backside of his thigh. Perfect. Michael let out a slight gasp at the contact, but more out of fear than anything else. He slowly reached around with his good arm as his grandfather had instructed him to do and retrieved it.

"Ow!" Michael cried out. His body shifted slightly at the weight of the pack, moving his body, and with it, his broken arm. This time Michael couldn't hold back the tears.

"Grandpa!"

The cries hit Callahan like an arrow into his heart. He stood up with a jolt of adrenaline and, contrary to everything he knew and felt, he was going to save his injured grandson by whatever means possible… or die trying!

He quickly turned around to look for tools or straps or anything they'd either brought with them or that could be found in nature to help him either get to Michael or pull him back up.

Alas, nothing. Callahan's heart sank as he started to lose hope. Just then, he suddenly heard the prop of the helicopter propellers.

CHAPTER 13

IT MAY HAVE LOOKED like the village was just barely kissing the shores of Lake Geneva, if you happened to be lazing on the top deck of a yacht or perhaps a small sailboat, yet either way, you couldn't help but admire the beautiful snow-capped Alps that loomed skyward at the foot of its enormous European mountainous base.

Montreux, the tiny resort town known more for its music festivals and as a weekend getaway for the rich and famous than for anything else, was really just a quiet hamlet, seemingly encased in history.

Chateau de Chillon, the 13th-century island castle, sat just offshore and belle époque buildings rose up through the narrow cobblestone alleys and walkways, giving the impression to any tourist that they'd been transported hundreds of years into the past.

The Riviera-Pays-d-Enhaut municipality was in the Canton of Vaud, one of the most beautifully sculpted and scenic parts of all Switzerland. The Alps had naturally wrapped themselves around and above it, as if cradling it from harm. People from around the globe were drawn to the wondrous place.

And, as typical Swiss fashion dictated, any tourist coming into this utopia would need to arm themselves with at least a working knowledge of

French, German, and Italian to converse with the locals. English would be tolerated, but only after the requisite three attempts were made to appease the longstanding residents in their own tongue.

"Oui!" said Callahan. He gestured to direct the chocolatier toward the other side of the glass case filled with assorted chocolates and tempting sweets.

The storefront was beautifully designed and immaculately sparkly and was lit up to enhance the endless options that would drive any sweet tooth into a diabetic coma.

The yellow and white lights inside and out reflected the warmth and color of the freshly baked confections, some topped with fresh fruit, others with crème, or some sort of exotic and secretive special Swiss recipe.

Callahan had been strolling down the pristine walkway on his way toward the lake when he was magically pulled toward, and then into, the small shop. The miraculous essences wafting from the little shop grasped him by his nose; scents so mysterious and so glorious, resistance was futile.

He looked up to see the sign and guessed that this quaint confectionary had probably been family owned for generations. As he pushed the glass door open, he was assailed with the full scope of aromas from Heaven. Smiling to himself, he imagined the bouquet of smells were the first foray in some sort of diabolical plan. It must have been created by the shop owners to draw prey in from the street before assaulting them with the magnificence of the pastries and chocolates. Artistically lighted to further work their evil wiles upon hapless consumers, the racks of decadent sweets and savories laid in wait, content in the knowledge that none could resist their siren call. They would lure every tourist in to spend their francs, gelt, yen, and dollars to satisfaction. Then, their plan would be complete. Callahan knew himself to be powerless in the face of such genius evil gastro manipulation.

"No, Monsieur, cinq Java, cinq Bolive, un, quarte cacao, s'il vous plait!" he said in his best French.

French that was surprisingly good for an… American, the candy maker guessed.

"Oui, Monsieur!" the chef responded, his tone cheerful and welcoming.

Having dealt with tourists in his town since he was tall enough to wear the long apron without tripping, the confectionary chef deduced the man in front of him was most likely from the United States, yet he had probably lived in France or another French-speaking country for many years. It was for this reason, and therefore nearly his duty to respond in kind, as Callahan was due the respect any Frenchman would give another on an egalitarian basis.

The chef liked that most of the Americans he had met on his trips abroad or during their visits to Montreux seemed to have had spent a good deal of effort to learn his language before arriving in his humble village. He always appreciated the effort, even though he himself spoke five languages fluently.

Pulling one of these languages out now for the comfort of his guest, he folded a sturdy box, preparing to insert the magical tasty treats. "These are for your wife, yes?"

Callahan smiled his appreciation; he knew the chocolatier had recognized that the French he had used was rusty and would probably be broken up after his next question, so he played along so as not to embarrass himself any further.

"Yes and no," he acknowledged ruefully. "They are for my wife and myself."

"Bravo, Monsieur, you know your chocolate and its usefulness when dealing with our lovely ladies."

The man carefully placed the remainder of the sweets onto a piece of wax paper. He then brought the entire sheet up and lowered it into a beautifully crafted box.

He finished the gift-wrapping by tying a single tiny red bow around it, carefully inspecting to make sure there were no blemishes or mars on the box. He then made a handle out of the remainder of the lace so that Callahan could easily carry it with him back to the United States.

"Vingt-cinq francs, Monsieur," the chocolatier said as he walked to the register and began to ring up Callahan's order. He pressed down hard onto the embossed keys of the huge brass antique cash register. Highly polished, it too had probably been in the family for generations, Callahan thought, imagining this same mature chef as a child, being allowed to polish the keys and carefully wipe down the brass.

It was this kind of historical relic, like most of the antiquities around here that he loved so much. He cherished the knowledge that there were still places on this Earth that believed in the old ways.

Callahan reached into his trouser pocket, realizing he didn't have the requisite 25 Swiss francs that would normally suffice; he only had larger 20 and 10-franc notes. He had no coins, nor smaller bills to give to the man, so he merely handed him 30 francs instead.

The chef smiled, took the Swiss francs and buried them in the bottom of the register for safekeeping, then he retrieved something from the drawer and handed him his change.

Callahan knew the transaction was completed, as the chef was summoned away by the quiet ding of a bell signaling some new exquisite treat was ready for his expert touch. With a cheerful wave, the chef returned to his display table to finish yet another handcrafted work of edible art.

Glancing at his watch, he suddenly realized he was running late for his meeting. He exited the confectionary as the tiny bells above the door sounded. He began to walk at a brisk pace, not just because he was tardy, but because the cold air in Switzerland tended to creep into his joints and the places he had injured himself when he was a younger man.

Hoofing it out across the square, he headed toward the park area, but not before passing and admiring the statues of both Freddie Mercury and B.B. King. Callahan had remembered that this little slice of Heaven was unlike many countries in that it honored its artists, and in turn, the artists went out of their way to return the honor.

For instance, he thought, it was no secret, yet still not widely known that when the rock band Deep Purple was recording their Machine Head album in 1971, a crazed Frank Zappa fan brandishing then shooting off a flare gun with a live incendiary round accidently burned down the famous Montreux Casino where the band was supposed to record the album.

The group was so affected by this wild and unforeseen event that they came up with their titular hit song, Smoke On the Water to honor their new favorite home away from home. Deep Purple would subsequently return years later to record another album there, as would many groups after them.

Callahan was nostalgic in that way and would often return to what he called his memory palace to recall and relive such events. .Yet that luxury was a momentary exercise, as he wasn't there in Switzerland now as merely a tourist; he had much more important work to do.

He, like his friends, was a precise man, and therefore knew how the others would have travelled and made their way to their destination. Without having to ever confirm whether he was right or wrong, Callahan figured that his friend Robert Miller had probably shacked up for the night somewhere near Montreux, probably in her sister town of Wiesbaden, West Germany, which wasn't very far away.

He further supposed that Miller had spent the past few nights there to shake any tails and avoid any prying eyes and would take train after train to finally reach a small town as to not arouse suspicion from border guards or nosy Krauts, as they often called them, especially the East Germans at the time.

And although the war had long been over, there were still plenty of nervous Europeans, not to mention Communists, and any one of them at any time could or would have misinterpreted his actions as being anything less than honorable.

Nassar Khumari, in turn, would have hired a discreet driver to take him by a small, inconspicuous Vauxhall or Renault from somewhere like Menton, France. They would pass unmolested, hopefully, through the border checkpoint and make it to their next destination.

Perhaps they had even posed as travelling buddies from the West, just in for the day to catch a rock concert or to meander around one of the many beautiful gardens this part of the world had to offer.

Nassar would have planned the trip down to the rust patches on the bumpers and would probably even make a few scrapes and dents and mud splotches on the windows to avoid any extra interest in the vehicle.

The three boyhood friends knew that by flying in and out of different countries, separately, and on different schedules, any government agency at that time would be waylaid, as Montreux was strictly a rock concert venue and gamblers' paradise for the rich and depraved.

Those governments relied on the kickbacks, bribes, and payoffs from their neighbor, so they knew better than to hassle too many Westerners, as Nassar and his driver knew not to call any unneeded attention to themselves.

As Callahan hustled up the stairs of the Territet, he suddenly noticed a man coming down and wasn't quite sure of his intentions, so he decided to throw the man off guard in case he were there in a clandestine manner. Callahan looked him straight in the eyes, then nodded.

"Wie geht's?" Callahan said in flawless German, with just a touch of Bavarian to throw off suspicions.

"Hallo!" the man replied, thinking him a kinsman, yet more modern and refined.

Callahan pushed the brass bar on the revolving door meant to keep the heat in and the cold at bay and pushed hard with his body to accelerate the motion. He admired the brass and double-paned glass that was virtually without flaw.

He refused to make eye contact and slipped his way past the concierge as that man never stopped talking and seemed so impressed with himself that he scarcely heard the needs of the other hotel guests. This guy was just a nuisance and more trouble than he was worth.

Callahan crossed the marbled-floor foyer and made a right around the large pilaster, one of many that filled the first floor of this ancient manor.

He barely had a second to smell the sweetness of the fresh flowers that bulged from the numerous vases in the lobby, as he was on a mission, and he didn't want to be any later than he already was.

It was still early, not yet dusk and too early for dinner, at least for the Europeans, so he knew the lounge would be relatively empty. It was the perfect place to meet up with his comrades and he suspected they had already started without him.

"Ca va?" Callahan said to the man cleaning a glass behind the bar.

Henri had always been his favorite bartender and he spent many an evening being entertained by the Frenchman. But, as it was, he had already marched on in and had no time at the moment to relive past pleasures.

Callahan's French wasn't as pure as it used to be, Henri thought, but one good thing about Americans is that they are filled with confidence, and therefore not afraid to attempt to speak a language, flaws and all. A Frenchman appreciated a foreigner's respect for his language.

Callahan had known Henri for decades, and as such, had earned the right to drop the "comment" as it would have been too formal for the friendly mixologist he had come to know through the years.

"Ca va, tres bien!" Henri responded as he began to dry a premium bottle of Russian vodka.

Henri raised his chin slightly to direct Callahan's eyes to a table in the back of the room in a shadowy corner past the dance floor. Callahan nodded in response and raised his right hand, extending only his thumb and two index fingers. This was deliberate on Callahan's part, the signal for three of something being delivered in the man's native language, so to speak. It took small efforts to make people comfortable, and he had learned early in his career that he was actually good at feeling out just what small things worked the best and how to use them to his advantage.

In addition, it threw off the eye of anyone watching for an American, as Callahan had made this motion in the German manner. He hardly noticed this type of thing; it was so ingrained into his behavior when he was travelling like this. But, many little things added up to a person's subconscious assumptions, and to waylay any suspicions about roving Americans from any local prying eyes that may have followed the men into the hotel took only the effort of a little tradecraft.

"Tres!" he mouthed.

But Henri was way ahead of him and was merely waiting for the last piece of the puzzle to appear before bringing the drinks to a darkened table at the back of the lounge where two men were sitting.

Callahan approached the table and quickly unbuttoned his fur-lined trench coat. He peeled it off and threw it onto the back of the booth. There in front of him were Nassar and Miller looking up and smiling back at him.

"My old friends!" Callahan beamed.

"I hope your trip was uneventful," Nassar said, smiling at his old friend.

"Any trouble?" Miller asked. It was something that Miller was known for, always asking it as his lead question. They were all naturally suspicious, especially in their respective lines of work, but Miller seemed more so than the others.

Callahan just shook his head from side to side, smiling at his predictable old friend.

"Al es clar, der Commissar!" Callahan joked in his best German.

Miller and Nassar rose to greet their old friend as they wrapped each other in bear hugs, no different than they had done as boys. Henri had just sidled up and was careful to slip in behind the men and carefully place the significantly large drinks onto the table.

Henri smiled at the camaraderie, the type of friendship and loyalty he had not seen since he was a boy back in his rural village in France.

At once, they reached for the drinks and raised them to each other in silent camaraderie. Callahan took the moment to really look at both of his friends. He could still see the boys they had been, and for a moment their age almost startled him. The rims of the heavy crystal glasses rang together and they swallowed a long drink. With a shake of his head, Callahan put his thoughts back on track and pulled a chair out to get comfortable.

"Okay, enough slobbering, gentlemen," he gestured that they retake their seats. "We have important work to do." Callahan took a moment to look at both these men, his oldest and dearest friends.

Nassar reached down and retrieved a custom briefcase, plopping it down on the seat next to him and snapping the two side latches open to reveal an unusual-looking monoscope.

"This, gentlemen, is the new X1000 Photo Scope—a creation we have talked about for years and now have as a new arrow in our quiver."

Intrigued, Miller immediately picked up the scope to take a closer look and inspect every inch of it.

"You say that you have tested this thing up to 1,000 yards and we can still develop high-resolution photos from the negatives?"

"That's right, and the three negatives can only be developed in our labs, by our own unique process. If anyone else tries to give them a stop bath or develop the photos using standard acids or agents, it will dissolve instantly."

"Good, we need that insurance policy."

"So now we have the clip that will only hold three rounds and the recoil causes the camera to take the picture."

Callahan sat back in his chair. "As we've agreed, this photo scope will be used to primarily test each other's security. It will prove that one of our members has compromised the security of another firm. In addition, I propose we go ahead and form the Kill and Release Hunt Club. From these shooters, we'll recruit our prospective shooters."

Miller interrupted. "We are going to have to fund this sufficiently to attract the best hunters."

Nassar picked up the scope from the table and turned it over. "We can have our respective office staffs and lawyers work out the details and start the promotion of the public part of this, but of course, the part where we recruit the winning shooters for our own services, we'll keep that part to ourselves."

CHAPTER 14

EVEN WITH THE SEAT belts, Will was being tossed about enough to thump his head lightly against the side window of the small helicopter, as the Rotorway fought its way through the turbulence toward the needed rescue.

"Can't you keep this thing steady?!" Will barked, rubbing his sore noggin.

He pulled the microphone attached to his headset closer to his mouth and shouted into it again. Sandy Little Bear was too busy to listen to Will's complaints, as she had her hands full trying to control the stick. The wicked crosswinds that were preceding the storm kept tossing and turning the helicopter like a kite in a hurricane.

She did her best to level out and steady the copter by finding calmer air through the patches of cloudless air while simultaneously checking her scope for any changes.

"We're in for a rough ride!" She didn't answer his complaints. "Double check your belt."

"We are ALREADY on a rough ride!" Will gave her a look as if she were kidding that it was going to get worse.

Sandy had a close friend at the National Oceanic Atmospheric

Administration and was talking to him on the other line, still cognizant never to lose contact with her own tower feeding her weather updates as well.

"Hey Nick, it's Sandy Little Bear!" Sandy shouted into her mic.

"Go ahead, Sandy!" A voice echoed in both Sandy's and Will's headsets.

"I'm with Sheriff Pierce, flying a Rotorway on a Search and Rescue. Can you give me the NOAA Doppler updates for Grid 471? It's getting pretty choppy up here!" Sandy relayed.

"Copy that, Sandy. Running it now."

With nothing else to do, Will decided to reposition the external flood lights in an attempt to find landmarks to gauge their position. But it seemed a fool's errand, as at that point the strobe was merely lighting up the vast, roiling darkness and reflecting off the dense clouds below them.

"Wow, it must be pretty choppy up there, Sandy!" the voice continued. "You won't believe the numbers I am getting here."

"Surprisingly, I would have no difficulty at all believing pretty much anything you have to tell me, Nick," Sandy continued, still monitoring the gauges as she juggled the stick and the twin lines of communication.

No wonder she was ignoring him, Will grinned.

"Well, according to this, you have some whiz bang storm clouds building up, certainly some heavy rain heading your way, probably some hail. Have to pray we don't actually get a tornado out of this one. Are you really flying in this?!" her friend's incredulous exclamation came over the speaker loud and clear.

Sandy nearly laughed, then gave Will a look, and they momentarily shared a smile.

"Anyway, Sandy, yeah, you're in for a whopper. I suggest you drop below the deck and bring the rails down."

"Negative, Nick, I've got an injured child that fell off the ledge on Eagle's View Plateau and his elderly grandfather. I've got no choice right now, so I have to follow this one through to the end."

"Roger that, Sandy. In that, case, head upstream into the headwind, then come in on the downdraft. Try and position yourself just above the plateau and sink slowly, cuz that wind is gonna pummel you like a tsunami crashing over your head once you start descending the cliff face."

"Copy that, Nick!" Sandy said, with the slightest tension in her voice. "I'm lucky I've got Will here with me as my lifeguard," she chuckled.

"Well, I'm smart enough not to try and convince you to turn around since there are lives at stake, so try and stay above the deck at least 5,000 feet since the big thunder boomers are just below that until you get above Eagle's View."

"Roger that."

"We're also showing super conductivity in the thunderstorms all around Grid 471. One piece of good news. If I have your flight numbers correct, you're going to get a small window of opportunity that will open up just about the same time you'll be hovering over the mountain, but you won't have a whole lot of time."

"Copy that."

"I'd advise you to come in from the north, northwest and drop down into it. That's your best chance of not hitting the really bad wind and hail."

"Thanks, Nick, I'm going to let Control take it over from here… you're the best! I'm buying the beer next time I'm up your way!"

"You got it, San…" suddenly the voice cut out and static interrupted the communication.

Will gave Sandy another look, this one more of a smirk as they were both in the soup now. He continued to search into the darkness to try and find something recognizable with the enormous light.

Sandy had lobbied hard for the new Devore Search and Rescue LED floodlights, which were pricey and normally reserved for larger Life flights. But because Sandy's emergency rescue team would be forced to occasionally use the two-seater Rotorway, she was able to get the requisite funding by lobbying both Homeland and the county oversight board to approve the system and have it installed in the smaller aircraft and the larger bird.

Sandy Little Bear was no novice, either at bureaucratic politics or flying tough missions. She had already completed three tours in two wars in both a Sikorsky HH-60 Pave Hawk as well as an S-70.

She had been flying search and rescue missions while still in her teens while her friends went to rave parties and got drunk every night in college. Sandy had survived some of the worst humanity had to throw at her and normally had nerves of steel, especially since the weather in Wyoming was so unpredictable and serious. But this flight gave her more than a few butterflies in her stomach.

"Okay Will, here's what I'd like to see happen," Sandy said into her headset, turning to face him.

Sandy, like Will, was all business when the time came and she was in combat mode now. And although Will didn't do well these days taking orders, since he was so used to giving them, he knew she was far more experienced than he at matters of search and rescue. He knew he would have to acquiesce… no matter how much he wasn't going to like it.

"Since we only have room for one passenger, it looks like you drew the short straw unless you somehow learned to fly a helicopter since we last talked," she said, half seriously.

"Really, Sandy, did you think I hadn't figured that one out already?" Will gave her a half-snide look.

"Well, that's not all," Sandy continued.

This was more to appease her sense of a safety check as well as the recordings at the other end of their headsets that kept records of every word spoken on each and every flight.

"I don't know yet if I'm going to just drop you at the top of Eagle's View or if you're gonna have to put on the harness and be lowered by the cable."

"In this wind, are ya crazy?" Will snapped.

"I'll take my chances rock climbing down from the top, thank you very much. Besides, the way you're flying, I doubt you'd qualify to drive a county school bus."

Will turned toward the window as he chuckled, not just because he actually made himself laugh with that last one, but the nervous energy he was now feeling caused a blast of adrenaline to his brain and he was feeling it.

Sandy didn't take offense, as she had always been one of the guys, especially in tense situations, as such, she was always allowed into the men's secret society of sarcasm. She knew Will was just saying goodbye in case anything was about to go south on them.

The green blip that they had been following on her screen was centering itself up ahead. They were coming upon their target: Eagle's View Plateau.

Sandy brought the stick back and to the right in an attempt to gain the higher ground into the headwind. She fought and pulled and the helicopter barely responded. It was ferociously choppy and the blasts of wind shear jostled them around like turbulence on a transatlantic flight.

Will quickly repositioned the flood lights as Sandy fought the heat rising up from the valley floor colliding with the cold air aloft to rise above the mountain and get into position.

She came about, bringing the helicopter right and settled into a small nook of calmer air, as rain suddenly began to pound the windshield. By now, all traces of daylight were disappearing under the mounting weather and the storm clouds overhead seemed to smother the helicopter, and with it, any chance of seeing the storm let up soon.

"We don't have much time, Will. It'll be hailing like hell any minute now and I know how hard-headed you can be, but this storm looks like it's gonna be a doozy!" Sandy shouted as the noise from the prop and the rain pummeled the cabin, making it nearly impossible to hear each other speaking.

Will snatched up his pack and unzipped it quickly. Inside, he pawed his way through bottles of water, vacuum-packed food, plastic rain ponchos, tarps, and carabineers, finally grasping what his fingers were searching for.

"I've got about 200 feet of rope," Will said as though he were counting inventory.

"Good, 'cause I don't know how far down he fell and the cable may be too heavy alone."

Sandy peered through the rain as the floodlights began to illuminate the top of the plateau. Suddenly, she could just make out a figure moving in the half-darkness. It was Callahan. He was jumping up and down, waving his arms as the rain battered him.

Cold, exhausted, and beside himself with excitement and terror, Callahan was trying to signal, pointing down the northwest face of the cliff. Sandy nodded her head, even though she knew Callahan couldn't see her. Still, she craned forward against the restraining straps as she tried to follow the light Will was playing over the ground below them.

"Target acquired!" Sandy blurted. "We have contact! I see the boy!" Will followed Sandy's finger and saw Michael lying face down on the rocky outcropping.

"Yep, I see him, and I don't like the way his body is positioned!" Will shouted. "Looks like I'm rappelling; just pray I can find something to tie off to."

"Negative, Sheriff, I'll go high and lower the cable down for you." Will gave Sandy another one of his famous looks of scorn.

"Are you nuts? What do you think comes after torrential rain and then hail…? Lightning, that's what!"

Sandy grimaced, knowing full well Will was right, but she didn't like the option he was proposing.

"I'm not planning on becoming a barbecued chicken wing for dinner if you lower me down on that lightning rod of a cable," Will laughed. He had already undone his safety harness and was trying to hang on and pull his pack forward.

Sandy gritted her teeth, as she knew Will was right, but didn't want a man of his age taking a risk like that, especially as she was the only one in that helicopter that had been specifically trained for just this type of emergency.

Having successfully pulled the pack onto his lap, Will dug out the climbing harness and squirmed into it.

"You and your women's lib," Will laughed at her expression and decided to poke at her some more, just for the fun of it. "Do you think I'm gonna let some Lakota squaw get all the glory for this rescue? Drop me off at the top and I'll have the old man help me get into position."

With that, Sandy maneuvered the helicopter around, giving it some lift through the chop, and bringing it back into the position where she had first seen Callahan.

By dint of years of experience and a bit of luck in getting a slight let up in the gusts for just an instant, she manipulated the helicopter over a flat part of the plateau and lowered it until the rails were just a few feet off the top of the ground. She knew this would allow Will to safely jump from that height. She also knew that one bad gust and they'd both need to be rescued.

"Radio check," Will said into his walkie-talkie.

Sandy nodded her response. He had already set both walkie-talkies to their emergency frequency, channel 9, and to the emergency channel dispatch, so the tower, the hospital, and anyone else concerned would hear everything he transmitted.

"Squaw, my butt, Will Pierce!" Sandy yelled back with a smile at Will.

Will turned the latch to the large helicopter door and pushed hard against it. Just then, the pressure vacuum yanked the helicopter door open, nearly pulling his arm off in the process as he fought to hold on.

Meanwhile, the prop wash forced Callahan to nearly flatten himself out onto the ground. He had started approaching the helicopter rails, then realized he'd have to back off. Nature quickly decided for him to keep low to the ground and merely await Will's arrival.

"I'm going to tie off somewhere up here and have that guy brace the rope," Will continued.

Sandy nodded.

"I'll assess the boy's injuries to see how bad he is and try not to break him up any more than he probably is when I slip the harness on him."

Will leapt out of the copter into the blackness of the storm, turning back to yell up to her.

"When I give you the signal, lower the cable and I'll hook him up." Pointing behind him to Callahan, he shouted, "Bring the copter back up here and he can load him into my seat. His grandfather and I can wait out the storm up here until you can get back and pick us up!"

Sandy was a little concerned now. She knew Will was no spring chicken and that this would probably be a taxing proposition for the veteran.

"Will Pierce, you best be careful or I'm gonna…!" Sandy shouted.

Will slammed the door hard and fast before she could finish. Will knew what Sandy was saying, but he hated the sound of a woman's voice when she was worried about him and would rather complain and nag than actually tell him her true feelings.

Will moved forward toward Callahan as the helicopter bounded up and banked over the plateau. If Will didn't know better, he'd thought Sandy was a goner as it looked like the downdraft had pummeled the aircraft down the thousands of feet off the top to the valley floor.

"Hi, I'm Will Pierce!" Will shouted. "I'm here to get your grandson back to safety!" Will had to yell even louder to make sure Callahan could hear him over the howling wind and rain, as he approached Callahan and extended his hand.

"Tim Callahan. Sheriff, he's over here!" Callahan guided him to the edge, the relief obvious in his voice. "Hurry, please! He's been down there for hours."

Will took out what looked to be a modified Maglite and searched the ground at the edge of the cliff. He strafed the growing darkness, moving the flashlight back and forth trying to capture some kind of outcropping or jagged rock with his eyes that could support his weight.

"He's down this way!" Callahan shouted, as he wondered why Will was lagging behind.

"I've got to find a perch for the rope. It needs to be strong, so it can hold my weight!" Will shouted.

"You? What do you mean, you? I thought the helicopter would lower down the cable," said Callahan worriedly.

Will finally saw something dark, wet, and solid. It was a chunk of craggy rock, jutting from the ground, just barely enough rock to wrap the rope around maybe twice, but he'd be damned if he wasn't going to do it anyway.

As Callahan ran on, Will knelt down on the hard surface and began to dig a small trough around the rock. He checked its strength and attempted to get more of a base. It looked good, initially, so he was able to wrap the rope around the stone twice, with a bit of it crossing over the top.

"You're not serious, are you? We're about the same age!" Callahan shouted at Will, who was motioning him to come closer.

"Put your foot here, one aside the rope, the other on top of the rock."

Giving up on his half-hearted efforts to talk Will out of his plan, Callahan followed Will's instructions to the letter, knowing it was his grandson's only chance.

"You're gonna wanna lean back and I'll pass the rope around your waist. You're not gonna be pulling or pushing me, but I gotta know that rope is taut and secure," Will instructed, giving a quick nod to ensure that Callahan understood everything he was saying.

Callahan nodded and did exactly as Will had told him. He passed the rope around Callahan's waist, handing him slack from the secured end. He then wrapped the rope through his rescue harness and checked that the vest was set.

Will then took another, smaller flashlight and attached it above where he had tied himself off. He knew this was a critical piece of equipment.

He handed Callahan his large flashlight, threw his pack over his shoulder, and without even a nod, walked to the edge of the cliff and began scaling downward. He disappeared as quickly as he'd arrived.

Will's footing was good, but he worried the rain would really begin to give him problems the further down he got. Just then, his boots began to slip, as if on cue. He pushed on the rocks harder in an attempt to gain more traction. He knew he was still 10-15 feet above the boy.

"Mother Grabber!" Will spat as he lost his footing again. He quickly regained it and righted himself.

Sandy was now also just above him and the propeller was just a few feet from the cliff side, which wasn't helping Will's prospects at all. He was grinning anyway. After all, it wasn't like this was some dumb video game that he could turn off and put down. He had to get this done; not just for the boy now, but for himself as well.

Will had no idea, but he was actually making amazing time, even though he looked like a drowned monkey, soaked head to toe from the storm.

He glanced down the side of the wall and realized he was now just above Michael, so he gingerly swung his body a few degrees to the side so his size 11 cowboy boots didn't land on the poor kid's head.

Will landed hard, tweaking his ankle in the process, but he couldn't be bothered with that now. It was about that time that Michael could now feel someone's presence behind him and called out.

"Help! I need help!" Michael cried, a cry he had been holding in for hours and really needed to let out.

"I know Son. I'm here to help you," Will said with the calm of an old nanny. "How bad are ya hurt, can ya move?"

With that, Michael slowly twisted his body as if to try and get up, then slid his bad arm against the ground.

"Ah!" Michael yelled in pain. "I'm pretty sure my arm's broken, Sir."

Will could see his arm was definitely broken in at least one place, but was more worried that the boy's back might be broken, too.

"Okay, wiggle your fingers and toes. Good. Now, slowly move your legs and the arm that ain't broke."

Will watched the boy's movements carefully to try and assess the damage.

"Good. You're doing great! Now, where else does it hurt?"

Will knelt down to stabilize Michael, but was careful not to touch his body.

"My back, it hurts a lot, but I think I just got the wind knocked out of me," Michael said bravely.

Just then, Will's walkie-talkie crackled to life.

"Will, we gotta move!" Sandy shouted from the helicopter above. "We're losing the window and that front is nearly on us. I'm afraid this bird might start cavitating in this deluge," Sandy continued.

Will looked up and gave her his signature sneer, not that it did any good. She couldn't see him. But he knew she was right. Whatever the boy's injuries were at this point, it didn't matter. He could only hope he didn't make them worse for the doctors to repair.

"Okay, listen," Will said to Michael. "I'm gonna pick you up cause I gotta put this harness on you. You go ahead and cry if it hurts, just tell me if one thing hurts more than another, okay?"

Then, with no further discussion, Will reached under Michael and picked him up as gently as possible. He knew the boy would be stiff, if not from spending the past few hours in one position, then from any damage to his body that had time to sink in.

Will also knew he had to use his considerable strength on such a small parcel of land, while also being as gentle as humanly possible.

"Umph!" Michael let a lungful of air.

Will thought, the good news is he didn't scream, so maybe he was gonna make it.

"Okay, I'm gonna wrap this harness on you."

Will's attention now jockeyed between his walkie-talkie and Michael, easing the harness around the slim body as quickly as he could. Finishing, he cradled the boy and looked up.

"Sandy, you're the bus driver up there."

"Roger that, Sheriff."

"I'm gonna lift Michael here up to the top of the plateau where his grandpa's gonna load him into the helicopter."

"Copy that!"

"Okay, Michael, you heard what I just said to Sandy Little Bear up in the helicopter. She's the nice lady who's going to take you to the hospital, understand?"

"Yes, Sir," Michael responded.

"I have to put you down for a minute or two, while I catch the cable when it comes down," Will explained to the boy, giving Sandy the signal to lower the cable.

Sandy steadied the helicopter as best she could, even though the wind was starting to whip up closer and closer to the cliff side.

"Steady, steady now." Sandy began to say to herself, unaware she was broadcasting it, as it came through over the walkie-talkie.

She knew she had literally minutes, perhaps only seconds, to get it right. So as soon as Will gave her the thumbs up, she would simultaneously reverse the cable as she went up top. She knew Michael was in for a fright from that action alone, but it was the only way at this point.

Will steadied the boy on the cable as it took up the slack, and just as Michael was beginning his ascent, the boy swiveled his head back toward Will.

"Don't forget my grandpa's rifle; he'd never forgive me if I lost that!" he shouted in a surprisingly clear voice.

Amazed that Michael seemed more frantic about some old rifle than his own injuries, Will just smiled and gave him a thumbs up.

CHAPTER 15

SMALL ROCKS AND DIRT had been kicking up around Michael's face, but as he rose high in the air, the debris gave way to rain and cold. Michael was even more miserable now and felt excruciating pain, but could hear all the commotion above him and knew that help was coming in the form of his grandfather.

He wanted to call out to him again, but equally wanted to tough it out as he knew he was at the age where the sign of a true man was shown by how much pain he could endure. After all, he had seen the action movies, the superhero movies, and the classics his grandfather loved so much and all the information he had ever received about men dealt with pain and sacrifice. He knew it was his turn to sacrifice.

As the flood lights illuminated his position, he realized just how close to the edge of death he really was. It must've been quite a shock to see the nothingness below him and only cold, wind, and rain above him.

He gritted his teeth against the whimper that desperately wanted to escape. Think of something other than the pain, had been his grandfather's advice when he had smashed his finger while helping pile firewood. Michael tried to think of something besides the pain and cold and fear and could come up with nothing. So he tried concentrating instead ON the pain. Where did he hurt? Well, his arm, of course. And his back felt bruised, and his chest hurt too. The inventory actually managed to keep him from screaming over the sound of the prop wash long enough to make it to the top. And he opened his eyes to the wonderful view of his grandfather's face.

CHAPTER 16

SANDY LITTLE BEAR SHOULD have been given a medal that night. She had somehow kept the Rotorway helicopter steady enough to bring Michael up off the ledge, saving him from death and simultaneously bringing him to the top of the plateau without bashing his little body against the rocks by the force of the wind and rain.

Callahan could only watch helplessly as the mechanical winch slowly pulled the cable Michael was harnessed to up at the same time the helicopter rose above the plateau and slowly cleared his body from the side of the mountain.

"Grandpa!" Michael shouted, his thin voice soaring over the sound of the whipping wind and propeller. Callahan could barely hear his grandson, but knew exactly how he felt.

"I'm here, Michael! I've got ya! I've got ya! Don't worry, you're gonna be just fine!" Callahan shouted over the din of machine and weather.

Callahan could see Sandy was taking great care as she watched every movement the copter made as the wind and rain pounded it relentlessly. She slowly maneuvered Michael's body as he dangled helplessly down from 40 feet, to 30 feet, to 20 feet, to 10 feet, to 5 feet.

"I got him!" Callahan screamed at Sandy, giving her a thumbs up from below as he reached his grandson. Sandy could barely see the two, but trusted Callahan would signal her the instant he unhooked the harness from the cable. Callahan was already scrambling to do just that and he threw up his arm in victory as the cable swung free and he had Michael safely tucked in his arm.

Callahan nearly squeezed the life out of Michael as the boy winced in pain.

"Ouwee, Grandpa!" Michael cried as his grandfather touched his broken arm.

"I'm sorry, kiddo, here, let me help you with that." Callahan knew he had to project calm to Michael as he slowly unbuckled and removed the harness from around his waist and shoulders. Suddenly he jumped as the shock of Sandy's voice emitting from a bullhorn-like speaker at the bottom of the helicopter nearly gave him a heart attack.

"Hurry up, Sir! We need to get him into the cab now!" Sandy barked. "Put your heads down, I'm going to land that way, at your 9 o'clock." With that, Sandy bravely fought the cross current of torrential wind and rain, and slowly, carefully, set the copter down. She knew she couldn't leave the cockpit, so she relied heavily on Callahan doing the right thing, whether he knew what that was at the moment or not.

Callahan swiftly carried Michael in his arms like a baby. Cradling him across his chest, careful not to bounce him too much and leery of his possible injuries. He raced toward the aircraft like a young man, as his adrenaline was pumping so hard, his heart was pounding louder than the sound of the helicopter in his ears. He had the erratic thought that now was really not the time for a heart attack and almost snorted at his own whimsy.

Sandy was pretty impressed as she watched the older Callahan wrangle Michael. She carefully eased one hand off the stick and reached way over while still buckled in, unlatching the door and giving it a little shove to try and help.

Callahan quickly swung the door open wider with his shoulder, to clear room, as he raised Michael up and swung him into the empty seat in one smooth motion. Before Sandy had said anything, Callahan found the V-shaped seat belts and carefully locked his grandson in. This man knew something about helicopters, she thought.

Sandy held up the headset Will had been wearing and offered it to

Michael. She gestured, and Michael nodded, and for just a moment, he forgot his pain with the realization that he was going flying in a helicopter. The thought of taking his first ride in such a miraculous flying machine AND getting to wear a headset just like a real pilot was enough to bring a grin to his pale, filthy face. Sandy opened the headset wide and softly placed it over Michael's ears.

"What's your name?" Sandy said quietly into her microphone. She looked at Michael and tapped on the plastic so he'd know he had to respond back into his. She mouthed words so he knew what to do.

"Michael, Ma'am," he said shyly. Sandy smiled, then looked up at Callahan, her expression morphing instantly back to serious.

"Okay, I'm taking him to Critical Access in Cheyenne," she yelled over the thunder. "We'll be back for you as soon as the storm dies down!" Sandy had to yell past Michael to get to Callahan, but everything seemed better now that there was a plan and an execution of that plan.

"Just get him somewhere safe and fix him; don't worry about me," Callahan said in a heartfelt timbre.

"You're gonna have to help Sheriff Pierce back up the plateau!" Callahan nodded at her instruction, but grew impatient for her to take Michael away.

"You boys are gonna have to hunker down til someone comes back for you..."

"Yes, yes, we will. Don't worry about us... just get my grandson somewhere safe."

"... Now step back 'cause I'm gonna launch this thing with the wind!" Sandy barked her final order, and Callahan slammed the door tightly, pulling down the handle to lock it securely.

Callahan only had a split second to wave to his grandson, but that was all that was needed to ease any anxiety he may have been feeling. He knew it had been a traumatic day for both his grandson and himself, but was comforted in no small measure when he saw Michael smile and wave back to him.

Suddenly, Sandy lifted the helicopter. It popped up fast and furiously, then quickly banked left with the tremendous wind and dropped out of view.

It happened so fast that Callahan could only see the lights of the aircraft for a moment in the storm before it disappeared into the blackness.

He suddenly felt a lump in his throat, thinking about his daughter and how she would feel now that he had put her son's life in danger.

It was precisely at that time Callahan began to hear shouting from below.

"Shit!" He swore to himself, scrambling over to the rope that stretched taut over the edge… nothing like forgetting the man who had saved his grandson's life. Dropping to his belly, he wriggled to the edge and peered over.

Will was struggling. He had the distinct feeling that he had already worn out his welcome on this mountain. With each step up, Will's footing was getting shakier and he had begun to think that maybe he should have had a bigger dinner, as his muscles were clearly running out of steam.

He dug his boots deeper and deeper into the side of the mountain, now considering it his enemy that he would have to vanquish if he were ever going to be able to get off this mountain.

Will could barely make out Callahan at the top of the plateau, but luckily both men had been smart enough to attach their LED flashlights to their chests for visibility in this wretched weather.

Will dug in his toe harder as his other foot slipped on a loosened rock as it dislodged from the side of the mountain, along with his last bit of energy. The harness was biting into him and even in his gloves, his hands were burning. Maybe he could just take a little breather. He panted, struggling to maintain his position, when he felt dirt and pebbles falling down on his head from above.

Maybe he wasn't that far from the top after all. He gave it one last effort.

CHAPTER 17

"IT'S ABOUT DAMN TIME!"** Will shouted at Callahan as the older man's silhouette came closer into view. "Hurry up and help me! I'm about to lose my grip!" the sheriff barked.

Will had already scaled 20 of the 30 feet, and his arms were giving out at basically the equivalent of pulling his own body weight for the past few minutes.

Callahan had spread-eagled himself on the ground, digging his toes in for greater leverage. He extended his arm over the edge, grasping not at Will's hands, which were fully occupied, but rather the heavy collar on Will's jacket. Wriggling backward as he pulled, he helped Will up the last few feet.

Will was swearing under his breath. The rope was sopping wet, he was wet, the mountain was wet, and everyone had seemed to have forgotten he was there.

With Callahan's grip taking some of the strain off his arms, Will stretched his tired right arm up and hooked it over the edge. Callahan's other hand snaked out and latched on above the wrist, anchoring the Sheriff as he wriggled against the edge of the cliff, trying to drag his exhausted body the rest of the way up and over the cliff's edge.

Neither man had to say anything as they were both doing what they were supposed to be doing in order to survive.

Callahan, whose adrenaline was still pumping madly from the exertion of helping Michael, was now showing enormous strength as he helped Will back up to the top of the plateau. Keeping his one hand anchoring Will's wrist, he let go of his collar and lunged out and down. Latching onto the sheriff's belt, with a final burst of frantic energy, Callahan hoisted him up and over pretty much by the seat of his pants.

"Phew!" Will coughed as he reached the top and lay in the muddy mess atop the plateau. "Thanks for the helping hand," he wheezed after a minute or two.

Having flopped on his side next to Will, Callahan waved one hand carelessly through the rain. "Think nothing of it, Sheriff. Anytime you feel like saving my grandson's life, you can count on finding me ready to give you any damn thing you might need," Callahan managed to say as his adrenaline finally ran out.

For a brace of minutes, the two men simply lay in the mud before trying to move again. The wind began to pick up in a powerful gust that nearly knocked them off the side of plateau. Callahan still had a hold on Will as they helped each other up. They moved as quickly as possible, toward the center of the plateau.

"Wait here!" Will yelled as he turned and staggered into the darkness.

Callahan did as he was instructed and crouched down to avoid being pushed around by the gusts. He peered into the darkness where he had last seen the sheriff and trained his eyes on that position. After a moment, he finally began to see a darkened figure coming back and realized the sheriff was carrying a pack.

Will knelt on the ground and quickly unzipped the pack, pulling out a large, lightweight tarp he had somehow wedged deep into his pack. He swung the pack over his back, then flung open the tarp in one motion. The fierce wind caught the tarp and unfurled it in the direction Will wanted it to go. He grabbed the waving edge of the tarp and sat on the ground just as the other corner flew upward toward Callahan's face.

"Come on, grab that side!" Will yelled.

Having no idea what Will had in mind, Callahan complied, but the curious look he cast at Will won him some instructions.

"Roll your end under your butt, then pull it up under your feet too." Will demonstrated, anchoring the tarp with his own weight.

Callahan nodded his understanding and again complied.

"We gotta cover ourselves before this rain finishes turning into hail. If it starts coming down any harder, it's going to clobber us!" Will ordered Callahan, shouting over the sound of the wind, rain, and snapping tarp.

Will didn't have to say that twice as Callahan followed his lead and dragged the free end of the tarp up and over his head. Pulling it down and wedging it under his heel, he instantly found relief from the pounding rain. Glancing at Will, he saw that he had also pulled the side of the tarp in and tucked it under his butt. Copying his moves, Callahan was amazed to find that they were tucked into an envelope of a tarp. A short bark of laughter escaped him as he observed their impromptu shelter. If it weren't for the fact that they were both soaked through to the skin, this wouldn't have been a terribly uncomfortable tent. Even as he thought it, though, he realized the tarp had even cut off most of the bite of the wind and he could actually feel his own body heat starting to warm the air around them.

"Damn clever!" he announced to no one in particular, and Will grinned his response.

And with that, almost as though Will was some kind of rain psychic, the rain, hail, and wind began to grow and pelt the tarp with all its might. But since both Will and Callahan had used their best efforts to stretch the lightweight but impermeable material taut, it protected them from even the most extreme elements.

"Here, help me with this," Will said.

Callahan watched as Will removed the rifle he had carried back up to the plateau from where he'd found it with Michael. Callahan pushed up against the tarp over their head as Will rotated the rifle and propped it up underneath the canvas to take some of the pressure from the tarp off their heads and necks.

Callahan immediately reached to steady the butt of the gun in the mixture of rocks and mud, like they were two boys playing in the back garden, then forced the barrel upwards higher and under the tarp. By wedging the rifle under the tarp, it created an inverted V effect so the rain and hail and anything else that nature might drop from the sky that night would wash down either side.

"Wow, great idea, Sheriff!" Callahan enthused. "You not only save my grandson, but then provide me with shelter from this storm."

"No need to Sheriff me. The name's Will, Will Pierce. As you've probably figured out, I'm the only one around these parts dumb enough to attempt a rescue like that."

"I'm Tim Callahan, Will. And I am darned glad to meet you. As well as being eternally grateful that you were dumb enough to attempt a rescue like that!" Callahan grinned as he wiped his rain-soaked face with his sleeve, as he finished introducing himself. "I own Callahan Security."

Suddenly, Callahan gasped. In the dark, he hadn't realized it was his rifle, or more correctly, Michael's rifle until he suddenly saw the scope appear when Will twisted and turned the gun into a solid position.

"You managed to retrieve Michael's rifle!" Callahan could hear the incredulous surprise in his own voice. "How on Earth did you manage that?"

"That's funny," Will said, looking as the older man stared at the prized weapon now serving as a tent post. Something in the tone of voice brought Callahan's head up to meet Will's eyes. His own voice was a bit stiff at the tone that had been addressed to him.

"Just what's funny, Will?"

"Your grandson told me it was *yours*!" Will noted slowly. "He was very concerned you would be mad at him if he'd lost it, very concerned."

"Mad at him?" Callahan said, his eyes welling up. "I could never be mad at him." His voice choked and he had to stop and clear his throat, looking away from Will while he tried to get himself under control.

Callahan looked down at the dark tarp and the mud that had joined them under the tarp from their boots and clothes.

"I gave him that rifle," he explained. "It had been mine. I told him it was one of my favorite pieces but that he had earned the right to it. He knew how much it meant to me. But it could NEVER mean more to me than that boy. Nothing in the world means more to me than Michael."

The quiet fervor in the voice coming out of the darkness convinced Will the old man was telling the truth.

"Sorry for the fish eye," Will dropped his own gaze back to his pack where he began to feel around as it was too dark to see anything. "But it kinda bothered me that he seemed more afraid that he had damaged some damn rifle than he was about his own injuries."

"My God." Callahan had lost that first euphoria from the successful rescue and was rapidly descending into depression. "That child was my responsibility and I almost let him die… His mother will never forgive me, as long as I live!"

Will's fingers had finally identified what he was looking for, darn thing had worked itself clear to the bottom somehow, and wrenched it free of the rest of the now-soaked tools. He fiddled with the buttons, then turned on his secondary larger LED flashlight. He depressed the larger rubber button on the top and it suddenly lit up the dim proto-tent. Will slowly moved the large light over the barrel, to the rifle stock and then toward the butt. Looking up, he interrupted Callahan's now-silent deprecations.

"You say you're in security?"

Startled, Callahan nodded. "Yes, why?"

"What type of security?" Will inquired, as he kept moving the light slowly over the no longer pristine stock.

"Well, Callahan Security deals with just about every security issue." Callahan leaned closer, his curiosity distracting him from thoughts of his daughter's rage.

"Could you be any more vague?" Will muttered sarcastically.

Stung, the other man pulled himself fully into the conversation. "Sorry. Stock answer. But, well, we deal with Middle Eastern contract work of all kinds: construction, private security forces, military training, government and cyber protection, you name it, Callahan Security does it."

Will rolled his eyes as Callahan was starting to sound like a commercial and not at all addressing the reason for his inquiry about the man's company.

"Here, look here," Will said, bringing the light closer to the rifle butt.

Callahan peered closely, squinting and wishing he had his reading glasses. Following Will's finger and the light to where a deep gouge appeared in the wooden butt of the rifle, Callahan could clearly see a bullet lodged into the wood, the dull metal just visible at the deepest end of the rough cavity.

"What the…?" Callahan actually tried to pull back from the sight, so great was his shock.

"Your grandson didn't merely slip and fall off the side of the plateau."

"You mean someone took a shot at my grandson!?" Callahan shouted, actually managing to startle Will for an instant.

Callahan's face flushed clearly, even in the poor light, as his blood pressure began to rise. He pulled his elbows down around his knees and rocked slightly, contemplating just what all this meant to him, as well as his grandson.

"I'll kill whoever did this to my boy! I'll chase that son of a bitch to the ends of the Earth if I have to!" Callahan's anger echoed as his voice dropped three octaves and the timbre of his voice became almost demonic and frightening. "There is no place on Earth he will ever find sanctuary, I swear to God!"

Callahan's bellow continued as Will began to realize this was a man who not only loved his young grandson dearly, but who was in the habit of getting exactly what he wanted, when he wanted it. And right now, it seemed that what he wanted was someone's blood. Will didn't have a problem with that, as long as they went about it Will's way.

The most interesting thing, though, was that the old man wasn't frightened. Oh, he was scared for his grandson, no doubt about it. But he wasn't physically frightened for himself. In fact, Will swore he could see the determination to get whoever did this coalescing in the old man's frame. Tired, cold, wet and aching he might be, but this was a man to recon with, Will grinned to himself. Good. Just the kind of person Will liked to work with.

Will's thinking had already switched gears without waiting for any conscious orders from his brain. This was no longer just a search and rescue party; this was now a crime scene. And it was going to fall into his lap now. A case of attempted murder and such a unique scenario, in such a remote place, was by no means an accident and not at all a coincidence. Could it have been a wild shot from another hunter? Sure. Was it? NO. Will knew with a visceral certainty that it was not.

He began to get that rumbling in his stomach he used to get when he was a federal agent newly assigned a suspect or killer. There's a feeling that all keen cops and good detectives get when they first start to formulate an idea of the perpetrator; a perpetrator who would stop at nothing to satiate his destructive urges, even snuffing out the life of a child.

Subconsciously, this was exactly what Will needed to wrench him out of the excruciating boredom of retirement and his self-imposed banishment into local law enforcement. Without informing his active consciousness that he was once more on the hunt, Will was already laying out the order of inquiries he would need to start.

"You say you're in the security business? You better start making a mental list of all your enemies."

Will could see Callahan was a lot like him as the wheels were in motion as they both contemplated what their next move would be... and the killer's.

"We may have to pay them a visit once we get down from this mountain," Callahan agreed.

Will slowly looked up as the hail beat down so heavily, it nearly tore a hole in the tarp ceiling. "... if we ever get off this mountain, that is!"

As Will took a closer look at the rifle, he swore he remembered seeing a rifle just like this one, somewhere, but he just couldn't pull the memory far enough forward in his brain to identify where it was.

CHAPTER 18

CLAIRE CALLAHAN WAS THE proverbial father's daughter. She was as beautiful as a woman could be and a redhead no less. She had model looks and a brain that could and would challenge and confuse most university professors, and a smile that could melt your heart.

Claire was as ladylike as a man could ask, yet she had an Irish beer drinker's sensibility with solid street smarts—the latter being a hangover of trading her Ivy-League status for a state school, then promptly backpacking through Europe as soon as her secondary education was completed... with honors.

She looked like a celebrity when she wore a ball gown to charity and black tie work events, but she preferred blue jeans and flannel shirts around the house with her son, Michael, and occasionally on casual Fridays.

She had risen to the enviable position of president of Callahan Security and had all but taken over the massive corporation her father had started and built from the ground up. He had made the decision to slowly ease out of the enormous responsibility of overseeing and maintaining the corporation and settle into his retirement years.

"Becky, call Singleton from Frazier Weapons!" Claire called to her assistant, as she exited the elevator. "And get me the status on the recall of those defective Kevlar vests."

Claire continued listing her demands to the tall woman who had appeared beside her, already making rapid notes on her iPad as she calmly kept up with the brisk pace through the widely spaced and ergonomically designed work spaces of the top floor of the Callahan Building.

"Yes, Ma'am," the young woman responded, not even slightly intimidated. She had come up through the ranks with Claire and could almost predict what the next thing to come up would be.

"Howard, can you get me the updated sales reports on the 50 caliber ammunition from Devon?" Claire tapped the desk of a tall graying man as she passed him, hardly slowing her march.

"You'll have them on your desk by 5!" the older gentleman agreed, without a pause in his discussion with one of their counterparts in India.

"Oh, and Jake, make sure you recalculate the figures on the Saudi burst transmitters." Claire actually stopped, and leaning over the space age-looking desk, put her face down closer to that of the occupant and noted more quietly. "Not everything is sold in U.S. dollars, you know. Try and keep that in mind in your next report." A slight flush colored the man's cheekbones, but Claire had already passed on with no more than a double pat on the man's desk.

Claire leaned into one of the few glassed-in offices that lined a wall on the floor. Glassed, because as she had told her father, if everyone else has to work in the open, so should the top guns. And it also allowed everyone access to some natural light rather than only the upper most echelon getting to see the light of day or night, as the case might be. Another reason for the wide-open space of the rest of the floor was the light from the huge floor-to-ceiling windows that spread out across the floor all the way to the elevator. No one should have to work in a cave, she had informed the architect.

Now she found the young Middle Eastern man unpacking his briefcase onto a boat-sized conference table.

"I see you got back safely," she grinned at him.

"No thanks to you," he grumbled mockingly. "Sending me over there with those numbers almost got me lynched."

"But it worked?" she was already pulling back, getting ready to head on.

"Yep," he agreed. "I will go over it all in the meeting at 3."

Her waved hand was his only answer as she was already heading to her own office, only two large glass partitions away.

Claire was young, not as young as she used to be, she had to admit. A single mother, hard working and hard playing, she took a quiet pride in the fact that her auburn hair and alabaster skin shaved at least 10 years off her real age.

Although she had a deep shade of red hair, she also had blonde streaks woven in throughout to give her an even more youthful look. Mind you, not the cheap and cheesy kind of streaks, like a lot of very young women like to wear in their hair these days, but tasteful, merely enough to enhance the red and highlight her enviable youthfulness.

Claire was a Pilates-hound. She exercised every morning to the point where she could hold her own in any bar fight, as most Irish-American girls (and boys) are taught to from a very early age. But she had long since given up her wild days of drinking and debauchery and had settled into being the best mother and successful businesswoman she could possibly be.

Her employees at Callahan Security loved her; she was that rare combination of tough but fair and always tended to give anyone a second chance, even if they had screwed up in a big way.

Flopping down in the ergonomically designed chair, Claire spun halfway around and took a deep breath. Time to really start her day. "Okay, first thing, cancel my dinner reservations."

Her assistant gave her a strange look as though she were trying to figure out why she would break her tightly regimented protocol.

"I'm gonna try and work late since my son is out of town this week," Claire said as she pressed the speaker phone on her desktop receiver and ran her fingers across the keys to initiate her voice mail.

Claire's emerald green eyes were kind and open, unless she was annoyed; then they would narrow like a snake's and anyone seeing that look would be better off running for the hills.

She had a lean, sharp jaw that could shred an unwanted man's gaze with a look if need be or calm an ocean of torrent with a smile. She wasn't hard to look at, but she did have a certain edge. After all, being a single mother in this day and age is no easy task, yet it was the one task she felt she was always meant to fulfill.

She was tall and lean, but with real muscle mass, not from years of purging or trying to fit some women's magazine's image. She was a feminist, in her own way, but didn't rattle a sabre or shove her beliefs down anyone's throat. She looked corporate when she wore a dress suit, elegant in an evening dress, and as sexy as a super model in jeans and a t-shirt. She was a paparazzi's perfect cover girl.

But Claire's life was no *cakewalk*. She had enormous responsibilities with running the corporation and somehow still was able to manage the thousands of employees in their worldwide offices. She was known to travel more than she'd like to foreign and exotic lands, but thought nothing more important than her own young son.

"I think we'll push that conference call back to 4:30, since Randall is running late from the airport," she continued in her day-to-day business tone.

"You have 47 messages," a computerized voice said as Claire ran through her daily routine. Her assistant had strolled out to the outer office, but Claire was still shouting her daily instructions, confident that she could still be easily heard.

Frowning at a voice mail as she jotted down the relevant information, Claire glanced up. Unusually, her assistant had just reentered the office, grabbing the doorjamb as she stuck her head inside to make sure she had her attention.

"Claire, you have a call on Line 1," she said with some urgency.

"Who is it?" Claire asked, looking up and staring at her over the tops of her bifocals. "I'm pretty busy."

"I don't know, but it sounds urgent. It's a hospital in Wyoming."

Wyoming. Michael. Her Dad. Claire stabbed at the blinking light on Line 1. "This is Claire Callahan. What can I do for you?"

"Yes, Ms. Callahan, are you the mother of Michael Callahan?" A sudden chill ran down the length of her medulla oblongata and continued down her spine.

"Yes, yes, Michael is my son. Why?" Claire shot her assistant a desperate look as her eyes began to well at the information about to be conveyed.

"Ms. Callahan, my name is Doctor Rajeed Gupta. I'm calling you from Critical Access Hospital in Cheyenne, Wyoming. Your son has been in an accident." The doctor's sympathetic voice on the other end of the phone resonated, as he knew any parents who were to receive a call from him would soon be in shock.

Claire nearly dropped the phone, but her mouth dropped instead. She was silent for a moment before stuffing her fist against her mouth to try and stifle the scream trying to claw its way out. It would do no good; everyone would soon know her pain.

Claire's assistant immediately raced to her side as Claire grasped her hand and squeezed it tighter than she had ever squeezed anything, waiting for the final answer to the status of her young son.

"Ms. Callahan? Ms. Callahan? Are you there?" The words droned through the receiver.

After a moment, Claire collected herself enough to be able to choke out. "Yes, doctor, I am here. Please give me the details." Pressing the receiver even more firmly to her ear, she listened intently to what the doctor had to say. She began to furiously scribble on her notepad, swiping the tears from her eyes with the back of her hand as she wrote.

Concentrating on the voice on the other end, she didn't hear her assistant leave the room and begin to issue her own set of orders. Orders for cars to be prepared for instant departure, planes to be readied for flights to Wyoming. Clothes to be immediately transported to said plane. Personal doctors to be notified of the emergency and to have them ready to answer any and all questions about Claire Callahan's young son.

CHAPTER 19

NASSAR KHUMARI LOVED HIS birthplace more than any other place he had lived in his youth.

Like his father, and ultimately his son, he had been born in Jordan, but had been raised in nearly every other Middle Eastern and Western European country that one could pronounce. Nassar was so proud, romantically perhaps, of Jordan that he ultimately decided to make his homeland the headquarters of his company, Falcon Securities.

He had built a solid business, employing hundreds, if not thousands if you included the many private global contractors and was considered a Favorite Son of not only Jordan, but of the royal family as well. Of all the local Jordanians, Nassar was treated like a king himself, as he brought much-needed modernization and employment to the region.

The only thing Nassar loved more than his country and his company was his wife and son, Ali. He named his son Ali, which means *on high,* and like Nassar's own name, it had a profound meaning in Arabic.

Yet Nassar knew, even decades before, that a simple Middle Eastern name would allow his son to travel and live among foreigners, even Westerners, without the slightest furrowing of an eyebrow, unlike his other brethren who chose radical names that had deep-meaning and contentious roots.

Nassar's son Ali was a handsome man. He was dark, much darker than his father, and that was certainly unusual, as he was half Assyrian. But, unlike his father, his mother's darker Egyptian complexion would ultimately win out.

He had jet black, thick hair, which he thought would never turn gray, as many of the elders in the region had nary a streak. He had dark smooth skin and dark brown eyes. He was a striking man who had had the luxury of not only schooling in the States, but having made many American friends.

He was highly educated and could speak numerous languages, like his father, who had purposely exposed him to life by keeping him by his side as he travelled the world.

Like his American counterpart, Claire Callahan, Ali was now in charge and running Falcon Securities. His father, much like *his* lifelong friend, had also built his security company from the ground up. And he, too, had built it from nothing into one of the world's finest security firms.

Falcon Securities' clients were comprised of mostly Middle Eastern millionaires and billionaires, but Falcon had a strict policy of dealing with only moderate Muslims and Middle Eastern governments as clientele. Nassar believed, and passed down to Ali, that they would never, ever do business with ideologues or radical Muslims or anyone for that matter, as that was, in his opinion, what was ruining the Middle East.

Ali, like his father, ran a tight ship. He was no prince, but he could certainly act like one. He could be a hard man to deal with since he was so spoiled, but he also enjoyed the finer things in life, like women and jumping into his Lamborghini Aventador and racing through the streets of Jordan.

Ali spent his evenings hitting every nightclub Jordan had to offer. He loved the nightlife and he had bragged to a friend once that he had probably spent more money on alcohol in those clubs than he had on his Lamborghini… at least last week, he would clarify.

Ali was the classic player; he was a womanizer, a reluctant misogynist, and cared less about the local gold diggers than the few homeless that roamed the streets, but he had one vulnerability: a hole in his heart.

His hole was not literally from a bullet or a knife, but from the loss of a woman in his early life. It was this loss that propelled Ali head first into a life of debauchery and endless hedonism in some vain attempt to stave off the pain and loneliness he felt for his former love.

A longing for a woman he had been in love with his whole life, but was never allowed to be with because circumstances dictated they never be together, at least formally or in any known way publically or privately. He ached for her endlessly but decided to turn his sadness into vice and excess whilst seeking comfort in the arms of other women around the world to ease his pain.

Still, Ali was determined to win her back. He had made a vow to her many years before that he would fight to regain her trust and love at any cost. He had made many promises and he was a man of his word, but life, family, and obligation had clouded their paths and left the two lovers scorned and bitter. He knew he would have to dig deep if he wanted to ever prove his worth to her again.

Ali knew if he put his nose to the grindstone and worked like a madman, this would truly impress his woman. So what if he spent his evenings in the embrace of other women? So what if he enjoyed his excesses in the form of drugs, cars, booze, lavish yachts, and wild trips to untold destinations with his friends that followed him loyally?

He knew all these things could be forgiven if he were pure of heart and dutiful in the fact that he loved her and she loved him and nothing could keep them apart forever. So for now, he would merely live the life that Allah had generously bestowed upon him and would worry about the other background noise when the time came to be reunited with his love.

But in the meantime, he would have to settle for being the most eligible bachelor in Jordan, let alone the entire Middle East. His star was on the rise like that of the late John F. Kennedy, Jr. He would become the darling of the press and paparazzi, splashed across the covers of all the Arabic and French magazines from Tripoli to Baghdad.

Ali thought about these things often, and as such, battled the feelings of both guilt and remorse, with excess and pleasures, turning his pain inward to cover the damage to his heart. He decided this day he would have to merely turn the wheel of his priceless Aventador hard as he quickly shot through the tiny streets of Amman. The old men watched as they smoked their hookahs and filter less cigarettes outside on the corner cafes as he flew by at ridiculous speeds. Everyone knew Ali Khumari would drive by this location every day at this time, and it gave them joy to watch such a proud man succeed in life as Allah would have wanted.

Ali crushed the accelerator with his foot as he simultaneously switched gears to ever-increasing and dangerously unsafe speeds. This way, he thought, it would be easier to forget her face.

CHAPTER 20

WILL AND CALLAHAN SAT Indian style on the cold ground with their legs crossed. They pulled their arms in tight and wrapped them around their chests. They had to lean forward to keep what little bit of heat was left in their bodies in order to survive their ordeal and knew they were in for a long night.

Even with the rifle acting as a support post, Will and Callahan had their heads slightly pinned down by the weight of the sopping wet tarp. From the outside, one might have thought it looked like a small circus tent as the barrel of the rifle held up the center, making a point at the top, but the two men's heads held up the two outer sides so there were a total of three humps.

This would prove effective in keeping the sheets of rain draining down the sides and protecting the men from getting their chest, clothes, and faces even wetter than they already were. Yet the problem they didn't predict was pooling below them.

As the rain was averted to either side of them by the tent-like tarp, it was still coming down and still going somewhere, and that somewhere was under Will and Callahan. A small pond had matriculated under their legs and feet as the top of the plateau was fairly flat, and as such, susceptible to flooding—which it was doing with fervor.

Even with the wet and cold miserable conditions, the two men had managed, surprisingly, to somehow get a few hours of sleep. This was even stranger in the sense that it was something neither of them could normally do on an average night in their own bed with soft sheets.

Perhaps it was the combination of adrenaline and testosterone first surging, then coursing through their bodies, then slowly leaving their brains. Or maybe it was the fact that both of these older men had just experienced a harrowing event and their bodies were ready to repair themselves.

Will awakened first. He reached up and put the palm of his hand up to the top of the tarp ceiling. His hand was dry, but still cold and he was surprised by what his fingertips were feeling. He expected more wet and cold, but instead, he was greeted with something completely different.

"Uhm," he said to himself.

The tarp was cool, but not cold. Water wasn't pouring in where he had placed his hand and the weight of water was no longer pushing the tarp downward. He passed his hand along the underside of the ceiling until it got close to Callahan, then stopped.

This was a good sign as it sounded as though the storm may have passed, and perhaps, if it had, the morning sun was beginning to warm the mountains and valleys, and hopefully, the top of the tarp as well.

Will slowly shifted in his wet jeans and lifted one of his posterior cheeks. He reached back and grabbed a corner of the tarp below him and pulled it out from under himself. He carefully pulled the tarp back up and over his head. He didn't want to dump a fresh load of water down his neck. He'd concluded that Callahan was already awake, as he had been watching his breathing. Will was still an expert at some things and reading if a man was awake or deeply sleeping was one of his strong points. He slowly uncrossed his legs and wiggled the stiffness out of his joints.

Will began to stand up slowly as every muscle and joint in his body was reminded of the arthritis that had crept into each fissure, break, and fracture he had ever had. He placed his hand on the ground and pushed himself upward and slowly stretched his back so as not to pop or strain anything as older men can do quite easily. He was hoping this would take care of all the kinks.

The sun had already risen above the higher mountains to the east and had begun to warm and dry the valley floor. Will stood up and surveyed the horizon. He let the morning sun warm his chilled face and took another scan of their locations. He figured it was about 7 in the morning.

The type of fierce storm they'd just experienced would have devastated any residential homes or local industry had there been any in the area, but as it was, this was the rugged Wyoming outback and a storm like the one they had lived through was just another Tuesday night in this part of the world. Will always loved Wyoming storms, as they seemed to offer a new beginning after each devastating torrent.

Will took a final inventory of his surroundings as he peered as far as his eyes could see. During his years as a city slicker, he'd forgotten how beautiful it got on the high plains. But now that he was home, one of his greatest pleasures was to simply stand in the dawning sun and watch the light spread across this magnificent land.

He guessed it wasn't the worst night of sleeping outdoors he had ever experienced. He had spent plenty of times sleeping rough as a kid. Though, since he was back on his ranch, he didn't have to sleep in the barn if the horses got colicky or a cow was in a breech labor. He had hired hands that could do that work for him. But at least, in those circumstances, he had made himself a nice bed of warm hay and stuffed his jacket to make a pillow.

Covering his eyes as the morning sun began to get intense, Will took a 360-view from the top of the plateau. He could see that there were still places that were a little waterlogged, but nonetheless, passable. He calculated the distance in his head of how long it would take for Sandy Little Bear to return with the chopper, and his fallback position of he and Callahan trekking back to his rental car.

He thought what better way to shake off the cold and damp that had crept deep into his bones over the past seven hours than a brisk five-mile hike down the mountain to the country road? He knew how quickly the blood circulating through his body would warm his core and get him back to normal. Of course, he wasn't so sure about his new partner's enthusiasm for the idea.

It was just about that time Callahan decided to make his entrance as he threw the tarp over his head and away from him. He too slowly stood up and stretched.

"How are you doing?" Will inquired.

"I'm okay, a little sore and I'm sure I've got a potent case of pneumonia coming on, but all in all, no worse for wear," Callahan responded.

"Okay, I think our best course of action would be to hoof it out with our packs the same way you and your grandson came in. What do you think?" Will asked in a gruff morning voice.

"Yeah, I was hoping for our ride to come back and pick us up, but I'm more concerned with getting to the hospital as soon as we can to make sure my grandson is getting the best care possible."

"I know Sandy Little Bear. She's a combat-tested pilot and has done more than her fair share of evacs and exfils. She's saved hundreds of lives and there's nobody I'd want taking care of my family more than her."

"You trust her that much?"

"Absolutely! Without a doubt!"

"… and the hospital?"

"Look, this is Sandy's job and she's the best at it I've ever seen. She probably made your grandson a cup of tea and fluffed his pillow before they even got to the hospital. And I'll tell you, Sandy herself is a trained medic, so if Michael had any problems whatsoever during last night's flight, she would have found a soft patch of ground and fixed him up right then and there, I kid you not!"

Callahan nodded. "That makes me feel a whole lot better to hear you say that."

"Look, I know you and your grandson have been through a lot, but I think you struck gold with the personnel that are now handling things."

"Are you including yourself in that statement?"

"Ha, hardly, I should've said, 'Michael got lucky, you got the shaft!'"

"Well, Sheriff, you've impressed me so far, from rescuing my grandson to keeping us alive through the night. That's certainly no small feat." Callahan smiled, then reached down in the crumpled canvas tarp and pulled out the rifle.

"Uh, uh, uh!" Will uttered. "I'll be taking that! I'm gonna need that rifle for evidence. After all, this is a crime scene now."

CHAPTER 21

CLAIRE NEARLY BROKE THROUGH the thick tempered glass, as the double doors couldn't open fast enough for her. She moved quickly, like a Heisman Trophy-winning running back as her eyes darted back and forth until they fell onto the right person and she saw someone she felt was in charge.

"Michael Callahan!" Claire barked in a panic.

The nurse immediately held up her hands to slow Claire's roll. This wasn't the hospital's first rodeo with a crazed mother of an injured child.

"Slow down, Ma'am. We'll get you to your son."

"He, he was brought in last night. Michael Callahan."

The nurse seemed to move as slowly as the double doors, so Claire made sure she heard her once again.

"MICHAEL CALLAHAN!!!" she shouted again to the head nurse at the station. The old nurse was a salty dog, and she knew the panicked expression of a mother's face. Whenever a child was brought in, the entire staff was alerted that there were going to be fireworks. It was protocol that each resident as well as every non-essential employee know where each child was and there were status updates distributed as best as they could.

This way there would be less stress on everyone concerned and no reason for any parent to lose it.

"He's this way. I'll take you myself," said the nurse, quickly rising to meet Claire at the corner of the desk, then deciding to slow her pace to allow time for Claire to settle down and breathe.

Claire had valiantly been holding back the tears, fighting them as she doggedly questioned the nurse. "How is he? The doctor was vague on the phone. I have to know, I have to know." She began to raise her voice.

But the nurse knew exactly how to play a concerned parent. She took her hand and waved it slowly toward a large open door to a patient room. "He's right in here, but you're gonna have to get a hold of yourself, okay?"

Claire wasn't used to being spoken to in this tone, like a drill sergeant addressing a batch of new recruits, but she was frantic and she knew the nurse was right. She stopped at the hospital room door, took a breath and tried as best she could to control herself, as she knew her son would need her strength.

The nurse led her into the room, but blocked the other figure with her body so Claire could concentrate on her son. She was careful not to alarm Claire as Deputy Jenkins, Will's right-hand man, was sitting just inside the doorway reading a *Field & Stream* magazine with his legs stretched out, as the two entered.

Rusty had been up all night, standing guard, as he had been radioed by Will the night before to make sure no one went anywhere near the boy. No one, with the exception of hospital staff, was allowed into his room or could bother Michael. Will had made it very clear that he thought someone had tried to murder the boy. He was now a protected victim of a potential homicide and Will Pierce took such things more seriously than just about any other aspect of his professional life.

Rusty, on the other hand, felt this was the most exciting piece of law enforcement he had ever experienced, and now he, and he alone, was the only line of defense between an innocent child and a cold-blooded killer.

Every action movie and police drama scenario he had ever seen was cycling through his brain to prepare him for his solemn duty, and he would implement the most heinous can of whoop ass anyone had ever heard if anything were to go down and jeopardize this little man again.

He had the opportunity to brief the head nurse and her staff, the doctors, everyone who was within earshot or would listen. He may have been a bit overeager, but he took his responsibilities seriously. He also knew as long as his sheriff, Will Pierce, was on the case, that bastard, son of a bitch was gonna get caught and face the consequences to the full extent of the law.

Rusty didn't see Claire or the nurse until they were just about upon him. He jumped to his feet quickly and was about to stop Claire when the head nurse shook her head. Rusty gave a deep nod and stayed off to the side as Claire entered the room.

As her eyes adjusted to the brightness of the room, there, lying motionless under a white sheet and durable comforter on the hospital bed, she saw her son Michael. Her self-control went right out the window.

"Michael!" she screamed. Michael's eyes flew open in alarm at a sound he had never in his life heard before, his mother's terrified screams.

"I'm okay, Mom. Really, I am okay. Really," he babbled desperately. He never, ever wanted to hear his mom sound like that again. Hearing this, Claire managed to slow and reverse her terrifying descent into madness. As she approached him, he shifted slightly in his bed, readying himself for the emotional assault.

Claire grabbed his face and began kissing it all over. She rubbed her fingers through his hair, squeezed his face, snuggled his neck. She reached down to squeeze his shoulders when Michael suddenly jerked.

"Ouch, Mommy!" he let out painfully. Claire jumped back, realizing she had inadvertently just caused her son pain. After a moment, she reached down and slowly pulled back the covers and sheet. There she saw a cast on his arm.

"Careful now," Doctor Gupta said as he entered the room. Rusty eased his defensive posture, allowing the doctor unimpeded entrance. The doctor walked past the nurse who was standing in the corner, now merely to observe and be there in case Claire broke down with emotion or madness.

This room is starting to get pretty crowded, Rusty thought. The doctor stopped at the edge of Michael's bed and pulled his chart off the hook that hung from the front of the footboard.

"His left arm was badly broken," he began to list, "and he has a bruised sternum and spleen." The doctor recited all the ailments, maladies, and injuries, not needing to look down at the chart he carried. He had been

Michael's trauma doctor when Sandy Little Bear had brought him in, and as such was one of the first to see him and had been the primary doctor for his treatment in the hours since.

"He's very lucky it was a clean break," Doctor Gupta continued, "and we didn't need to put pins in."

"Oh thank God," Claire whispered to herself as the doctor continued.

"But, I'm sorry to say he's not gonna be playing baseball for a few months." Claire's eyes welled up and tears began to flow uncontrollably.

"That's it?!" she said crying happily. "He's okay other than that?"

The doctor nodded. "Yes, as I said, he was extremely lucky. A fall like that could've killed him."

Claire nearly dove at the doctor as she wrapped her arms around him and gave him a big kiss on his cheek. Doctor Gupta, a devoted family man, could only blush and pat her back in response to her sudden effusiveness. As if realizing his discomfort, she released the poor man, and almost instantly there was a change in her expression as a look of realization slid into place over her features.

"So help me God, I'm gonna kill somebody," she murmured under her breath. Rusty took notice and began to rub the top of his service revolver that was tight in his holster out of sheer subconscious habit.

"And not just any somebody; I'm gonna kill my father!" she actually looked at Rusty for a second, and he took a step back in case she decided to use him as a warm up.

"No Mommy, you can't be mad at Grandpa," Michael tried pushing himself up in the bed. Clumsy from the cast and still sore, he only managed to wriggle around.

"Of course I can," she said, as her blood began to boil.

"Don't be mad at Grandpa. It felt like something pushed me off that cliff, like the wind or something." Claire listened to her son's tale. "Grandpa tried to help me. He called the police and they came and took me up in a helicopter and everything. Can you believe it? I got to ride in a helicopter!"

Claire palmed Michael's head with her hand and brushed his hair with the tips of her fingers. She smiled, as her tears flowed, listening to the adventure of her young man. How could she not respect the wishes of her son?

The hospital room was set up for two beds, but since Michael was being treated like a celebrity patient, albeit for all the wrong reasons, he basically had his own suite. Rusty wanted to sit down on the other bed, but knew he had to stay alert and at the ready. Doctor Gupta smiled at the mother and son reunion, then turned back toward the door to finish his rounds. Suddenly sounds of slogging and squishing filled the room.

Michael and Claire heard it too, and everyone trained their eyes on the door. Callahan appeared, muddy, pale, drained, and exhausted, his boots nearly shredded by the quick hike back to his rental through mud, thickets, and waist-deep water in some spots. Will, just behind Callahan, brought up the rear and doubled the squishing and squashing sounds. He also wanted to see how the boy was doing.

"Michael!" Callahan shouted. He ran, or what he thought was running, quickly to his bedside. Before Callahan could reach his grandson, Claire jumped into his path.

"What the hell did you do, Dad?" Claire screamed, digging her perfectly manicured nails into her father's chest with the rage of a demon. If she could have, she would have penetrated his heavy vest, flannel shirt, and skin and reached all the way to the bone.

"He's my son, my only son, and YOU took him to that place where he almost died!" Callahan lowered his head in sorrow, knowing full well the situation had been his responsibility.

"He could've died!" She shook him, or tried to, her death grip on his thick vest only managing to shift the material around his thick body. Letting go suddenly, Claire began to pound her father's chest, and all Callahan could do was drop his head in shame, as tears began to well in his eyes.

"I… I don't know what to say, Claire!" Callahan forced out the words, even though his throat felt like a large pair of hands was constricting it. Knowing his daughter, that might just be her next assault. He still struggled to explain. "I don't know what happened. We took all the precautions. We followed all the safety measures. I just don't know what could've happened."

"You son of a bitch!" Claire screamed. "It should've been you at the bottom of the cliff, not my sweet, sweet, boy!" She started beating Callahan's shoulders and chest again with her fists clenched as tightly as a professional boxer's. She knew how to make a fist. He had shown her himself when she was young. It just hadn't occurred to him that she would ever have a reason to use it against him.

Rusty, seeing Claire's attack on Callahan, felt like he had to step in, but was hesitant as she was in Mama bear mode, distraught and emotional, and he would have to approach with extreme caution.

"Ms. Callahan," Rusty began to interrupt as he put his arm across Callahan's chest to slightly protect him. Before Rusty could draw the distressed woman's rage down upon his own head, Will stepped in and firmly put his hand on Rusty's shoulder.

"It's okay, Rusty, I'll handle this," Will said in a fatherly voice, so as not to embarrass or pull rank on him. Stepping past the pair, Will grabbed Claire by her shoulders and turned her anger away from her father. He wasn't particularly gentle with her as he hoped he was right about what she needed right now. Turning her sharply to face him, he put his face close and hissed harshly, but in a soft voice, so Michael couldn't hear.

"You are scaring your son! Is this the way you want him to see you behave?" Nothing could have stopped her in her tracks faster. Eyes wide, she gasped as her brain snapped back onto track and she shuddered at the actual physical effort it took to pull herself back from the edge.

Will couldn't help being impressed by the speed that Callahan's daughter brought herself back under control. A slight flick of her shoulders shook his hands off and he gave way, stepping back as she turned to her son. On the bed the boy laid, mouth open, eyes wide in surprised shock.

Claire dragged a grin up from somewhere down in the vicinity of her shoes. "Remember how many times I told you, you don't want to make me mad?"

"Well, yeah," the boy answered honestly, in total awe. "But who knew you really meant it?"

That actually managed to pull a real laugh out of her. "Now you know. That should pretty much take care of any discipline problems til you go away to college."

His irrepressible smile blazed away at her. "Yes, MA'AM!" And that finally broke the tension in the room, as everyone managed at least a smile at his cheeky answer.

Appreciating the sanity and becoming aware of the intelligence in her eyes, Will spoke again, sternly but in a flat normal tone. "Ms. Callahan, there wasn't anything your father could've done. It wasn't his fault."

With a quick glance at her father that promised him words would still be said at some point in the future, Claire straightened the blankets over Michael and managed with her body language to open up a space for her father next to the boy and herself.

"What do you mean, it wasn't my father's fault? How can that be?"

Callahan was holding his breath. Not quite ready to believe the storm had passed, but Will nodded to him to carry on toward his grandson, awaiting a hug from his grandfather.

"There was someone else there," Will said, his voice deepening to a baritone timbre.

Claire looked at him, cockeyed.

"I'm afraid someone, we don't know who yet, but they took a shot at your son."

Callahan had made his way with some caution over to Michael's side, and now he cradled the boy's face in his large hands. Looking deep into the young eyes, the relief and normality he saw there almost took his breath away. He quickly looked back at Claire and knew he was in for a serious ass-chewing… but first things first.

"Grandpa, did I get the shot? Wait, what do you mean? No one shot me. I fell off cause something pushed me," Michael said innocently. Will turned his attention toward Michael in case he could shed any light on the incident. "Something hit me hard and knocked me over. I'm just glad you were there to save me, Grandpa!"

Hearing this, Rusty gritted his teeth at the thought of someone taking a shot at this young boy. He thought of his own younger brother and how if anyone had ever taken a shot at him, he'd be wrapping his hands around their throat, before slapping the cuffs on his and dragging his sorry ass to enjoy the incarceration of Wyoming's finest penitentiary or a long nap from an extended sleep hold he'd gladly provide.

Callahan broke down, grabbed his daughter Claire by the shoulder, and huddled in toward Michael for a family hug. He pulled them close, as he knew they were the only things left in his life that made living bearable and he would move hell and high water if that was what it took to protect them.

Michael poked his head out between his mother and grandfather to see Will conversing with the doctor. He watched as he saw Will nodding his head and smiling at the answers. Will suddenly caught a glimpse of Michael looking at him and winked back.

Will shook the doctor's hand, then slapped his mitt down on the doctor's shoulder to illustrate the good job he'd thought he'd done. After that, he decided to approach the other three who were commiserating. He couldn't help but scratch his day-old beard and smack his dry lips for a good glass of water.

"… Yeah, I wanted to talk to you about that, Michael."

"What's that, Sir?" Michael asked.

"That something that hit you hard and knocked you over, that's what I want to talk to you about!" Will answered as his detective instincts kicked in.

CHAPTER 22

WEAPONS INTO PLOWSHARES WASN'T just an idea, but a philosophy and a lifelong dream that started in Lebanon decades ago by three young boys who grew into successful men.

Their unique ideology to somehow try to curb the out-of-control arms race as well as war, which, ironically they all contributed to, was a brainchild of Callahan, Miller, and Khumari.

It was no secret they had all made their fortunes off the sales, manufacturing, application, training, and sustainability of weapons of war to the highest, and sometimes lowest, bidders, yet they knew this was a necessary evil they alone would never be able to stem, so why not try and control as much of it as possible?

And, as such, they had decided, even in the innocence of their youth, to offer the world an alternative to the use of weapons for violent purposes. It was a small contribution, but they felt it was something that met the basic needs of men: hunting, killing, and the satisfaction of winning.

All of which, of course, meant no one or nothing would be harmed in the process of what they had turned into a contest. A contest, like many contests, where men and women of all shapes and sizes, ages, and ethnicities would utilize their evolutionary talents within the ancient art of hunting, albeit with rifles, and cheating just a little bit by using sniper scopes and modern technology to hunt and ultimately kill their prey.

Like many philanthropists that chose to spread their considerable wealth, influence, and affluence, Callahan, Miller, and Khumari had a favorite in their Weapons Into Plowshare Foundation. A foundation that celebrated the real hunter, one with an eagle eye and light trigger finger; the primal man that sought to satiate the age-old desire to track his quarry and use his instincts to fell it.

The WPS Foundation Annual Awards banquet was one of the finest events of the year and the best ticket in town. That is, if you knew it existed or were one of the lucky few in the past decades to be invited to it.

The WPS Hunting Club, as it was known in tight circles, was the most prestigious club a shooter could ever be asked to join. It was invitation only when it came to the WPS Hunting Club, and the three founders would only allow specially designated and handpicked recruiters to seek out and find the top shooters, snipers, and hunters the world had to offer.

Weapons Into Plowshares seemed like a strange and ironic name for a hunting club annual dinner, at least for new members, but it drew the very best talent in the area, and by word-of-mouth, gun enthusiasts, hunters, ex-military, and, surprisingly, even nature photographers.

Callahan, Miller, and Khumari's brainchild started when they saw the devastation of many of their homes, Lebanon being one. They were also drawn into the same industry they saw destroy cities, by the stories of heroism, the honor of serving their country, and the glory of defeating their enemies. It was truly a dichotomy for all three, but they knew it was part of the yin and yang of their lives.

Since they were raised around the world, all three with military, paramilitary, or Special Forces training, they had various forms of post-traumatic stress disorder and knew that by exorcising their demons in the same way they were created meant the possibility of peace in their lives.

This night, there were hundreds of men and women meandering about the enormous ballroom. They chatted, commiserated, drank, laughed, and reminisced about those better days when they were at their best. Then, of course, after a few libations and the loosening of ties and tongues, they began to discuss their favorite hobby.

The breezeway just outside the banquet hall was choke-full of sponsors of every kind: camouflage clothes, gun manufacturers, military advisors, government "contract" workers, armament representatives. If it had anything to do with hunting, outdoor living, camping, fishing, military, or the great state of Texas, it had to have a booth in the halls outside the WPS dining hall.

The prerequisites to be a sponsor or hawk wares at this private annual affair were the same as the requirements for being a member: exclusivity and discretion. Callahan, Khumari, and Miller had known, even decades before the cult classic made it a cultural mantra, the number one rule is, no matter what, *You Don't Talk About Fight Club!*

The only way they knew to keep their society secret, for all the right reasons, was to keep it hush-hush. It had to be invisible from the prying eyes of the NSA, foreign governments, ne'er-do-wells, Al Qaeda and other terrorist groups, and perhaps the least of their fears, from the overwhelming mediocrity and inquisition.

By all accounts, the WPS was not just a sportsman's paradise, but a way of life for its members. It looked like the elite side of an RV Expo, high-end military contractor convention or outdoor enthusiast camping sale, but there was something very different about the WPS, and only those exclusive few, be they sponsors or invitees, knew the real reason the men kept it shrouded in secrecy, and that was all that was needed to keep everyone from ever uttering a word about the WPS.

Yet there were also others in the room this night that made themselves less conspicuous, less engaging, less ready to brag about their accomplishments. These men and women seemed more interested in honing in on certain younger guests. Guests who may have proven themselves outstanding, not only on the field of battle or even in the trenches of weekend war maneuvers, but perhaps when others weren't even looking. Someone involved with the WPS was always looking.

These lookers weren't just the elite alumni or wandering hucksters they may have appeared to be in the hallways among the looky loos; they were the hand-picked recruiters Callahan, Miller, and Khumari felt could do the job in their stead.

These recruiters were tasked with one job and one job only: recruit the best of the best. And their assignments weren't to be easily ignored, no, they were to be approached with caution of course, but nonetheless brought into the special fold that would offer them fame and fortune… of course, the former would only be for the chosen few.

"What do you mean, the best of the best?" one of the young potential recruits could always be heard asking in the middle of the crowded banquet hall.

"You'll soon find out," the recruiter would inevitably answer.

CHAPTER 23

WILL HIT THE BRAKES with both boots and skidded up to
a long stop, eventually landing perfectly in front of the sheriff
station. He watched as the dirt flew forward, then upward like
a mini-dust devil. He loved doing that. Not because it gave him some
superior feeling of invincibility or entitlement, but for the fact that he still
had that little kid inside him and he liked to exercise that from time to
time—and utilizing government property for his own entertainment, well
that was just gravy!

He was still covered head to toe in muck from his night of involuntary,
impromptu camping, and now his cruiser was putting its WeatherTech
rubber floor mats to the test. The same couldn't be said about the now
tragically stained upholstery, as the muck and moisture that had covered
Will's clothes had transferred nearly everywhere, but especially to the
driver's seat, where he'd been sitting for quite a while.

The mud and mess had practically become one with the fabric, ground
in by the weight of Will and the shifting of his body, particularly while he
and Callahan were racing to the hospital after coming down the mountain.
He was certainly going to put the boys down at the motor pool in for

overtime, as it would take hours to clean the interior of his government-issued vehicle.

Will reached into the back seat and grabbed a long, mud-covered canvas-wrapped object. He carefully maneuvered it from the back seat to the front without scraping the fabric on the car's ceiling or banging any of the windows. This was a very important piece of evidence and he would be damned if there were any, or at least any more, damage done to it because of an error on his part.

Before he'd even exited his vehicle, he looked up and saw movement: heads bobbing up and down in an attempt to be sneaky inside the station. It seemed to be bustling as though they were preparing for their yearly Christmas party. He knew word had probably already gotten back from Rusty, the hospital, Sandy Little Bear, or all of them to create a rare feeding frenzy of excitement and gossip these parts only get from time to time.

He looked down and smiled, knowing everyone was going to be running back to their desks and pretending to be doing what they were supposed to be doing. He wasn't going to deny all his hardworking employees and deputies the one piece of human interest that even he found compelling.

Will jumped out of his SUV and made enough noise to wake the dead slamming the car door to give everyone enough time to get back to their stations. He headed up the handicap ramp as it always seemed to be easier on his knees in winter than the stairs and made his way to the station's front entrance. He opened the door, carrying the canvas-wrapped package under his right arm and with his left hand at the bottom as though he were about to begin rifle drills for a surly Marine sergeant. Normally by this time of day, Will would have already stumbled into the office before everyone else, but today he was arguably allowed the tardiness he had never as yet exhibited.

After all, he thought, he'd already risked his old bones jumping out of a helicopter in the dark, wind, and rain, while being pelted by hail, to save the life of a young boy. All this because those younger, more experienced paramedics had shirked their duties while they were off to the big city to party and chase girls under the guise of "helicopter repairs."

Additionally, he had to climb down a rain-soaked mountain to secure the boy in a harness, climb back up alone, slipping every step of the way, spent the whole night out in the wind and the rain and the morning hiking, then driving to Cheyenne and back to the hospital. What he really wanted was a fresh cup of coffee and a little shut-eye.

They didn't have to say anything, but everyone in the office was surprised Will would even think about coming back into the station for the rest of the week. But not Will Pierce; he had work to do. And this was the kind of work that put a kick in his step and brought out the detective he was always meant to be.

Deputy Jenkins leapt from his desk as Will entered the station. He had already assigned another guard to the hospital to watch over Michael and the Callahan's and had somehow, in his zeal, beat Will back. He must've been doing over 90 on the back roads in order to get there. Will was gonna have to have a little chat with Rusty about that, he thought.

Rusty banged his large black leather belt against the side of the desk as he shot forward toward Will making his way down the front aisle. Will had seen Rusty get his Taser pistol and pepper spray canister caught up on the corner of the desk and took an extra step to ensure he'd be in front of his deputy before they crashed into each other.

This of course, put Rusty directly behind his sheriff, so he doggedly pursued Will all the way to his office with a line of questions. "Is that it, Sheriff? Rusty sounded like an excited puppy. "Is that the evidence?"

Will could've chastised Rusty for his overexcitement, but he needed Rusty to get more experience, more involved, and felt he had to pass the torch in some way or another and bring his deputy into more cases and on newer and more complex issues relating to crime and the law.

"Yep, this is it," Will said. He continued toward his office unabated, knowing full well Rusty would nearly be climbing over his back to get an extra peek at what he was carrying.

"Man, Will, I mean Sheriff, I am here to tell ya that I'm so excited!" Rusty continued to flank Will all the way inside the doorway to his office. "It's like my birthday and Christmas all wrapped up on the same day."

"Clear a space on my desk, would ya Rusty?" Will said with deliberate calm. He knew full well he could've made it an order, but he actually liked Rusty a lot and was only seemingly hard on him when it was needed.

Rusty immediately began to clear an area where Will would usually put his boots up for a nap in front of his chair. He took a long sweep of his arm across the desk using his shirt and the fabric covering his forearm to literally mop up any dust or debris. Then snatched open the cupboard next to the desk to pull out a clean cloth that he carefully spread out, making sure it evenly covered the whole surface.

Will saw him consider the paper jumpsuits they kept to use at crime scenes that needed to be kept free of contamination. Anything to keep from corrupting the evidence before it was even brought to the forensic lab in Billings for testing. He was nothing if not obsessive about procedure and that put a smile on Will's face... metaphorically speaking.

Deciding for him, Will simply lay the canvas onto the desk and slowly, carefully, unrolled the package, keeping one end up and the other balancing on the edge. As he unfurled the material, it began to reveal Callahan's rifle.

Still dirty from the fall, wet from the rain, and beaten from the elements, it was not really much worse for wear, as its basic quality of manufacture had pretty much protected it... with the minor exceptions of some new scuffs and scratch marks, courtesy of the Wyoming open range.

"Okay, you remember your forensics training?" Will asked, standing and turning toward Rusty. "I want you to start from the beginning and try not to forget anything."

"Yes, Sir, ah, yes, Sheriff!"

"Take your time, it's not a race. It's more important to be thorough and take longer than it is to rush through it and forget important details, understand?"

"Yes, Sir, Sheriff, I remember," Rusty answered as excitedly as a schoolboy as he suddenly reached into his back pocket to retrieve something. "Got 'em right here, actually I've got quite a few of them."

"Hell, Rusty, you're only gonna really need one, but go ahead."

"I carry 'em with me now everywhere, since when you told me to last time. Remember when old man Smithers went missing and we couldn't find his body until the snow melted after he got drunk and tried to walk all the way home from Chico's Lounge and fell asleep in the snow bank?" Rusty pulled a pair of latex-free surgical gloves from behind his back and began to quickly put them on as though he'd been practicing for weeks.

"I remember."

"Poor old guy, why do you think he laid down in a snow bank, Sheriff? I mean, after all, it would've been colder than the air outside, don't you think he would've felt all that cold and jumped right up and sobered up?"

"I don't know, Rus, let's get back to the task at hand, shall we?" Rusty began to run his imaginary checklist in his head as he placed the gloves on.

"Check!" Rusty stretched his fingers to conform into the gloves and looked back at Will for instruction. He was tempted to pull the plastic back and snap it like they did in the medical dramas his girlfriend liked so much, but decided this wasn't the right place or time.

"Get your flashlight ready so we can illuminate anything."

"Copy that, Sheriff!"

"And here's a magnifying glass to check the details." He waited til Rusty had finished with the gloves, then handed it to him, not gently, but like a doctor handing another surgeon his scalpel.

"This is just like Sherlock Holmes," Rusty said.

"Nope, this is real," Will reminded his deputy through slightly gritted teeth. He reached over and turned on the desk lamp, then moved it over the top of the rifle. "Now start from the back and cover every inch of surface on this side first."

Rusty nodded in compliance.

"I want you to describe everything you're seeing, like a doctor would, and call out anything of note so we can log it." Will was trying to be as professorial as possible in order to give his deputy the benefits of a federally trained, albeit former, special agent.

One thing Will understood clearly was protocol and that the chain of custody was nothing to trifle with. A single error, one omission, a forgotten detail, something overlooked, a tiny mistake and all could be lost. If you were hung-over from the night before, fighting with your wife or having trouble with your taxes, your sloppiness, your lapse in judgment, could set a killer free. Nearly worse than that, the department could get a black eye from a vigorous defense attorney out to crucify cops or the law enforcement office they hold, whether or not they deserved the scrutiny.

By this time, Rusty could hardly contain himself. He took a long, deep cleansing breath, then exhaled for composure. He steadied his hands, then took the magnifying glass and leaned closely toward the rifle to begin his reconnoiter.

"Here, you're gonna need this!" Will reached across the desk and opened one of his top drawers with a single motion. He rummaged around with his fingers and stopped when he found what he was looking for, quickly pulling out a small, digital recorder and popping open the back to make sure it had two triple A batteries. He clicked the *on* button once and saw that it was in working order.

"One thing I've always learned, it's better to document each and every inspection both in writing and on tape. This way if anyone ever calls into question what you did and how you did it, you've got audible verification of every step you took. It's basic CYA."

Rusty gave Will an odd look as though trying to figure out what those letters meant. His mind was wandering as he squinted, attempting to come up with the right answer and impress his boss.

"… Cover Your Ass!"

Rusty smiled and got back to the task at hand. He took the microcassette recorder from Will and depressed the *record* button as he began. He arched his body carefully in order to get as close to the evidence as possible, without actually touching anything.

"Okay, I see an older weapon, a rifle, bolt action," Rusty started. "It has a nicely polished wood grain, a couple of lateral scratches and two deep gouges in the butt, from the top extending at a downward angle." Rusty stopped and stood back up with a quizzical look on his face. "I'm guessing these are new striations from the fall and all," Rusty said intellectually.

Will's eyebrow furrowed at Rusty's obvious command of the English language. Where did he get such a good vocabulary? Will wondered. He may want to use more of that in his day-to-day conversations.

"Good, go on," Will nodded.

It was tedious for Will to watch because he had the ability to spot something amiss a mile away and hours before, but like a teaching hospital, he knew he would have to take the time to pass on his skill and expertise. Rusty would, after all, be taking over his position… sooner rather than later.

"It still has a smell of gun oil." Rusty had already leaned down closer and began to sniff the rifle. "Whoa, what's this?!" Rusty blurted out. He ran his finger over a deep indentation in the stock and looked closer as he crossed over a hole in the wooden stock of the rifle.

"Wow, Michael is one lucky kid!" he said to himself, but loud enough to be caught on the recorder.

Will stepped in closer to prod his young protégé. He wanted to help Rusty and nearly whispered the clue into his ear: "*and* why's that?"

"That's a bullet hole there, alright!" Will pretended not to have already seen and calculated the indentation for what it was. "... and by the looks of it, I'd say it's a 7.62 round!" Rusty looked back at his mentor, as he was now ready to be tested. Will would certainly not be letting him off the hook that easily; now was the time to apply a bit of pressure.

"How do you know it's a 7.62 round?" As confident as Rusty was with his discovery, Will had just shattered that sense of accomplishment. "Why couldn't it be a 7.35 Carcano, or a .222 Remington Magnum, or a 7 x 57 Mauser?" Will began to challenge everything Rusty was going to say as well as his observational skills, but more importantly, he was trying to force Rusty to use every part of his God-given brain.

"I, I don't!" Rusty answered quickly, not waiting for Will to answer or give a physical gesture of acknowledgement. "On account I haven't yet X-rayed the rifle!"

Will nearly smiled, but held it back so Rusty would keep digging through his mind to come up with different and alternate scenarios.

"I haven't done a 3D CAD design and rotated it 360 degrees to get a full ballistics spectrum." Now he was cooking with gas, Will thought.

"I have yet to carefully dig the projectile out to see if there are any identifiers left somewhere on it..." Rusty ran the sequences and itemized a forensics list in his mind, then repeated to Will as though he were bucking for student of the year.

"So yes, Sheriff, I can't say with any conviction, as yet, if that bullet is, in fact a 7.62."

"Excellent, Rusty!" Will said as proudly as any father. Will dropped his smile and lowered his eyes as if to say that wasn't enough. "Now what else?"

Rusty ran the length of the gun with his eyes, then carefully picked it up and turned it over to inspect the opposite side he had yet to see. "Well, it wasn't a through and through shot."

Will stood there like a stone, not giving Rusty a single clue with this poker face.

"So we know young Michael Callahan's little body absorbed the entire force of the bullet near his chest."

"And how do we know this?"

"We know this because he told us by making a declaration from his hospital bed when he recalled that as he was setting up his own shot at the sheep and was about to pull the trigger, he had pulled the rifle up to his chest and the stock up tight against his chest and ribs."

"Good," Will said.

Rusty nodded, but he knew he was only at the beginning of the process, so he wasn't about to get overconfident.

"That's why the doctor's report states he had a bruised sternum and spleen. You were correct to illustrate the fact that he had absorbed the bullet's energy and thus his injuries, combined with those of his fall, are in line with being shot."

"Should I talk about the fall? I mean, maybe it's gonna be important?"

"No, don't cloud the issue. Right now you're making observations and opinions about the rifle, the bullet, the shot, the boy… *cause and effect.*"

Rusty nodded again.

"His additional injuries *could have* come from the fall, but it's more likely that the force of the bullet hitting the wooden stock of the rifle then driving it into Michael's chest and he absorbing the full force of a bullet from a sniper's rifle knocked him over the cliff like a sledgehammer hitting him squarely in center-mass."

Rusty listened intently to his hero's dulcet tones as though he were the Messiah speaking from on high. Suddenly a strange look came over Rusty's face, the same look he had when he had first heard the news of Michael Callahan's victimization.

"That poor little boy," Rusty said, shaking his head. "If I ever get my hands on that shooter, I'm gonna wrap them around the neck of that bastard who tried to kill an innocent child." Rusty looked at his hands as he brought them to his face, then simulated a strangling as he gripped them together and shook them violently. "Better yet, I'm gonna…"

Rusty had lost himself in the bloodlust as he wrapped his hands together as though he were strangling the life out of the imaginary perpetrator.

"… you're gonna arrest him and turn him in!" Will quickly interrupted. "Because that's what we do!" Will said again, matter-of-factly.

"We in law enforcement are not in the revenge or vigilante business. We're in law enforcement."

Rusty snapped out of it and practically stood at attention as Will recited his creedo.

"We're gonna bring this guy to the judge. We're gonna hand over the District Attorney all the evidence we've collected. We're gonna give him all of our theories, opinions, and our best hypotheses and observations."

Rusty nodded in agreement like a dog that had just wet the carpet.

"Then we're gonna let a judge and jury of his peers decide his fate. Why?"

Rusty was too terrified to answer.

"'Cause it ain't up to us!" Rusty nodded at Will's correction and gave him a look like it would never happen again. Suddenly Will reached over and turned the recorder to the *off* position.

Will's stern look began to melt as he contemplated something. "That said, of course it all depends if the son of a bitch gives up or not!"

Will made sure that even though he said it under his breath, Rusty could still hear. "… cause if he don't give up peacefully, well that's a whole different ballgame!"

Rusty cocked his head and was now confused and certainly a little curious.

"If he wants to go out in a blaze of glory, I think we'll be able to accommodate him, don't you Rusty?" Will tilted his head and smiled sinisterly at Rusty. "A wink's as good as a nudge, they say."

"Copy that, boss!" Rusty said. He now knew his primal feelings for what had happed to Michael were being mirrored by Will. Men have an unspoken language and it was screaming at both of them right then and there.

"So Rusty, you know what we've got here, right?" Will concluded.

Rusty nodded.

"Now, go and write up your report and don't spare any details."

Will reached over to the microcassette recorder and turned it back to the *on* position so Rusty could begin taping his forensic examination. With his other hand, he picked up the rifle with the canvas underneath it and handed it to Rusty. Before letting go, he quickly pushed a hidden quick release button on the side of the scope. The monocular suddenly popped off and Will set it back down on his desk.

"Here." Will's timbre changed and his tone became all business. "Take this to your desk and examine it some more so you're completely accurate in your report."

Rusty took the microcassette recorder and the rifle back from Will, but had a curious look on his face.

"I'm gonna take a closer look at this scope. Something seems a little off about it," Will explained.

With that, Rusty nodded and smiled, then carefully took the rifle, cradling the weapon and carrying it like a newborn calf out into the bullpen to his desk.

Will turned around and began to admire and inspect the monocular. It was about this time when he decided to sit down at his desk that he thought about the fact that it was the first time he had sat down since the day before and was about to close his eyes for a well-deserved nap when he heard a familiar voice approaching his office door.

"Hey Sheriff, look who's the talk of the town today!" Molly Volta was the local newspaper reporter, and an enthusiastic one at that. Because in Wyoming, the state still had a vast readership of periodicals and Molly was considered at the top of her game.

She entered Will's office with a big grin on her face, as the excitement of the previous night's events were palpable around town, and being the local newsy, she took great pride in getting all the salacious details of a potentially deadly event straight from the horse's mouth, as it were.

Will continued to close his eyes regardless of Molly's presence, as he knew it would take her about 20 seconds to figure out he was faking it and that was the only 20 extra seconds he was gonna have of shut-eye that entire day.

"Come on Sheriff, Ben Founder and Natalie Bernstein overheard Sandy Little Bear at Sam's Diner, and you know those two couldn't keep a secret if their life depended on it." Molly kept talking as though she had his attention, even though Will kept pretending to sleep.

Molly was very pretty, especially for a woman who had grown up in this part of Wyoming where life can be harsh and take its toll on a person's skin, and for that matter, their mind, body, and patience. This included Will's, as he really wanted to sleep.

She was a single woman in her late 30s, who had been married once to a man who was killed in a wreck out on the interstate and she had never tried it again. She had a huge crush on Will, one that had held pretty steady for a long time. The trouble was, she wasn't afraid to show it. Molly was smart enough and knew all his games and, even though journalism was a fast-dying profession, she was the only reporter in the tri-county area worth her salt, so she wasn't going to give up without a story that would include her byline attached to the top of it.

"Molly, give me a break," Will said, opening one eye.

Molly folded her arms in an obvious show of annoyance, bordering on anger.

"I've hardly slept in two days, can we do this another time?" Will said as he shut the one opened eye.

Molly looked back out into the office and saw that everyone seemed occupied, so she quietly shut the office door so no one would notice. She decided to approach Will, creeping closer and closer to him until she was right up to the side of his head and close to his ear.

"You know I'm not going away, Sheriff. You're a big hero now and everyone wants to know what Will Pierce is thinking, wearing, and eating for supper. Just like on those reality shows like *Housewives of Beverly Hills*."

Will opened one eye again. He knew Molly would continue her barrage of annoyance if he didn't concede and give in to her demands. "Look, first, I'm no damn hero. I just did the job I'm paid to do, same as anyone does!" Will said half-awake.

A big smile crossed Molly's lips, as she knew he couldn't resist her charms.

"And I'm no spring chicken. I didn't set any records by getting that child off that mountain quickly."

Molly gave him a sympathetic look; she knew he needed to vent and if he was going to vent to anyone, it was most assuredly going to be her.

"Hell, if we'd had the paramedics here, like they were supposed to be, instead of off for God knows what reason and where, he'd been treated and taken care of up there on the plateau instead of being drug all around Hell's half acre in a two-seater puddle-jumper getting his little body battered even more than it had been from side to side worse than when he was laying on that cliff side in pain.

Will looked up and noticed that Molly had been taking notes the whole time.

"What are you doing? This is off the record!"

Molly's lips pursed and she gave him a look like a disgruntled wife whose husband forgot to take out the trash.

"You can't print that, everyone involved with that rescue is gonna read it, especially those paramedics that were up in Billings getting the helicopter repaired!"

"Will Pierce, you know I got a job to do and like it or not, you're a public servant and I need to have you debrief me on just what the heck happened," Molly said sternly.

"Wha!" Will began to say before he was cut off.

"And if you try and stonewall me or give me some BS two-sentence answer, I'm gonna publish that *unauthorized* Will Pierce retrospective and then everybody will *really* be clamoring to get a piece of you!"

Will smacked his lips and slowly reached into one of his lower desk drawers and retrieved a bottle of water. He looked at Molly, still standing in a highly defensive position, and chugged the liquid down. *Clug, clug, clug.*

"Now Molly, I could give you some line, like 'no comment' or 'it's still under investigation,' but that would just make you even more mad than you seem to be, which is pretty mad, wouldn't it?" Will said teasingly.

"You bet your ass it would, Will Pierce!" Molly retorted, nodding her head furiously.

"You mean, Sheriff Pierce, don't you?" Will returned, calming her down quickly. "There's one thing I learned when I was at the Bureau, and that is keeping crucial information from the public does not help a case, especially a case of attempted murder!" Will said, waiting for Molly's reaction.

Molly's eyes widened and her jaw went agape. "Did you say '*attempted murder?*'"

"… of a child!" Will finished as Molly's face flushed red from the way Will had presented his statements and the fact that she may possibly have just stumbled onto the story of her career. This was the type of story that every journalist spends their lives trying to find.

"Go on now, get that recorder out of your purse. We have a lot of information to cover and I don't want you misquoting me again," Will said playfully.

"Misquoting?" Molly barked, digging in her purse and retrieving her own microcassette recorder and fumbling with the *on* button.

Will chuckled as he knew any reporter would take umbrage with that statement, but Molly was especially sensitive to the idea of misquoting someone.

"Don't get your panties in a bunch, I was just kidding," Will laughed.

Molly shot him another annoyed look.

"But in all seriousness, I'll give you the exclusive, but you're gonna have to get it out onto the wire services and the Internet."

Will lifted his arms up as he stretched away the tightness from the night before. "I want this story published far and wide, if you know what I mean? This is gonna upset a lot of people." Will reached down and picked up the riflescope on his desk and began to examine it. "Yep, a lot of people are gonna be unhappy about what we've got here!"

CHAPTER 24

CLING, CLING, CLING COULD be heard as the room full of invited guests began tapping their fine polished silverware against the Waterford Crystal goblets that circled the table in front of each guest.

The lights were dimmed and suddenly a bright light burst forth onto a screen at the head of the room above everyone's head. Slowly, a series of slides began to appear on the screen, but this was no ordinary slideshow; this was the slideshow that would determine this year's winner.

The large high-definition display showed every photo in crisp, clean detail and each image was even more unique and rare than the last. Oohs and aahs could be heard rising like cigarette smoke in the air as the occupants were spellbound by the complexity of each shot. Ironically, a single shot would be the defining term for this awards banquet.

The first image was of a buffalo on the plains with the center of the shot nearly perfect with the animal's eye. The image was black and white and grainy, even though it had been put through processor after processor to enhance the image and bring out the pixilation to highlight the bison and the surrounding images. But each image had a specific flaw, as some might say, or overlapping image on the photo.

The white dotted lines looked like crosshairs of a rifle's scope, but in fact were actually the camera's own aperture that was seen as you looked down the length of the eyepiece. Each and every image was merely a photo from a photographer's lens: an image or headshot here, a glamour shot there, all were in perfect focus and most difficult to get.

As the recruiters eyed the room of guests, looking for their prey, they scanned everywhere as they watched each and every guest train their sophisticated eyes on each picture, or target, as they saw them, and salivated over the idea that theirs might just be the next WPS Award winner.

The recruiters would walk amongst the guests, going from table to table examining each person's attention to the photo and the shooter's ability to capture the image before that image would be erased from history, or at least never be in the same place as it was when the shot was taken.

The recruiters had a vested interest in their special recruits because they too received remuneration: a percentage of what the award winner would receive by the foundation. So it was incumbent on them to use all their knowledge, talents, and experience to be wise enough and bear witness to study their quarry, measure their effectiveness, and choose wisely.

Each image remained a moment captured in time, like a genie in a bottle with quite literally a jury of their peers judging how expert they were that very moment. And, although the judging was certainly considered subjective, each shooter had to abide by specific, and most certainly stringent, rules and regulations the club dictated or they would be disqualified from not only the contest, but from the hunting association as well.

Each guest knew the rules and could recite them verbatim. It was one of the many conditions for being a successful club member.

CHAPTER 25

WILL WOKE FROM A long night's sleep and had just begun to feel the cobwebs clearing from his head after an unexpectedly busy couple days in law enforcement.

His body and mind weren't used to all the rough and tumble of late. And the attempted murder of a child by a sniper was something he'd hadn't seen in quite a while. Violent acts of terrorism were usually relegated to the federal level.

Will hadn't seen action like this in quite a long time and he'd forgotten how his instincts used to naturally kick in during challenging events. He was certainly not feeling like a spring chicken today, but he was beginning to grow a logic tree in his mind. He liked to test himself with various scenarios to keep his mind sharp and get closer to his unknown subject, or UNSUB as the Bureau had an affinity for calling them.

He had awakened early that morning, like all mornings, but this day would prove to be different from the past few, as he was off duty and looking forward to spending the day in his arena, tending to his livestock and other animals, and of course, getting a chance to ride his favorite horse.

Will had already risen, dressed, made himself a light breakfast, and was out the door toward the stables before his other wranglers had finished their morning coffee. He would get a good start on the day, as he wanted to inspect the progress of a pair of beavers he had brought in to repair an old spring at the back of the 40-acre pasture. He also hoped to ride and train his horses. While tending to his affairs, he hoped his brain would start organizing the evidence currently running loose in his head.

Will did his best detective work when he was on the back of a beautifully trained horse, as he could clear his head of everything else except what he needed to focus on. Although normally tractable, Will had learned the hard way the need to keep his attention on the job at hand. Even a small horse could weigh over 800 pounds, and he had worked with a couple probably closer to 1,300 pounds. He'd learned never to take his mind or eyes off the horse.

It was cloudy that morning with a slight breeze from the northeast, just the way Will liked it. Will was proud of his ranch, aside from the dirt and dust that got into everything and settled everywhere, it was as neat as a pin. All boards in good repair. All fences maintained. Weeds knocked back and trees trimmed.

He knew the value of learning hard work early and he wanted to impart his knowledge to the next generation. So he'd made a deal with the local high school. In return for students' help on the farm, he gave them hands-on education on the business of running a ranch like his. It wasn't all just chasing cows. There was a lot of work that didn't involve shoveling manure. Sales to be prepared for, breeding to arrange for horses, cows, and sheep. Getting the hay in on time and the next year's crop planted. Planning the rotation of the crops. Sure, some of the local high school kids came out every day and cleaned up after his horses, but he made sure they got a chance to make use of their brains as well as their brawn.

He paid them good wages and did the same for the wrangler who worked for him full time. It was just good business and kept everything on an even keel. There had been one or two of particular promise that he had gone a little further with, helping with college recommendations or referenced to employers. And every once in a while, money that was needed for tuition to a university would appear. He didn't talk about it and would just glare at anyone who tried to bring it up. For the rest, he knew they could get a jump on things they needed like trucks, movie money, or just a few bucks to take out their girlfriends on a Saturday night. It also didn't hurt that he was quietly helping out in a depressed economy.

Will entered the barn and his demeanor changed. He softened his hard edges and began to use a lower voice and timbre to address his flock. One of the great joys in Will's life, he thought, was that he was blessed with being from Wyoming and was raised to respect and care for animals. After all, most were helpless in the wild by today's standards, but more importantly, they gave unconditional love to him and any other human they encountered.

He passed down the barn aisle, coming up on the stalls that housed animals anxiously awaiting to greet him. He walked by and spoke to each and every one of his animals, as was his custom to make sure that each of them felt as loved as the other.

Rufus shot past Will's hip as he walked. Rufus was Will's canine, and therefore best friend, as the saying goes, so he took precedence over the other animals and affection would be showered upon him first and foremost.

Since Rufus was an indoor and outdoor dog, he got the lion's share of Will's attention, so there wasn't any need to stand on ceremony with him. Besides, Rufus was a Labrador and labs are like big kids; they just can't stop running and playing, demanding their master's attention, hugs, and pets.

"Come on, Rufus, let's go say hi to the kids," he said, slapping his hip hard.

Rufus ran and jumped in front of Will and shot in and out of the stalls until he could figure out which one Will would stop at first.

"Hello, Petey!" Will approached the stall of his white and brown tobiano Pinto, his naturally quiet walk easing himself into the animal's space. He let the animal smell his hand first, then began to stroke the horse's long nose with a tender hand. Petey, like most horses, enjoyed that immensely. Will continued to scratch him under his chin and rub behind his ears.

Petey liked this, as it reminded him of something his mother did when he was just a foal. She would lower her head and rub the top of her large head under his chin. Will brought Petey's head up to the side of his face and let the horse caress it. He snuggled the large animal's muzzle with his own.

"Petey, why the heck would someone want to kill a young boy?"

The horse knew when his master lowered his tone that it was some kind of question and he also knew to make a sound as though he were responding. Petey whuffled at Will's hair, as Will continued his line of questioning to the horse.

"A boy who was just out hunting with his grandfather in the back country of Wyoming?" Will said in a low, kind voice so the horse would feel comfortable as he pondered the elements of the crime scene. After a moment, Will stopped with Petey and walked toward another stall where an anxious horse awaited. Rufus had already made his way up the aisle and back a number of times, announcing the arrival of their master to the barn.

The horses and other livestock were restless and excited and making a great deal of noise at the prospect of a head scratch, rub, or perhaps a cube of sugar or a tasty apple.

"What do you think, Rocket?" Will approached the stall that housed a beautiful black and white American Paint. The horse knew his mind was elsewhere, but all he wanted was the human's attention and affection.

"Why would someone go to all the trouble of sighting in a human target, at nearly 1,000 yards no less?"

The horse began nodding his head, as if he too agreed that it was certainly perplexing, but nothing a piece of apple or carrot couldn't solve.

"There were only a couple of higher perches even remotely near that plateau." Will continued thinking out loud as he petted and strummed the whiskers of his Paint. He looked around for the sturdy brush he normally kept on a nearby shelf, but it was nowhere in sight and, since the horse didn't seem to mind his hand stroking him, he kept brushing his face gently.

"So the sniper follows Callahan and his grandson for over 100 miles to a remote area, easily over an hour away from any major town, then makes an even harder hike up a mountain?"

Rotating his body, the horse made it easier for Will to reach that wonderful spot just in front of his withers.

"So this bad guy stays still enough and remains out of sight of a CEO of a security company. How does he get away with that, I wonder?"

The other animals raised their cries of attention even louder as Will was seemingly spending too much time with only one animal.

"So Callahan never sees he's being hunted, he has no suspicion of his presence, then out of the blue, *BAM!*"

The other animals stopped momentarily as it sounded as if their master was now cross with them. Suddenly, his deep voice continued. "So the sniper decides against a head or chest shot, certainly more challenging than anywhere else on the body and decides to shoot the wood on the butt of young Michael's rifle and nowhere on his body?"

The horse shifted his weight and nodded his head wildly, wanting more of his attention and scratches when Will stopped petting him for a moment.

"Sorry, old boy, of course, you come first," he laughed at the gelding's antics. Will knew horses could be like children when they wanted attention, but Will was free with his love and he never had a problem being kind to an animal or giving it what it naturally desired from a human.

Will reached into a barrel of oats just out of reach of the horse's long head and scooped up a handful. He raised it to the horse's muzzle. A few hand treats never hurt a horse, he believed, though he had been told by many that it led to nipping.

"So a lone gunman, a dedicated lone gunman, who has a chip on his shoulder or is out for blood or is trying to prove something, but why a boy?" Will wondered as he continued to stroke the long nose.

Suddenly, Rufus began to bark as the other horses in the barn began to nay loudly—Will's signal to move on and attend to the other animals.

"Okay, okay, I'm coming!" Will shouted down the aisle at the rest of the animals.

Meanwhile, Rufus shot into a stall and could be heard playing in the hay.

"Rufus, git out of there!" Will barked. "Leave Lonesome George be."

As Will approached one of the last stalls, a beautiful bay stallion appeared as Rufus shot out into the aisle at Will's command. His mind was clearly on the case at hand as well as the shooter, but the horse didn't take offense; he as well as the others just wanted Will's love and attention.

"How ya doin' this morning, Lonesome George?" Will talked to his favorite as though he were speaking to a child. Across the barn was the young stallion's dam. Rosa had yet another youngster currently prancing around by her side; a sister to Lonesome George. Will was grateful every day for the beauty and strength she passed down through her powerful bloodline.

What made Lonesome George, as well as his relatives, so special to Will was that he was a Peruvian Paso. Pasos, as they were called, were unique in their way of travelling. Instead of a trot or a canter, they had a four-beat lateral gait that could carry a man for hours and still leave him ready to dance the fandango at the end of the day.

Lonesome George was by far Will's favorite horse, and everyone knew it, even the animals, and especially Lonesome George, who appeared to accept it as the way it was supposed to be.

"Okay Lonesome George, what do you think about this whole plot to kill a boy?" Will said, leaning over the rail into Lonesome George's pen.

The horse rubbed his head against Will's arms and nuzzled Will in different areas, in order to get his full attention.

"So we have what could arguably be one of the finest shooters I've ever seen, out in a remote part of the prairie. Okay, we've established all that, but to what end? What's his end game?" Will asked Lonesome George as he heavily contemplated the situation.

Suddenly Will had a flash of genius. It was so obvious, even Lonesome George observed Will's body and facial expressions change with his big brown eyes.

"It has to be Callahan!" Will said excitedly. "Nobody is that stupid as to line up a shot from nearly a mile away and try and kill a boy for no reason! What's the point?"

The horse made sure Will expelled at least a modicum of concentration on him with a flick of his tail and a nicker to keep Will stroking him.

"Callahan was either the target or who the perpetrator was trying to make suffer for something. But for what?"

Will opened his hand to reveal a cube of sugar he'd been hiding and slipped it into Lonesome George's mouth before the other animals saw.

"Why would a world-class sniper try and get the attention of an old man who runs a security company?"

Giving it up for a moment, Will gathered his equipment from the tack room and led Lonesome George out to the hitching rail, preparing to saddle him. The grooming, saddling, and bridling took no time at all.

George was a well-trained horse. Will had trained him himself, so if there had been a problem, he knew it would be his fault, not the horses.

Lonesome George nickered and bopped his head as Will eased up the cinch.

"So a top sniper takes a shot from an impossible distance as a calling card for what… a job interview?" Will continued thinking out loud in the hopes of sparking another realization.

"I certainly wouldn't be interviewing for a job from the man whom I just tried to cancel his heir apparent!"

George followed Will out of the barn and waited while Will slipped a boot in the stirrup and swung on.

"So who is this guy? Why is he after Callahan? And what does he need to prove to get his attention?"

Lonesome George shook his long mane, as Will was getting too introspective for the horse's liking.

"Alright, alright!" Will said. He couldn't help smiling at the horse. As Will shifted his weight and gave George permission to head out across the fields in his ground-covering stride, Will saw his wranglers were up and dressed, scratching their heads at how Will could've possibly beaten them up and out that morning.

Leaving the reins draped on the horse's neck, Will let George pick their path and pulled his cell phone out of his holster-like crib. He called a 202 number, which was the area code for Washington, D.C.

"Hey Charlie, it's Will Pierce," Will said in a business-like tone.

"Hey Will, long time no hear! How you keeping out there in the Wild, Wild West?" a voice on the other end of the call said happily.

"I'm good, how about you and the kids?"

"Well, Nancy's been taking care of Ann, our little one, as she's been catching all her colds, seemingly at the same time."

"Sorry to hear that. Listen, I'm gonna be sending you some ballistics and other evidence and I'd like you to run them through SWGDAM."

"SWGDAM? Sure! Do you want this on the books or off the books like the old days?"

"Definitely on the books! I appreciated everything you did for me when I was at the Bureau, that's way I'm entrusting you with this evidence… it's pretty weird."

"Weird is my middle name, the weirder the better, I say."

"Okay, I'll run it through CODIS here on our end. I've got a rogue sniper who took a pot shot at a young boy and I've got a strange feeling he's a professional and this isn't his first long-range pop."

Finishing his call, he picked up the reins and looked around.

"What do you say we check the back fields on the way, George?" he asked. "They should be due for cutting soon."

CHAPTER 26

N NEARLY EVERY POLITICAL thriller movie and on every conspiracy theorist's lips is the omnipresent, overshadowing, secret society. For thousands of years, man has been enamored and in fear of a small powerful group that wields power beyond a normal man's control to effectuate an outcome that would suit the few and have their way with the many; a cadre that could act in its self-interest that was merely a shadow and rarely seen. The truth is, secret societies do exist, far from the scrutiny of the general public and government oversight and interference.

In a beautifully decorated dining hall outside Denver, Colorado, a nearly identical dinner to that of the WPS Awards had just gotten underway. It, too, began with a slide show, and as such, was also being presented to the small group of invited guests. These guests were part of a super elite group, hand-picked for one reason.

And their skills not only put the camera-eye to the test, but required nerves of steel because of the numerous dangers of getting caught hunting their prey, as getting caught was *not* an option in this game.

The lights dimmed just as they had at the WPS Awards dinner and the beam from the LED projector burst bright, but what appeared on screen weren't natural shots of beautiful animals in all their pageantry, but photos of humans, some famous, some infamous, others just people. All the photos had one thing in common. Perhaps it was an abdominal shot here, a little chin muscle there, or a shot behind the ear, every one had a precise intersection of two lines and each was arguably the fatal shot. Which would prove to be the overall winner was still a subjective matter.

As image after image from recent history appeared, no longer did the audience see the white dotted lines over the photo center, but the red or black crosshairs and intersections that grew more and concentrated for maximum reaction and for the highest degree of difficulty by the shooter.

The first image was of the late President John Fitzgerald Kennedy. The image was grainy, but oddly enough, the next image was crystal clear, showing the grassy knoll and two well-dressed men: one behind a tree, the other behind a fence, both holding scoped rifles trained on Kennedy's motorcade. A hush fell over the room. The incredible, never-before-seen shots not only told the *true* stories of some of history's great mysteries, but would prove to the world that indeed, secret societies are out there and they can control the fate of an awful lot of people.

Each red or black crosshair of a sniper's scope appeared as the shooter looked down the length of the eyepiece, not the white dotted lines of the camera aperture, which were eerily similar. Each and every image showed what a human would look like lined up ready to be assassinated.

After nearly an hour of the jaw-dropping slide presentation, the lights slowly lifted and a single individual stood up from one of the front tables and walked to the podium. After a moment, another followed, then another. Three men appeared behind the podium, the heads of the organization.

Callahan, Miller, and Khumari, childhood friends who had started the Weapons Into Plowshares organization, and also designed this labyrinth of a society within a society.

"Welcome, ladies and gentlemen, all of you elite shooters, and thank you all for coming to this year's annual meeting of those select few who take our sister foundation, Weapons Into Plowshares, to an entirely new and exceptional level," Miller began as he addressed the audience.

"We three conceived this organization over half a century ago and we always make it a point to reiterate the rules and regulations we follow and that you *MUST* follow in order for you to become the greatest shooter you can be," he went on.

Callahan chimed in, "From our forefathers like Teddy Roosevelt and hunter heroes like Daniel Boone and Davy Crocket, it was realized hundreds of years ago the importance of hunting conservation, after they witnessed pioneers and land barons opening up the frontier and the consequences of overhunting that nearly destroyed this country before it could even get started... and hunting for no other reason than killing for killing's sake."

"These forward thinkers created the first rules and regulations to hunting that ended the idea of commercial hunting as well as the emptiness, counter productivity, and pure waste of sport hunting," he continued.

Nassar stepped in between the other two men and began to orate. "Yet, man, as we well know, is a hunter! He thrives on the hunt, his heart races at the quest, and his blood boils at the idea of taking another life. This, my friends, is as old as man himself, and our DNA is coded to become excited at the idea of the hunt."

"The blood that courses through our body is billions of years of primal, uncontrollable lust for the hunt and we salivate, somewhere in our memory at the challenge."

"So when we three realized you can only harm yourself by trying to deny your basic nature and instincts, why couldn't we find a way to satisfy our primal urges, to at the time satiate our hunger for the killing of another creature?" he asked.

Miller smiled and patted the other two men on the back as he leaned in toward the mic. "That's when the light bulb went off. We knew what paths we were each on and that we would quickly have the ability to facilitate a way for not only us, but for those special few who shared our outlook as well as the thrill of the hunt."

The audience began to settle back in their seats and absorb these titans' words.

"So we first created the Weapons Into Plowshares Foundation as a way to bring hunters, gun enthusiasts, and other outdoorsmen and women together, and as a cover for our true goal."

"A goal I might add that only the select few of you here tonight can enjoy. Through the philanthropy of the foundation that our three respective companies produce worldwide to help children and families around the world, we can offer the exceedingly large purses to you fine individuals as former winners of the Elite Shooters Award," Nassar continued.

"Purses that have allowed you to become *specialists*, if I may take a page out of the military's book." Nassar looked at Miller, as if he meant a mea culpa to the former Marines.

"And as Weapons Into Plowshares continues its missions, we gain greater and greater acceptance, thus getting greater and greater access to the highly specialized individuals that will make this group grow and flourish for decades to come," Callahan said proudly.

Each of the three men momentarily stopped and looked at each other, then gazed upon the crowd of onlookers staring back at them, hanging on their every word.

"Although all of you know the Fair Chase statement of hunter's ethics, we also felt the need to add these other rules to limit any ambiguity or exploiting technicalities."

"…yet unlike our counterparts like the Boone & Crocket Club, Elite Warriors do no harm!"

Nassar continued, "As each and every one of you knows, we three have dedicated our lives to the preservation of life, but that doesn't mean we can't challenge ourselves, keeping ourselves and others on our toes in order to remind ourselves how precious life really is."

"We established this annual awards ceremony to honor those men and women who have shown the greatest ability to prove to us that they have what it takes to challenge themselves to pick the highest-value target, shoot that target at great risk to themselves, and prove to the selection committee that had there been a real bullet in the chamber of their rifle, that individual, no matter how famous, how powerful, how terrible, would be dead," Callahan orated with the presence of Mark Twain.

"If an outsider were to see these photos or our photo albums, they would most certainly believe they'd have stumbled onto an evil organization bent on the assassination of the world's most important figures," Nassar described. "Yet that would be the farthest from the truth since, as you all know, we keep tight controls over your shots to ensure that not only no harm ever befalls one of our subjects, but that it is *YOU* the shooter, who is in real danger!"

"The more dangerous the shot, the more dangerous it is for you the shooter. You have been outfitted with nothing more than a sniper's rifle, one of our tightly-controlled, high-powered single-direction, wireless camera scopes whose signal only comes to our standalone server, and our specially designed three-bullet blank cartridges," Miller detailed.

"Blanks!" Callahan reiterated. "We're shooting blanks! Why would someone be dumb enough, nay, I say bold enough, to take aim at a human subject, lock onto the perfect kill shot, snap a proprietary, and dare I say one-of-a-kind photo, at the exact split second a single round of ammunition reports to anyone within earshot that a bullet has been shot?"

A pin could've dropped and been heard by the attendees as they listened intently.

"In this day and age, the instant someone hears a shot, not only does everyone duck and cover, but authorities and citizens alike will attempt to chase down and capture the perpetrator."

"Satellite tracking has been able to pinpoint the report and reverberation of a single bullet and then instantaneously send that location to local law enforcement as well as military," he continued.

"Yet what have you really done?" Nassar interjected. "What crime have you committed? None! What you've done is remind those souls that were in and around the area that every second of their life is precious, every second a blessing. You've reminded them that the truly important parts of life are always there and they have the power to regain them if they could just survive the sound of a bullet!"

The crowd was riveted, hanging on each and every word like they were sages who had an insight to a mindset that has been lost through mindless technological upgrades, loss of true communication with each other, and the loss of love for their fellow men and women.

"So let's all review them again out loud!" Callahan, Miller, and Nassar all yelled together like a finely choreographed dance. They raised their arms and pointed to the audience.

They rules followed from a chorus of voices:

1) "A shooter MUST follow all United States state and federal law regarding the use of firearms as well as ammunition, even if they reside in another country and their prey is caught there.

2) A shooter MUST follow all federal and state Fish & Game Rules and Regulations.

3) Under NO CIRCUMSTANCE will the animal be stalked or harassed. Absolute quiet and clandestine movements must be made to ensure the prey is not alerted or startled or impeded from its natural habitat or environment.

4) ALL firearms MUST be legal under United States federal and state laws as well as those laws governing Fish & Game.

5) The GOALS of WPS include conservation and sports-person-ship."

The three men at the podium nodded their heads in appreciation of the members' recall.

"Now I'm sure you guys can do it again as we recite the rating system," Nassar yelled out.

The rating system followed the rules:

1) "Brain Kill shot = 3 points

2) Lung Shot = 2 points

3) Head Shot = 1 for 1."

Callahan, Miller, and Nassar were truly inspiring the audience as though they were gurus on stage with the power of Steve Jobs combined with the mysticism of the Dalai Lama.

"Now, as each and every one of you knows, from personal experience, we limit this group to the chosen few because of the demanding rigors of our unique vetting process," Miller began again.

"The psyche evals, military records, local law enforcement flags, down to your last parking ticket and what type of baby formula you used for your last child were scrutinized while we kept you under glass," Miller continued.

Callahan interjected. "It is only after the exhaustive two-year process that we make the overtures, the light contact, as we like to call it, to feel out whether you would even consider undertaking what I know for you is the most exciting mission on Earth."

"That is why we first introduce you into the Weapons Into Plowshares Foundation and let you get comfortable with other like-minded sportsmen while we focus and observe your movements, and more importantly, your motivations, until we finally reach out to you and offer you the chance of a lifetime to fulfill that deep, dark fantasy that lives in all of us," he said with a deeper timbre.

Nassar continued. "That is why *no one* in the WPS has any idea that this organization—an organization within an organization, if you will—even exists. Their only goal in the WPS is to challenge themselves with taking photographs, albeit the most difficult and dangerous photographs, after ours, of course, of animals for trophies."

"It is their goal to feel the thrill of the hunt and capture the animal's image just at the point in time where it would be dead if they had been using a weapon to end its beautiful life."

"It is your goal to go beyond even their goals and get the kind of rush only our primitive realities did tens of thousands of years ago by not only hunting and stalking their prey, but capturing their pseudo last moment, but then the added rush of alerting everyone of what you may or may not be trying to do, then getting away quickly and quietly before local law enforcement or civilians have a chance to stop you."

"It is for this reason our little organization can not and will not ever be breeched by a bad guy or ne'er-do-well, as you know, we keep incredibly close tabs on you through an array of NSA-based cryptography, eavesdropping technology, and satellite tracking systems," he finished.

"So it is with a heavy heart that I announce that someone has tried to kill a young member of my family... and we believe they may have come from this organization!"

The hushed crowd became uneasy and voices began to mumble to each other at the thought that one of them, perhaps the man or woman sitting next to them, could be an actual cold-blooded killer.

Each Elite Warrior turned to the other, then the other, then another. After each one had given a narrow eye to their neighbor, they each, in turn, began to look over their shoulders and back at the other members at each of the other dining tables and the suspicion began to grow.

"Please, please, we had to mention this unfortunate event to reiterate the importance of secrecy for what we do here," Miller yelled over the burgeoning noise of the crowd.

"We have our security teams investigating this heinous act as we speak and we can assure you this perpetrator will be caught," he finished.

"Now let's get to the awards... somewhere out there is a winner and their lives are about to change forever!"

CHAPTER 27

RUSTY HAD SPENT ALL night dissecting Callahan's rifle, with the would-be-assassin's bullet embedded, down to the tiniest of details.

The large metal laboratory table had a portable thin light board on it that Rusty had used for back lighting so he wouldn't miss the smallest clue. It wasn't Rusty's forte, but he knew weapons as much as anyone in Wyoming and certainly what to look for in terms of anomalies.

Rusty had carefully disassembled the rifle into a dozen large pieces and several other smaller ones, while placing each and every piece on the light board so it would be illuminated from the bottom up so as not to miss a detail.

He even went so far as to examine each piece with a jeweler's lighted magnifying visor. He studied each and every scratch, dirt cluster, and oily smear, but was frustrated at the lack of anything concrete. Before he reassembled the weapon, he made sure to recall what he had learned from Will.

He took great pride in the responsibility his mentor and hero had bestowed upon him, but he also felt he may have let him down. Rusty had fallen asleep sometime after 6 a.m. in the tiny makeshift lab, his face and head buried in his arms that were crossed on the polished stainless steel table as a slight stream of drool flowed out of the corner of his mouth.

The wire-framed desk chair had hardly squeaked all night because Rusty was a damn good sleeper, so much so, in fact, his girlfriend despised his ability to sleep through anything while she could be up all night from jealousy of his nocturnal relaxation.

Rusty had carefully taken apart the rifle, followed all the requisite mandatory forensic guidelines, worn proper attire on his hands, feet, and person, and had the patience of Job as he worked well into the night, eventually surprising everyone with his tenacity and diligence.

It was still early when Will quietly entered the lab to see Rusty's hard work and ultimate surrender to the sheer exhaustion he must have felt since Will had not received any urgent phone calls with that Eureka moment scream that Rusty was so prone to do.

Will decided to save Rusty's dignity and quietly back out of the laboratory, then make a commotion outside in order to wake him from his slumber. Unfortunately, this effort would take Will three or four times before Rusty awoke from his deep and well deserved slumber.

Will added a layer of believability as he pretended to talk to someone on his cell phone, when really it was merely for Rusty's benefit, but suddenly his cell phone did ring. It was the call he had been waiting for.

"Yeah, I know what Fish & Game said, what I want to know is who was the ranger or administrator who actually issued Callahan his permits that day to narrow down if anyone else had gotten one around the same time," Will said loudly and with the Will Pierce sense of urgency.

Rusty popped up and squinted. It took a second for him to realize that there was a small puddle of drool on the table, so he took his shirtsleeve and wiped it up as he tried to compose himself. What he didn't realize was that the hair on one side of his head was sticking up, making it very obvious that he had been asleep for some time.

"Hey Sheriff, just finishing up the first round of forensics on the rifle here," Rusty said, his voice coarse from only a couple hours of sleep.

Will walked up and looked at the table. It was obvious Rusty had torn the thing apart and put it back together a number of times, but he hadn't been able to see what Will had.

"Good work, Rus, now head on home to your woman and get some shut-eye, you're no good to me exhausted," Will said in a fatherly voice. "I'll make sure I sign off on the overtime for you as it looks like you worked all night."

"Well, I tried, but I think I fell…" Rusty said as he lowered his head.

"Okay, so now it's my turn to take a pass at it!" Will said, interrupting Rusty before he could admit he'd fallen asleep on duty, well, it wasn't officially his shift after all. The young deputy looked so dejected Will decided to give him a boost before booting him out the door to get some real sleep.

Will, not actually forgetting, but more like ignoring protocol, scooped the rifle with one hand and began to disassemble it, starting with the magazine.

"Look at this, Rusty. What do you see?" Will said as he turned the smallish clip outwards toward him.

"Sheriff, I tore that thing apart six ways to Sunday and dang it if I could find anything other than the bullet hole lodged in the stock," Rusty said, scratching his head and not realizing he was adding further to the shock of hair already standing straight up.

"You've been around guns your whole life, haven't you?" Will questioned.

Rusty began to get tingles as he knew Will was about to drop some knowledge on him that would probably shock and bewilder him like he always did when he began to sound like a college professor asking a simple question only to give an elaborate and profound answer.

"Sure, Will, you know I have," Rusty responded, trying to fight off the grin that was appearing.

"Well, okay, doesn't this clip look a little shallow to you?" Will asked.

Will began to hand it to Rusty, who quickly fumbled with a pair of latex gloves so as not to corrupt any evidence Will was obviously already corrupting.

Rusty began to inspect it as Will pointed into the feed mechanism that stored ammunition to be inserted into the magazine by a spring-load or slide. Rifle clips usually housed over a dozen shells with tips that might be as long as a few inches, but this particular one seemed too small, too light.

"Well, Sheriff, now that you mention it, yeah, it does look different," Rusty said, realizing he may have missed what could possibly be a major clue. But he just couldn't see it. He tried feeling his way through the answer.

"It looks way too shallow, like it might only fit a couple of shells," he theorized carefully, watching Will's body language out of the corner of his eye. "Why would someone want to use a clip that only fired a couple of bullets?"

Will took the clip back out of Rusty's hand and poked his finger in. "Exactly, Rusty!" Will answered. Placing his finger inside, he held it up for Rusty to see. "That's less than two inches deep," Will continued. "You could get maybe three rounds in there if you pushed it, but you'd probably have to rely on putting one up the spout in order to get a decent number of shots."

Rusty immediately realized he needed to write this information in his log as he looked down at the blank sheet in the spiral notebook next to the evidence.

"Hold on, Sheriff, don't say another word. I gotta write all this down!" Rusty said excitedly.

"So that's suspicious, isn't it?" Will said professorially, as Rusty scribbled into his notebook. Rusty nodded in agreement. He felt Will was embarking on a roll and all he could do now was listen, write, and learn.

"So you might think, okay, I'm letting my young grandson shoot today and we're gonna use a small clip with just two or three bullets, just to give him a taste," Will volleyed. "Rus, I want you to call up a bunch of pro shops and gun stores and ask around to see if there is some new type of magazine clips that only carry a couple of bullets, try the NRA as well because I'm not up on all the new products, but it seems pretty counter-productive to make a clip that only holds three bullets, as it'll keep you reloading more than actually shooting."

Rusty wrote furiously, only looking up when Will stopped. "Got it, Chief!" Rusty said, nodding his head as though he were the smart kid who sat in the front of the class.

"Now, there's something else I saw, that you didn't have a chance to look at." Pulling the scope from his pocket he placed it on the light board and spun it lightly for emphasis.

"This is some kind of high-end sniper's scope, but it's got a lot of pops and buzzers on here I'm not too familiar with," Will said as he inspected it. He pressed one of the tiny buttons on the side of the device and the scope went infrared. He pressed another and the night vision application began. These things he was familiar with, although nobody he knew could afford such an expensive piece of equipment, even the most avid hunter.

Rusty hung on every word as Will, too, was intrigued and attempting to work out the special features in his head as he eyed every conceivable angle.

"But what you've got here," Will said as he pointed to some small golden squares on the side of the scope, "they look like WiFi or Bluetooth wireless transmitters."

Rusty's eyes bulged, as he didn't see that coming. Now his brain was abuzz with all sorts of conspiracies and shadowy figures around darkened corners.

"Now look here!" Will picked up the rifle and pointed the scope in his other hand toward a part of the rifle that was newish-looking on such an older rifle. "This here looks like a receiver chip," Will surmised. "So, okay, we have a high-end, probably custom-designed, sniper's scope with a quick-release mount..."

Rusty was fully engulfed in what Will was saying as he continued to write.

"... we have what looks like a transmitter chip, among other things, attached to the side of the scope, then we have what could arguably be considered a receiver chip on the side of the body of the rifle."

Rusty finished writing what Will was saying, then placed the pen on the table momentarily while he began to formulate his own ideas.

"So the scope is talkin' to the rifle?" Rusty said, immediately regretting his statement.

"No, no, but, you're onto something there, Rus!" Will barked, as he tried out different concepts, rolling them at high speed through his brain. "So whatever is in the crosshairs of the scope could then be transmitted to the rifle, but for what purpose?"

Rusty took a deep breath and attempted to come up with an Earth-shattering revelation, as he had almost done moments before.

"Well, they've got those kind of GoPro cameras that capture pictures and video, but why would anyone want to connect that to a sniper's rifle?" Rusty said.

Rusty barely registered what had just come out of his mouth when Will blurted something out.

"Right again, Rus! Why the hell would someone want to capture a photo of something through a sniper's rifle? We're not talking pictures of game or sport hunting; this rifle is made especially for snipers."

"I'll call down to Cabela's and ask one of their geeks if there is such a thing," Rusty said in a fervor, convinced something was amiss.

"No, Rusty, you go home and get some shut-eye," Will said, worrying about his protégé. "I can do the grunt work on this one, since I got a good night's sleep."

Rusty smiled widely and began to gather up his notes before running for the lab door. He forgot one thing, ran back, ran back again to get another, while all the while Will watched as his excited deputy got more and more worked up.

"No way, Sheriff, are you kidding me?" Rusty laughed. "I'm not gonna be able to sleep for days now that we're onto something."

Will knew he had to bring Rusty back down to reality before he got out of control. "Okay, but remember, this is Callahan's rifle, not the sniper's," Will cautioned. "I'll admit there's a couple of unusual things going on here, but that doesn't mean there's any connection to the two men or even the boy, for that matter."

Rusty placed his hand on the lab door just before he burst out of the room. "Yeah, Sheriff, but this is sure beginning to smell like a proper mystery, if you ask me," Rusty said excitedly. "And I for one am not gonna sit on the bench while some perpetrator is out there training his sights on another target."

Rusty kept shouting as the glass door slammed closed behind him. "No, Sir, not on my watch! No Sir!" Rusty yelled as the other employees were arriving to begin their day.

Will took one last look at the rifle, then the scope, then the rifle again.

"You might be right, Rusty," Will said to himself as he exhaled. "We might've just stumbled onto something bigger than we think."

CHAPTER 28

CLAIRE TURNED OUT THE light in Michael's room and eased the door closed behind her. She suddenly stopped and realized something, then reopened the door slightly so she could hear if Michael decided to call for her during the night.

"Mom?" Michael's voice floated out of the darkness.

"Yes, sweetie?"

"I wish I had a dad I could tell my story to," Michael said as exhaustion took over.

Claire looked back into the room and watched as Michael rolled to one side and was out like a light.

"I do too, little man, I do too," she said, sighing as she wrapped her arms around herself as though to keep out a draft.

Claire walked back down the long hall of her condo and headed into her study. As she strolled in, she saw a pile of mail on the credenza and picked it up. She ran through each letter, trashing most of them in a receptacle at the foot of the desk, but came across one piece that seemed interesting.

She passed by her library of books on the custom-built shelving units and glanced at her computer as if to sit down in front of it and begin some late night work.

But instead, she walked past the busywork that haunted her and plopped down on her green chenille couch that sat just next to her home working area.

A fresh glass of white wine had been poured moments before and she picked it up for a quick sip. She leaned back, then sank into the plush goose down and foam pillows that made the couch so comfortable.

Just before she closed her eyes, she looked at the book cabinet at a framed photo of her on a jet ski next to a man whose face was blurred due to movement at the time the photo was snapped.

A slight tear formed in the corner of her eye and she swallowed deeply. She took a final breath, then fell asleep, the letter still clutched in her hand.

CHAPTER 29

WILL'S SIXTH SENSE, IF you believe in that type of thing, was kicking into high gear. He knew he didn't possess any real ESP, but much like a detective, or journalist, or any mother for that matter, Will had a sense that not only was this case going to get bigger and cause a lot of people pain, but that it was getting way too big for him to do on his own.

He decided to call a former colleague of his that he was quite fond of at the Bureau for some much-needed profiling assistance.

Will dialed the 202 area code and waited for the call to go through. It would still be before lunch on the East Coast, as Will was certainly aware of the time change as he had lived it for so many years. He called the main line because he had forgotten the extension.

"Yes, Mohinder Prabhat, sorry, Doctor Prabhat, please," Will said, correcting his error.

"Who may I ask is calling?" the exchange operator asked in a placid voice.

"Will Pierce, I'm a former Special Agent that had the great pleasure of getting to work with Dr. Prabhat on many occasions," Will said, establishing his bona fides.

Will thought the words "Special Agent" sounded strange coming out of his mouth, as he had not only physically resigned himself to one of the furthest outposts a man could exile himself to, but he realized that he had mentally resigned, or more like extricated himself, from the Federal Bureau of Investigations.

"Please hold, Mr. Pierce!" the operator said. Will nodded, although there was no one around him to see it. He felt a little foolish when he realized no one on the other end of the cell phone could see him nodding in acceptance either.

"Will Pierce, my goodness. To what do I owe the honor of a phone call from you, my long lost friend?" Dr. Prabhat said in a heavy Kerala accent.

"How are you, Mohinder?" Will asked happily. "Well, I've got something here that is right up your alley."

"Oh that sounds interesting," Dr. Prabhat answered. "But first things first. Where are you and what have you been doing with yourself these past years?"

Will wasn't comfortable talking about himself, but this man had always been a good man and a friend and was one of the first people Will had met when he was going through training at Quantico. They had actually gone through the academy together and were roommates at one point. Will had taken it upon himself to look after his friend Mohinder, newly arrived from India on a law enforcement exchange program. Since then, the good man had decided to adopt America as his new home.

"Well, Mo, I'm back out here in Wyoming. Remember you came for a visit in the 90s?" Will said, thinking about the events of his past.

"How could I ever forget that beautiful place, my friend?" Dr. Prabhat said joyously. "I will cherish that trip for a lifetime. You put me on my first horse and showed me how to ride like a cowboy with the hat and everything! My family back in Kerala still asks me about the cowboy who looks like Clint Eastwood."

Will chuckled. Mohinder always made Will chuckle, as it seemed that Indians could see the good, fun, and joy of all the things in life and relay it back to typical Americans with renewed eyes.

"It was fun just watching you trying to stay on the horse, let alone seeing you in chaps," Will laughed, loosening up as he conversed with his old friend.

"Yep, I'm back here on the prairie, but I got bored after a few weeks of retirement and decided to take a job as the local sheriff," Will said, easing into the nitty gritty of the conversation.

"Oh my God!" Dr. Prabhat yelled into the handset. "You are telling me that you are actually the sheriff… with the white hat and everything?"

"Ha, yep, and the six-shooter on my hip!" Will laughed, realizing his friend was making a mental picture.

"I'm going to have to tell Naja that, she always thought you were born in the wrong century," Dr. Prabhat laughed. "Now you're truly living the life you were meant to live, I think."

"Well, that's kind of the reason I called you, Mo," Will said, getting back to business. "I've got a shooter on my hands and I'm gonna need a profile worked up on this guy, because I don't think he's in our system yet."

"You are speaking my language, my friend!" Dr. Prabhat said, chuckling.

"I'm just a little worried since I saw you on Fox News a few months ago talking about the Kentucky case and knew you were the only man for the job, but was worried all that fame may have gone to your head!" Will said, ribbing his friend.

"Ah, I think we're all safe I won't get a competing reality show with the Kardashians," Dr. Prabhat responded, then changed his tune. "Okay, give me the details."

"I've got a shooter who took a shot from at least 1,000 yards in high wind, in a remote area, from a high perch. A single shot, weapon is unknown at this time. Ballistics should match the ammo to 7.62 or better, but it's my guess that the bullet was custom made," Will read off like he was going down a list.

Will knew how good his friend was as he was fascinated by the darker side of mankind and the evil that some men did.

"Hmm, okay, go on," Dr. Prabhat said as he wrote notes on the important points.

"The shooter took careful aim and shot a young boy who had his rifle trained down into a valley," Will continued. "The shooter shot the butt of the boy's rifle, causing the boy to tumble over the side of a cliff."

"What?" Dr. Prabhat said shocked, although he had seen and heard much worse in his day. "What kind of sicko shoots a child?"

"Yeah, right?" Will answered in agreement. "Okay, so the shooter aims at the only place on the gun that would absorb the impact and not necessarily kill the boy, but the energy and G-force did drive him over the edge of the plateau, which would suggest that perhaps the shooter was trying to cover his tracks and not leave a bullet in the head of the child and raise suspicion."

"Uh huh," Dr. Prabhat grunted in agreement as he continued taking notes.

"We're still in the preliminary stages of the investigation, but I believe he tracked his prey over several states, perhaps even flying on the same plane, as we think he'd have had to have gotten a permit from Wyoming Fish & Game like the victims had already done."

"Cold, calculating, yes, yes, I'm beginning to build a picture," the doctor said as he wrote.

"It's my guess he either knew the victim's grandfather and was either trying to prove something like how great a shot he was or was trying to get his attention for some reason," Will said, pondering the details of his own recounts. "I can't imagine a sniper as highly trained as he was actually going out of his way to kill a young child, unless he was motivated by money, perhaps a custody issue, maybe that child was related to him. I'm having trouble with that one."

"That's the Will I know and love," Dr. Prabhat said affectionately as he listened to Will's list of evidence.

"But there are two more things I think I should tell you," Will said hesitantly.

"What's that, Will?" Dr. Prabhat responded, more curious than professional.

"It has to do with the bullet clip and the sniper's scope from the victim's rifle," Will said, recalling the items. "First, the magazine was short and shallow. It could probably only fit two or three 7.62 shells, which is extremely odd."

"Why is that odd, Will?" the doctor said as Will had now piqued his interest.

"Well, clips are used to hold ammo that is very hard and frustrating to load," Will pointed out. "It's counterintuitive to use a small magazine, that's why the big banana clips are so popular. And this clip had some weird software in it, a chip, you know, like a transmitter."

"Yes, yes, I understand," the doctor said, following Will's logic. "And what of the sniper's scope?"

"That's a weird one too!" Will answered, scratching his head. "It's like the clip and scope went together as some kind of camera... but for what purpose?"

CHAPTER 30

STEPHANIE MILLER HAD BEEN married to Robert for more years than she could remember. She had borne him four beautiful children and raised them almost on her own, especially when Robert's Marine training led to him being called up for numerous engagements in undisclosed countries.

Then it was Robert's Special Forces promotions that were more like prison sentences, Steph thought, as it would take her husband away from her family most of the year, every year, for decades.

But now things were finally getting better; the kids were through with college and grad school, and since Robert had settled down and built Miller Strategic Management in Colorado, the only times he was gone was a weekend hop here or a midweek conference there. He had stayed true to the promise he'd made her; a promise to which she would add that if he didn't start showing his face at home more and settling down, she would leave him.

Robert Miller was true to his word and, having lost friends and loved ones literally around him his entire life, he wasn't about to lose the best, and most stable, friend he had ever had.

Steph thought about how happy she was and how lucky she was

often. She thought about it when she watched any of the *Real Housewives* shows as she chuckled at their antics and miserable rich lifestyles, and she thought about what a good man Robert was and how hard and painful his life had been in the service to his country and to other countries and people of the world.

But Steph especially liked to enumerate her love and luck with her husband Robert when she went shopping. She had recently converted Robert, after a cholesterol scare, to eat better, and a little more vegan. Robert obviously objected at first, but Steph was able to work in baby carrots here, some kale there, and ultimately, slowly, she added more and more, removing the artery-clogging grease and grimy food he had typically eaten to pack on the pounds for strength and power.

She pushed the small cart through the aisle of her local Trader Joe's and reveled at the new coconut oil bases, the sweet potatoes, and pickled-flavored popcorn. Some of the options actually made her laugh at the new, clever, but ultimately healthy foods that were never available to them so much as they were in this day and age.

She happily filled her basket with dinner items, as she knew Robert would be home a tad bit early this particular evening because he was ordered by his commanding officer (her) to ready the barbecue for the marinating chicken breasts.

Phil, the cashier, carefully packed Steph's groceries in a brown paper bag. He was an amputee missing his arm below the elbow. Steph often talked with Phil and knew he was a combat veteran who had been hired by the chain after he was released from the VA and given what they referred to as a clean bill of health.

Phil had fallen on hard times, both financially and emotionally, after his injuries and the U.S. government wasn't holding up its end of the bargain at a rate that would help Phil recover in an adequate amount of time.

Steph knew all too well the trials and tribulations that our Wounded Warriors endured and that is why she had recommended Phil to her husband for a job, training his soldiers on weekends and his days off from the store. Phil was never more appreciative, since he was now flush, feeling good about himself and his life and truly wanted for nothing.

"Any phantom limb pain these days, Phil?" Steph asked, as she pulled out her checkbook.

"Nope, Mrs. M., I took your advice and propped my arm up with a pillow at night and it sure helps," Phil said, happily grinning as he separated the can goods from the fresh vegetables.

"...My doctor's got me doing Mirror Box Therapy, biofeedback, acupuncture, and of course, TENS," he continued.

"Oh my, that sounds interesting, what's TENS again? I can't keep up with all the new high-tech therapies," Steph said, laughing and she dropped her pen and reached down to get it off the sparklingly clean floor. "I'm pretty clumsy as well!" she added.

"Oh, yeah, Mrs. M., it's transcutaneous electrical nerve stimulation, and it's great!" Phil enthused, as he placed the last of the groceries in a second smaller paper bag. "I can't believe Uncle Sam is paying for all of it. I get massages, too, don't have to pay a dime for it!"

Steph looked up proudly at him. "And well you shouldn't, not for the rest of your life, Philip!" she said in a fiercely motherly way as she fought back a tear. "And if anyone at the VA ever gives you another hard time, you let me know and Robert will have them cleaning bed pans for the rest of their bureaucratic lives, I kid you not!"

"I believe you, Mrs. M.," Phil said, realizing her protective nature. "I can't thank you and Mr. M enough; you've really helped me pull things together."

"Don't you ever thank us, Philip; we are the ones who should be thanking you for all your sacrifice," Steph said sternly, as to not allow any unwanted, or for that matter, unneeded, gratitude to approach her ears.

Steph grabbed the two bags and tried to balance her purse at the same time. She struggled for a moment as Phil walked around the cash register to help. Steph immediately righted herself and sprung up as to not allow Phil to attempt to help her a second more.

"Did you call Doreen, you know the girl whose number I gave you last week?" Steph said as she covered the embarrassment of her blunder.

Phil gave a big smile as his cheeks turned red as though he had a secret that only he and the mysterious Doreen shared.

"I did Mrs. M., and again, I can't thank you enough," Phil said humbly. "She's a real cool girl and at first I was like, *'She's not gonna like a dude with one arm,'* but then she told me what happened to her in Fallujah and it was like we'd known each other since we were kids."

"I told you, Phil, you need to trust me on this one: she needs a man like you every bit as much as you need a woman like her!" Steph said and noticed another shopper queuing up in Phil's lane.

"Okay, have a nice evening. I'll probably be in again tomorrow," Steph said as she juggled her two grocery bags and oversized purse at the same time. Suddenly, unbeknownst to Steph, two limes popped out of the bag and round toward the display of two-buck Chuck red wine.

Steph had the luck to get an open parking spot next to a handicapped one. Although Steph had osteoporosis as well as a host of other maladies, she would think it insulting, rude, and perhaps illegal if anyone were to suggest she take a spot reserved for the handicapped. By the grace of God, she could still walk, albeit much slower than she used to, but she would never allow herself to be considered needy.

Steph depressed the remote twice, unlocking the doors of her Ford sedan. Her trunk slowly opened as she approached to put the two bags into the spotlessly clean car. Just then, she heard her name being called.

"Mrs. M., you dropped your limes!" Phil called out as he hustled toward the Ford.

"Oh, I'm such a klutz!" Steph said, turning to see Phil coming her way. Just then, one of the grocery bags she was balancing on the edge of the trunk fell, spilling all the contents into the path of an oncoming car looking for a spot. Steph lurched forward to grab the bag and as she did, she felt a slight pressure above her forehead as her body seemed to be pushed backwards.

She crumpled at the foot of the rear of the sedan as she saw a shadow pounce upon her. It was Phil. He had lunged on top of her to protect her body. He had seen what had happened and decided to sacrifice his body to protect the friend he'd known and loved.

"I gotcha, Mrs. M., just don't move!" Phil said in a voice as calm as an angel.

The flash had come from blocks away at a very high angle. The other shoppers never heard the report, but saw Steph's blonde hair fly backwards and heard the *thump* as the bullet passed across the top of her head, flying hard and fast through the steel top of the raised trunk lid.

Phil, having seen this scenario play out too many times as it still played out in his head when he slept, or at least attempted to, knew if he dove on

Mrs. M. he was large enough to cover all her vital organs and most of her body and he'd be able to absorb the impact of a long-range bullet being shot from a great distance from a high perch. Many of his fellow veterans had suffered the same fate, but Mrs. M. wasn't going to be one of them… not on his watch!

The sniper quickly bolted another round into the chamber and pressed his right eye up against the eyepiece. The scope had barely moved a centimeter, so the crosshairs caught all the commotion around Steph and her car.

Some heroic, one-armed grocery clerk, he thought, was now covering his target.

"Well," Gaius said to himself in a smug manner, "if he wants to be a hero, let's grant him his wish, shall we?"

With his heart rate barely above 70, Gaius slowly exhaled, as he pulled his finger softly on the trigger and aimed at his target… the *pop* from the outgassing at the end of the perforated muzzle was barely perceptible.

CHAPTER 31

L ONG BEFORE THE PATRIOT Act was enacted, federal agencies under the Echelon Program had federal authority to wiretap, eavesdrop, and oversee any activity of any law-abiding American citizen it chose at anytime, anywhere.

The National Security Agency, or NSA, was tasked since the late 1960s to, among other things, scour communications, be they phone, telex, teletype, newspaper, or of late, cell phone calls, texts, emails, the Internet, any form either connected to a hardwire, Ethernet server, shortwave, ionospheric, atmospheric, Bluetooth, wireless, WiFi, in absolutely any form for certain red flags.

A red flag was used to signal actionable intelligence and was designed to collect and analyze communications coming in and going out of the United States as well as hundreds of other countries, both friend and foe.

Originally designed to spy on the former Soviet Union and other Eastern Bloc countries during the Cold War, Echelon took both the military and diplomatic lead in eavesdropping in the hopes of countering every move the West's enemies may make in order to keep stability, not only in the region, but on the shores of this free country as well.

Additionally, this software system had the frightening capability of controlling downloads and dissemination of the intercept of commercial satellite trunk communications. Yet that was still pre-21st Century technology; today, that program and other hybrids like it have gone global up to and including following every keystroke you make when writing on your laptop or emulating every instant message.

The Secret Service, the FBI, and other federal agencies stayed in close contact, working together with the NSA to deal with potential events that may "pop up," only after certain words are addressed. Those words, some 400 plus, will red flag the program to actually go back and record the entire conversation and follow any of the language to possible sinister ends.

Words like "assassination," "bomb," "dirty bomb," "drill," any of the federal agencies, "radioactive," "powder," "gas," "power lines," "rail lines," "cartel," "China," even "the president," were flagged. So one could imagine, if they really thought about it, Big Brother was watching (and waiting for) their every move.

It was this program that alerted a low-level tech at the NSA. Bart Cooper was a young, hotshot analyst and recent graduate from MIT who was about to have his day made.

"Oh, Red Ball coming down the pipe," he yelled to another analyst behind the next partition in reference to the film Minority Report.

"Yeah, watcha got?" the other analyst asked as he leaned way back in his chair and threw his head around the padded half-wall that separated them.

"Combo-nacho platter, dude!" Cooper said, relishing his find like a prospector in a new mine shaft digging for gold. "12, no 15 DHS no-no's."

"Dude, 15?!" his coworker said with skepticism and concern.

"You know whatcha gotta do, don't you?"

"Yup, I'm covering my ass by sending out a Blanket BOLO to all the top agencies," Cooper said as he furiously typed on his wireless keyboard.

"Okay, Homeland, FBI, Cyber Warfare, hum, hum, ATF, SWAT," Cooper said as he continued typing as though it was just another function of his position, which it was.

"SWAT? What the hell would you copy SWAT for?" his colleague laughed as he took a long pull off a red vine from the clear barrel filled with the gelatinous candy.

"Some sheriff in Wyoming is describing a killer that matches over a dozen DNA characteristics the feds are looking for," Cooper said in mundane fashion, almost sarcastically jabbing his colleague at his discovery. "Looks like someone's in line for a promotion!" Cooper said as he put the final touches on the security-coded emails.

"Please, give me a break," the coworker laughed as he listened to Cooper.

"I'm telling you, this killer is wanted at the highest level. I expect to be..." Cooper was interrupted by a shadow darkening his computer screen.

He looked up and saw three security officers standing above him and he was suddenly no longer in a jovial mood.

"Cooper, come with us!" The smallest of the three guards said. "And take his laptop with you," he barked at the other guard as they began to lead him down a long corridor.

CHAPTER 32

WILL HAD DECIDED TO take an early lunch in the hopes of gleaning more insight into the mind of the killer and perhaps enjoying a piece of hot apple pie in the process.

Cora's Diner was packed this time of day, but normally people kept pretty much to themselves as the lunch crowd usually consisted of long-haul truckers, cowboys heading in or out of town for the rodeo, or German tourists who seemed to love the vast openness and tranquility this part of Wyoming had to offer.

Will had ordered a greasy pastrami sandwich, the kind he used to get at Froman's Deli in lower Manhattan, one of the last vestiges of his time in the big city. He knew it wasn't good for his arteries, or his waistline, but sometimes a man just has to eat meat... and lots of it!

"You want more coffee, Sheriff?" Cora said, her bifocals dangling from a thin silver chain around her neck.

Cora always served Will herself. He was particular about his food, but he also had a big heart and although Will Pierce was a tall lawman cut out of wood, he was still very approachable and kind. He often talked to the locals and was easily accessible to children who would come up to his table in awe of the colors and majesty of a gold sheriff's star, the radio cord that ran up his back and attached under his epaulet, or the one thing any little boy or girl would be mesmerized by, his service revolver.

Will had just not quite gotten the peace and quiet he was longing for as Cora came back to refill his old weathered cafeteria-style coffee cup after he'd given his last gold star sticker to a young couple's children who were too shy to ask.

"Here ya go," Will said, to the amazement of the two kids. "If you ask your mom and dad, they might let you stick them on the wall in your bedroom or you could stick 'em on your bike helmets."

"Wow, really?" the boy said, as he glanced at the identical one his sister was holding.

"Sure!" Will said with a smile. "Is that okay with you, Mom and Dad? They aren't really gluey; they have a light adhesive on the back and can easily be pulled off and replaced onto just about any surface."

The young couple nodded, then looked down, beaming at their children.

"What do you say to the sheriff?" the mother asked as her husband placed his hand on his daughter's shoulder.

"Thank you, Sheriff!" the two children said in unison, then quickly ran down the aisle as excited as could possibly be at their surprise reward.

Cora hadn't finished filling Will's cup when he saw a figure plop down in front of him in his peripheral vision as it bounced slightly on the red vinyl bench.

"I get the feeling you're avoiding me, Will," the most definitely feminine voice said. "You wouldn't want a girl to get the wrong idea by that, would ya?"

Will did his best to hide the smile he was keeping for this very occasion. It seemed to be quite the cat and mouse game he and Molly were playing. It was like a G-rated version of a romantic comedy, but this RomCom was taking years to finish and Will seemed to be in the driver's seat.

"Come on, Molly. Does it look like I'm trying to avoid you?" Will said, chuckling.

"Hiding in plain sight is the strategy of all brilliant criminals, Will Pierce," she retorted.

Will leaned back and raised his long arm in the air as Cora passed behind him by another table of diners.

"Cora, get Molly a coffee, black, two sugars, and some half and half and put it on my tab."

"Oh, Will Pierce," Molly teased, "you really know how to treat a lady, don't you, you ole' devil, you."

Will turned around and smiled. It seemed that he and Molly could almost be considered an item, by their causal way when around each other.

"Now look, if you're gonna start asking follow-up questions and revisiting everything for that exclusive I just gave you, then your paper is paying for lunch," Will said, half jokingly as he sipped his coffee.

Molly looked slightly dejected, but since it was a reasonable concern for a man in Will's position, she decided to put him out of his misery.

"No, Sheriff, this is a social call," she said, then suddenly lowered her voice to a whisper. "The truth is… well, the truth is, I've missed you."

Will sunk back into the deep air pocket wrapped in vinyl that Cora had just reupholstered, smiling like the cat that just ate the canary.

"You missed me, huh?" Will said teasingly.

"Will Pierce, you lower your voice," Molly said as she yell-whispered at him. "It's bad enough I've got to chase you over Hell's half acre just to get a few minutes alone with you."

Will smiled widely, the kind of smile that can't be controlled and certainly the kind that showed his true colors and what he really thought of Molly.

"Cora, could ya get me a piece of apple pie?" Will asked as Cora walked across the café floor. "…and make that à la mode, and two forks!"

"Two forks?" Molly said, smiling as she slapped her face with both hands. "I do declare, Will Pierce, I think you may be a romantic."

"So what have you been doing with yourself?" Will asked, contemplating reaching out and touching her hand.

"Well, I've been writing that amazing story you gave me and all the wire services and Internet sites are picking it up," she said, changing gears, but nonetheless grateful.

Cora could be seen in the background cutting a larger than usual piece of pie from the hot box and placing not one, but two large dollops of vanilla ice cream next to it.

"And Rusty tells me the tip lines have been on fire with leads on the sniper," she said, excited as a little girl.

"Yep, and it's all cause of your story," Will said humbly. "Well, ya play your cards right, ya might just get an even bigger story by the end of the week."

Molly's interest piqued. "Well, Will Pierce, what did you have in mind by me playing my cards right?"

Just then Cora returned and interrupted Molly's inquisitive moment.

"Ah, pie!" Will nearly shouted in the hopes that the subject might change.

Will picked up one of the forks and began to dig into the pie and ice cream as he looked up and gave Molly a sort of evil grin as he put the forkful of sweets in his mouth.

"I take that back, what I said about you being romantic," Molly said, picking up a fork and gritting her teeth at Will. "I think you're really just a tease."

"Ha!" Will laughed, with a mouthful of apples and ice cream.

"You better not be getting yourself in trouble again, Will Pierce," Molly said, suddenly concerned.

"Whadda mean?" Will asked as he chewed, realizing he had, in fact, bitten off more than he could chew.

"I know how you get all obsessed with these types of important cases and you probably intend to take on all the heavy lifting trying to find this guy," Molly said, squinting one eye and pointing her fork directly at Will as she enunciated each and every word.

"Don't worry, I'll probably never get anywhere near that guy," Will said, attempting to reassure Molly. "Besides, he's probably halfway across the country already or even overseas for that matter, if you ask me."

Will lowered his eyes and smiled at Molly just as he dug his fork deep into the apple pie for a second helping when he suddenly felt a presence next to him.

"Are you Sheriff Pierce?" a deep, forceful voice said as three men in suits appeared looking down hard at Will and blocking any exit he or Molly may have had. "We're federal agents with the FBI; please come with us."

Will stopped chewing, as Molly glanced up with a worried look. "Cora, put this in a to-go box for me, will ya?"

CHAPTER 33

WHEN ROBERT MILLER GOT the call from emergency responders to meet them at Saint Luke's Hospital, he was in the middle of a training exercise with his gunnery sergeant, Willie Combs. Miller always kept a satellite phone in his cargo fatigues and it was his main line. He had often been so far away from any civilized culture during his deployments, he just felt more comfortable with it on him at all times.

"Go, for Miller," Miller said in an unusually jovial voice for mid-afternoon drills.

"Sir, your wife's been injured and we're taking her to St. Luke's. Sir, I am sorry, but it is serious," the voice of the paramedic said as Miller could hear the sirens and tire screeches in the background.

"Copy that," Miller said as he fell back into his military training, not yet truly affected by the information.

Sgt. Combs heard the conversation as he was standing close to Miller and putting their soldiers, or employees, as Miller put it, through their paces. *The Only Easy Day Was Yesterday* was Gunny's motto, even though he had adapted it from the Navy SEALS Special Forces.

"Class dismissed!" Sgt. Combs yelled to a confused line of trainees.

"Sgt. Shapiro, take these maggots and run through the Odyssey Obstacle course."

"Copy that, Gunny!" Sgt. Shapiro answered quickly. "You heard the sergeant, double time to the Odyssey."

The soldiers fell in quickly as the sergeant turned toward Miller, who was just starting to fall into shock at the news of his wife.

"Sir, we're gassed up and ready to roll!" Sgt. Combs barked to snap him out of his own head. Sgt. Combs grabbed Miller's arm under the elbow and began to lead him toward the motor pool as Miller suddenly snapped back to reality.

"We'll beat those slow-ass paramedics, Sir. I know a shortcut that will get us there *riki tik* with *beaucoup didi mau!*" the sergeant said as he opened the passenger door to one of the first generation Hummers that the military often used for combat deployment.

"My wife, Gunny?!" Miller said, the weight of guilt suddenly rushing over him.

"I know, Sir, I know," the Sergeant said as he roared the engine to life and headed for the guard gates.

CHAPTER 34

GAIUS ARRIVED AT DENVER International Airport within a few hours of his last hit, carrying only a long, triangular FedEx cardboard parcel that had all the telltale signs of drafting blueprints or movie posters to be shipped.

It carried his sniper rifle and he always checked his parcel because he could break down and package the firearm in such a way that the TSA, even on their best day, would never suspect it was a gun, unless they actually tore the package apart and inspected it.

Gaius thought most of the airport transportation security officers were lazy and getting fat on their union pay. Their nearly guaranteed lifetime positions were handsomely funded by the government in order to protect the citizenry from terrorists, not unlike himself.

Gaius walked up to the counter and handed his e-ticket, boarding pass, and blue United States passport to the airline counter agent. She inspected the document, gave him a quick look, then another, and one more since his eyes seemed to draw her in, then forgot any questions she might have had for him and gave him a receipt for his checked weapon, or luggage, as she saw it.

"Thank you very much!" Gaius said to the blushing counter agent. "That blue really brings out your eyes," he added as he turned to walk away.

Gaius knew himself to be safe. His brilliance kept him totally and utterly impervious to capture. After all, he'd had a British mother who held dual citizenship as an American and a father who was a Greek Cypriot with multiple citizenships, including Spain, France, Hungary, and Lithuania. Gaius had more passports, both real and doctored, from so many different countries, it was hard to choose which passport to use in which country at any given time.

He took an ear bud out of his shirt pocket that ran the length of his shirt to his iPhone. He always had it programmed to local law enforcement scanners and followed the progress of any given disaster in order to go the opposite direction or create a secondary decoy disturbance in order to stay free and in flight.

He strolled past the duty-free shop and momentarily admired the magazine rack.

"Oh, I wish someone would contract me to take out that family!" he said to himself as he saw several separate magazine covers with the Kardashians smiling back at him.

What is this world coming to? he wondered, as he heard the boarding call for his flight.

CHAPTER 35

"THIS IS NO COURTESY call, Will. I could jam you up for obstruction!" the federal agent threatened. Will leaned back in the office chair, for all intents, ignoring the rantings of yet another ambitious bureaucrat.

Special Agent Oscar Cordoba knew Will Pierce very well; they had come up together in the Bureau, yet were assigned to different divisions early in both of their careers.

"Damn it, Will!" Cordoba yelled, getting the attention of everyone else in the sheriff's station that hadn't been spying on the event from behind Will's closed office door. "You can't hang on to crucial evidence and not report an assassination attempt to Homeland or the Bureau," Cordoba continued.

"He was a young boy and we haven't got the reports back from Forensics up north, yet, Oscar," Will pointed out in his best bored voice.

Will contemplated taking his Emery board from out of the top drawer and filing down the piece of cuticle that had been bothering him. Instead, he reached into the drawer and fiddled with something the other men couldn't see. Yet it was obvious that Will was blowing them off and having fun doing it.

"… And you kept the rifle for two days before sending it through to ballistics?" Cordoba continued.

"Oscar, you flew all the way down here and darkened the doorway of my little patch of Heaven, you interrupted my lunch, and you're basically accusing me of screwing up *my own* investigation!?" Will barked.

He was now beginning to get angry and slowly stood up to advance toward his much shorter former colleague. Tensions were rising.

The three other federal agents quickly closed ranks in and around Cordoba to ensure Will wasn't going to get too close and perhaps overpower him… or them, for that matter.

"That's right, *my* investigation!" Will said, metaphorically planting his flag between the men.

"This happened in my county, under my jurisdiction, and I don't remember any of you pasty pencil-pushers flying through a Wyoming storm or hauling your lazy asses up the side of a mountain to save a child's life. And retrieving crucial evidence, while spending several hours huddled under a tarp in a hail storm all in the same night!"

Will loved the theatrics and was certainly making his point as the other agents had heard stories of the great Will Pierce and had good cause to be concerned for their immediate, yet unknown, circumstances.

"So don't come into my town and think you can piss all over my fire hydrants," Will barked. "Ya get me?!"

After Will finished, there was a moment of silence, except for the giggles that were coming from outside Will's office through the thin, tempered glass. He was really hoping not to crack a smile or look into one of his other staffer's eyes and lose it, as he was putting on his best John Wayne and Clint Eastwood character voices.

Cordoba loosened his collar, as his tie suddenly felt damp from sweat and tight, as the blood coursing through his jugular and carotid arteries seemed to swell his neck three sizes.

He knew Will was right in asserting his authority, but Cordoba had been pushing around civilians and local law enforcement in D.C. for so many years, he had forgotten that outside the Beltway, he didn't always make the rules, and most people didn't care who the heck he was and that his authority meant little to nothing, especially in the wild and wooly regions of Wyoming.

"You're right, Will, perhaps I've overstepped my boundaries a tad bit, but here's a writ from the U.S. Attorney that grants the DOJ authority over this case now," Cordoba said, loosening his collar.

Cordoba produced a blue document that was folded over twice and handed it to Will who was still standing tall in front of the other men. Will swiped it out of Cordoba's hand and walked back to his chair, but didn't bother to look at it as he had already seen hundreds, if not thousands, of writs, court orders, and subpoenas in his days as a federal agent and he knew how the other guy felt when the feds took an important case from them.

"So, who was the hottie you were lunching with?" Cordoba said in a feeble attempt to lighten the mood.

"She's a reporter..." Will answered without looking at Cordoba. "... and a damn good one at that. I've half a mind to sic her on you!"

The other agents looked at each other a bit confused at this statement.

"Okay, Oscar, what the hell is this trump card all about anyway?"

Will took a deep, unnoticeable breath in order to equalize his blood pressure, which had risen more out of the comedy of what he was projecting than from any real anger.

"What could possibly be so important to cause you to get off your ass, drive to the airport and get on a plane to fly all the way to Wyoming and grace us with your presence?"

Cordoba turned to the other agents. "Okay guys, take 10. Go get some coffee or a snack at that diner down the road. I'm gonna need a few minutes with my old friend here."

"You sure, Sir?" one of the federal agents asked. He straightened his belt like a peacock ruffling his feathers to ensure greater attention.

Will gave him a look as though, yes, he was the idiot he was acting like.

"Oscar's a big boy, he can handle himself," Will said before Cordoba could finish.

"Yeah, it's okay," he answered. Cordoba waved his arm to lead the men back out of Will's office and through the station, then slowly closed the door behind them.

Rusty, Martha, and the other employees were wide-eyed as the large, well dressed, coifed, and well-heeled federal agents marched in unison back through the bullpen and out of the sheriff's station. It was obvious the men were now hungry and since being ordered to relax and disregard their duties for a few moments, they happily complied and headed straight for Cora's Diner.

Meanwhile, Molly, who had already snuck in, sat down and made herself comfortable at an empty desk. She had been taking notes as the others gossiped and she knew something juicy would eventually emerge from Will's office.

She sat low and made herself almost invisible in order to write down everything she heard and observed. She smiled to herself as she recalled Will yelling at the special agents that she was a *damn good* reporter. He might just get that home-cooked meal after all.

"Holy cow, did you hear what Sheriff Pierce just said to those federal boys?" Rusty giggled. "He has balls bigger than Mr. Murdoch's prize longhorn bull, you know, Dangler?!"

Martha and the others began to laugh, while Molly went back to being as serious as she could in that moment about the story at hand.

"Y'all keep it down now!" Molly whisper-yelled. Molly was a bit of a control freak and was trying to control the others in the room. "Don't you see Will's got himself into a big case and now the feds want to take it from him? Now that just ain't right, and I'll stand by him if he needs me to!"

Cordoba sat in front of Will's desk as he began to explain the reality of the situation. "Look, this shooter just popped the wife of a very prominent military advisor and the head of one of America's largest and most influential security companies," Cordoba said, trying to ease the situation.

"He capped her at over 1,000 meters and put a punctuation mark on it too by capping a clerk who was trying to save her life."

"Security company CEO?" Will blurted out, suddenly realizing he may have said it a little too quickly and given away his advantage. Oh well, in for penny, in for a pound. He covered his gaff by demanding, not waiting, for the information he needed.

"What security company? What's the name of the company and who's the military advisor guy whose wife was shot? What's his name?"

Cordoba shook his head in frustration, knowing it was an exercise in futility to try and stonewall this FBI Special Agent in his county sheriff persona.

"It's no use me invoking the classified statement. I know you'd get around it somehow," Cordoba said, grimacing as he shifted his collar again.

"Okay, his name is Robert Miller. He's the *Miller* in Miller Strategic Management. It's a big outfit out of Colorado near Cheyenne Mountain. You know, Blackwater-type of security stuff," Cordoba answered.

"Well, hell, Oscar, all ya had to do is say that instead of coming in here all puffed up and assholey."

Will could hear tiny giggles coming from outside his door in the outer office growing louder, but thankfully, he knew Cordoba had a bad ear from a fire fight in the 90s and hadn't yet caught on that the others were making him a laughingstock.

Will misdirected Cordoba for a moment, then stretched his neck high to look over the wainscoting and through the glass above it. He saw Molly looking back at him with that look that he knew he would be in trouble, somehow, sometime soon, but when or why, he didn't know.

"What you boys in blue suits haven't yet gathered, from the mere fact that you're not dialing the director's private line yet, is that the young boy who was shot was the grandson of Timothy Callahan." Will set up for the other shoe to drop as he waited for Cordoba's reaction. "… And *he* puts the *Callahan* in Callahan Security. Now, how's that for a coincidence, them both being in the security business?"

Cordoba leaned back in the old office chair and contemplated for a moment.

"…and I would suspect that Miller Strategic and Callahan Security have at least one or two other things in common to make them *not so* coincidentally targeted… wouldn't you agree, Oscar?"

Cordoba began to relax as his body language settled in and he allowed Will to develop the theory for him. He knew Will was always smarter and more cunning than he, but he also knew that he controlled the neck, even if Will had a better head on his shoulders.

"Go on." Cordoba was gaining interest and mapping a future strategy in his head.

"And if you read the transcript of my phone conversation with Dr. Prabhat, which I know you did via NSA, you'd know this guy shot the rifle in the boy's hand, not the boy himself. That may be an important distinction."

"So what, the kid was as good as dead for all the shooter knew when he fell off the cliff!" Cordoba barked loudly as the two men began to come together within their collective professional hypotheses.

"True, but then why not put one in the kid's skull?" Will posed the question.

"If he were going to tumble off a mountain top, surely the coroner wouldn't even suspect foul play, as the rocks would've made a mess of things all the way around."

"So what are you saying?" Cordoba said, pondering the information.

"First, how bad is Miller's wife?" Will asked, leaning forward in his desk chair, excited about getting closer to evolving his strategy.

"Bad! They don't know yet; there was a lot of blood in her hair, so the doctors aren't sure if it grazed her head or took a chunk out of her skull." Cordoba motioned with his hand to the top of his head and circled it. "She was lucky, his shot was thrown off by Miller's wife ducking at the last instant. So, it only touched her on the top of the head."

"Clearly, your idea of *lucky* and mine differ, somewhat," Will muttered.

"God bless her, I guess she was always a klutz and just at the instant our shooter popped off a round, she'd bent over to pick up something she had spilled," Cordoba said, nearly laughing. "You know, even at a thousand meters, without any headwind or tailwind, for that matter, that bullet is gonna drop a few inches. It looks like he was going for a center mass shot, and she just had an angel on her shoulders."

"Yeah, a dark angel! Okay, I'll give you that for a moment, but what about our hero clerk?" Will wanted to know, not seeing the humor in Cordoba's statement. Will took matters of civilians or anyone getting shot as serious business.

Cordoba suddenly stopped as though a realization dawned on him.

"Damn, that grocery clerk who tried to save her was also one of Miller's combat trainers out at his farm," Cordoba realized as he continued his thought. "Huh, and if you can believe this one, the clerk's also a war veteran with PTSD, a Wounded Warrior who was an amputee to boot."

"So, our shooter took out two separate civilians, is that what you're saying, Oscar?" Will did his best to recap, trying to pry more and more information from Cordoba.

"Ah, maybe they were just having an affair and Miller contracted the hit to one of his own employees? After all, they're probably all a bunch of *ex-jarhead* snipers, anyway." Cordoba knew if he kept things light, he might be successful in sweeping the whole matter under the rug.

"Come on, Oscar, can't you see what's going on here?" Will demanded, losing patience and getting frustrated at Cordoba's lack of originality. "We've got a sniper that's going around killing innocent family members of two prominent security company heads. Security company heads, I might add, that facilitate government contracts around the world. That means these companies command a lot of authority and a lot of secrets. They employ a lot of ex-military, a lot of ex-snipers, well-trained, well-armed gentlemen who have probably seen more action than any five of us."

"Oh, our shooter made a mess of the clerk!" Cordoba said honestly. "… but the damnedest thing happened. Some shopper let go of her shopping cart after seeing the aftermath of the wife being shot and damned if it didn't roll right in front of the clerk who had already covered Miller's wife just as our boy decided to take his second shot."

Will's eyes lit up as he heard this incredible tale, but he hesitated to classify it as a miracle.

"Of course, all that did was force our shooter to take more shots."

"So Oscar, are ya getting Alzheimer's? More shots equals more evidence; more evidence means a broader profile!" Will shouted, as he threw his arms in the air, beginning to wonder if he was going to have to hand-hold and walk Cordoba through the investigative process.

"Oh, yeah, our shooter couldn't get the head shot at first, so he blew our boy's prosthetic arm all to pieces. Plugged him in the legs, then finally, when I'm sure the man could no longer stand the pain, he finally put him out of his misery by tapping him in the back of the skull."

Will took exception to the cold and callous way the sniper picked apart the man who tried to save the life of another and made him suffer. He began to formulate his own manner of execution if the opportunity presented itself in the near future.

"Turns out, the clerk, I mean, our Wounded Warrior amputee, was following Miller's wife outside for some reason and when he saw her drop, I expect he heard the report after a second, he dove on top of her…"

"Yeah, I'm following ya," Will said, growing increasingly impatient with his counterpart.

"Okay, so he's covering her up with his arms and body, cradling her to absorb the next shot, if any, and our sniper blasts our vet's prosthesis to kingdom come."

"He's frustrated! Our shooter has a bone to pick with someone and he certainly doesn't like anyone acting like a hero trying to save his target's life."

Will looked and mumbled something quietly to himself so Cordoba wouldn't hear.

"He had his target dead to rites, but chose to mutilate our hero instead?"

"Well, either way, the VA's gonna have to cough up a new way of honoring another heroic veteran!"

Cordoba couldn't stop making himself laugh at the thought of another bureaucratic administration trying to stay ahead of the press that would soon be consuming them over this particular human-interest piece.

"Hell, after the TV news gets a hold of this story, the next presidential candidate better take a trip out to see this man's mother!"

"So you're telling me you really think for one minute that this long-range sniper, this probable contract killer, actually missed, not once, but twice?" Will asked, attempting to coax Cordoba into catching up.

"Uhm, I guess when you put it that way, it does seem a little odd." Cordoba began to run the question around his brain. "Yeah, but come on, this could also be coincidence as well, Will."

"This guy is a professional," Will answered. "He gets paid, more than likely big bucks by ugly thugs to end people. I'm sure you guys have already linked him to a dozen other hits and it doesn't look like he's gonna be stopping anytime soon."

"More like three dozen," Cordoba said, exhaling at the thought of this criminal on the loose. "And it's not just here in the states; we've linked him to shootings all over the globe. So far, we've just been able to match him by the killing profiles, not yet by a single photo or through any DNA left at the scene."

"So that means he's well-funded, well-protected, and well-documented!" Will continued. "He's got friends in high places and he travels freely without interruption or molestation. That's some serious juice."

"Well Homeland…" Cordoba began to say as Will suddenly interrupted.

"Homeland's gonna have a photo of him!" Will said quickly as he stirred in his chair.

"Just task-in their facial recognition software geeks and use the parameters like facial matches of men under 50, traveling to and from Wyoming, Colorado, and the other places, probably checking some kind of single long tube or bag or packet that holds his gun."

Cordoba gave Will a curious look as though they had never thought of that angle.

"And that gun is going to be special. Who knows, maybe it's collapsible; maybe it breaks down like the old Air Force-issued .22 long rifle? Either way, you cross match with those parameters, and we're gonna get a hit!"

"That's kind of a tall order," Cordoba said, running the endless bureaucratic authorizations and whom he'd have to go to get them in his head as he counted.

"Oscar, this guy is sending a message to someone for some reason. Don't you see that?" Will said, frustrated. "He's toying with us. He's toying with them. He's flaunting it in our faces and he's doing it to distract us. This is some kind of decoy, some kind of ruse to keep us chasing our tails."

Cordoba was going to interrupt Will, but let him continue his thought process.

"And our shooter is about to ramp it up and do something epic that will solidify his place in whatever screwed-up Hall of Fame he thinks he belongs in."

"Okay, Will, get me everything you've got so far; all your notes, all the reports, every bit of evidence and I'll pass it up the chain of command."

Oscar quickly stood up as if to leave as he rattled off orders to Will.

"Are you back on the crack pipe again, Oscar?" Will said facetiously.

"There's no way I'm turning everything over to you and the Bureau. At the very least, we're working together on this one, *amigo*. So don't try pulling rank on me at the eleventh hour." Will pointed his finger at the agent. "You know, I still have the director's private cell number on speed dial, too!"

Oscar knew the second Will made his first point that the two men would be working together again. What he was doing was buying time to figure out what Will knew, before he deputized him back into the loving embrace of the federal government. Cordoba wanted Will on his team, in order to make him look good again to the Bureau, as well as the higher-ups.

"Jeez, retirement must really be killing you, Will."

Will gave Cordoba a look.

"What about your cushy sheriff's job and your soon-to-be double pension? If you're this desperate to jump back into a young man's game, I don't think there's any hope of you staying here in cow pie county."

Cordoba rushed toward Will's office door in case Will took umbrage with his last statement. Everyone just outside his office quickly jerked around in their chairs and pulled them up closer to their computer screens as they pretended it was work as usual when Cordoba flung open the door... everyone, that is, except Molly.

"Okay, okay, consider yourself back on the payroll. I'll set up an Inter-Agency Task Force for this shooter and have you assigned as one of the leads, next to me, of course!" Cordoba continued to try and regain what little control over the situation he had.

Will nodded. "Okay, I'll compile all the data we've got here, get the assessment from Mohinder, and collect everything from Cheyenne... I'll be in touch."

"Looks like we're gonna have to come up with another stupid name for this guy as well as an even dumber name for the operation."

Cordoba walked out of Will's office, through the bullpen and toward the front entrance.

"Oh, yeah, by the way, does anybody know of any decent hotels in town here?" Cordoba announced to the entire staff, as though they were his to command.

"Nope, you boys'll have to head all the way back to Laramie if you're gonna want something comfortable. There's nothing around here in cow pie county that would meet with your approval, Special Agent!" Martha was already ensuring that Cordoba and his men would be far enough away from Will to let him work the case his way.

"I'll call down to the Double Tree and make you boys a reservation, if you'd like? It's only a little over an hour back down the road."

Cordoba smiled as he passed Martha's desk. "Well, now ain't that mighty kind of ya, Ma'am!"

Cordoba was a patronizing putz, but Martha was no lilting flower, either.

"Anything for you and your brave men, Special Agent Cordoba!" Martha batted her eyes at the federal agent, but bit the inside of her lip to keep herself from laughing any harder than she had been since he'd arrived.

Cordoba nodded in Martha's direction, then headed toward the exit. He took a quick look around the sheriff's station and grinned in that East Coast, snootier-than-thou, pseudo-intellectual way. Just then, Will stepped out of his office to follow behind Cordoba as he left. As he walked into the bullpen, he caught a glimpse of Molly sitting quietly and lowered in her chair so as not to be noticed.

He looked down into his hand and had Molly follow with her eyes. Suddenly he tossed something at her in the air. She knew Will had been up to something, so she reacted quickly and as quietly as could. She reached up out of Cordoba's view and caught it with one hand, almost in defiance.

She slowly opened her hand and there she saw a tiny digital tape recorder. It was still running.

"I think you owe me one helluva home-cooked meal, little lady," Will said, walking past Molly, still following Cordoba as he left the station. "Oh, and I like red wine with my dinner, too, so open it up and let it breathe a little first!"

Molly smiled as Will headed toward the exit behind Cordoba, who was by now already in the parking lot and getting into his chauffeured government rental.

"And don't be afraid to use that good china your mother gave you a long time ago to try and hook a man. You know the nice plates with the blue clovers on them?"

"Will Pierce, you'd be the luckiest man in town if I'd ever have you over to dinner, and everyone in this station sure knows that to be the case!" Molly tried her best to protest, but it came out more like foreplay.

"See ya at 6!"

CHAPTER 36

ROBERT MILLER'S IPHONE VIBRATED at the predetermined time, as his alert went off. It was after 10 p.m. and he awoke from a light sleep in an extremely uncomfortable hospital chair after a hard day of helping ensure his wife was stabilized and as comfortable as she possibly could be.

That was the term doctors used to describe his wife, *stabilized*, when in actuality, she was in a coma and most likely would be for the rest of her life. Her head wound was just good enough not to kill her, but bad enough for her to ever rejoin society in any other state than vegetative.

She had a long row of train tracks and an innumerable number of stitches that covered most of the top of her shaved head. She might eventually need a new carbon-fiber skullcap, the doctors told Miller. It would be inserted and formed around the skull to protect what little was left of her brain after the surgeon had extracted the bone fragments, torn tissue, broken veins, arteries, and clots as well as other brain matter.

Stephanie Miller was intubated with a breathing tube and had not yet been put through an apnea test, as that would be a last resort after Miller would be told there was no more hope and that she would be better off being taken off life support and having her organs donated to someone who might just have a better chance at life.

If that were the case, the doctor would remove the breathing tube and watch the monitor for any independent breathing activity on her own. If she did continue to breathe on her own, they would continue to feed her, change her, and care for her as long as she lived. If she stopped breathing, she would be brought immediately into surgery and have her precious organs and tissues harvested and removed to be donated to other souls that could continue on with their lives.

Miller was beside himself, and for one of the first times in his life, he didn't know what to do or whom to turn to. He and Stephanie had nearly made it all the way through their lives at each other's sides. They'd raised their children and saw them succeed and go on to have families of their own. They'd survived a career as a soldier and soldier's wife, respectively, and made it through the toughest part of their marriage, only to recently recommit to each other and plan for their leisure-filled future. Their bond had become stronger than ever and they were determined to live and die by each other.

By this time, liaisons from the Pentagon and the Department of Defense had arrived at the hospital to support Miller just before the melee of reporters and TV news crews arrived to cover the growing story of a local woman and a wounded veteran murdered in cold blood at the hands of an evil and sadistic sniper.

Miller's own men, without orders from him, combined with those Marines assigned by the local base for his protection, formed en masse in and around the hospital waiting on any move he may make and to protect and secure him if he did decide to go anywhere for any reason.

There were already three teams to secure his home with electronic surveillance, heavily armed personnel, even bomb-sniffing dogs to ensure Robert Miller continued with his life. At least that was the wish of the highest-ranking members of government.

Miller felt his cell phone vibrate again and swiped his index finger over the face of it to unlock the call feature. He was careful to keep his voice low, thinking that would somehow not wake his comatose wife.

"Callahan, it's Miller. This is a Level 1 priority now!" Miller had desperation in his voice that Callahan had never heard before. This was very real. "I don't care about myself, but this thing is somehow connected to all of us and I don't want me or you to lose anyone else."

Miller listened for a response at the other end as the line stayed curiously silent.

"I concur." Callahan's voice was deep and resonated. He knew the gloves would have to come off now.

"We've got to alert Khumari ASAP; it looks like he's next on the list."

"Roger that!" Miller wanted to raise his voice louder, as his anger for what the assassin had done to his wife was raging just below the surface.

"He could be going after Ali, or even Nassar, for all we know," Callahan reckoned.

"How could anyone hurt a child or a defenseless woman, for that matter?"

Miller bit down and closed his eyes, trying not to think of what his beautiful wife had gone through and the silent prison she was now in.

"Innocents are always off limits. Everyone knows that. If they weren't, there would be chaos and anarchy across the globe."

"You know this has something to do with *us*, don't you, Miller?" Callahan asked in a low voice. "You know it deep in your heart."

"But how could such a harmless project produce such a psycho?" Miller wondered aloud, looking at Stephanie as her chest heaved up and down from the pacing of the life support system.

"It has to be one of our own members, but for the life of me, I couldn't tell you why."

"It doesn't matter why, it only matters that it is happening now, in real time."

Miller felt something odd rolling down his cheek and he quickly wiped it away before a nurse or a doctor doing his rounds might walk in and catch him.

"We have to alert everyone! We can leave *no* stone unturned, for everyone's sake. We need to send out a bulletin, a BOLO to all parties to be on the lookout!"

"I know we have to, but that could seriously jeopardize everything we've worked so hard to build," Miller lamented, as he knew the time had come to expose what they had kept secret for so long, in order to flush out their quarry. "If we start calling so much attention to the club, we'll risk losing some, if not all, of our members. Not to mention drawing unneeded scrutiny onto ourselves."

"We've already done that without even realizing it." Callahan knew he didn't have to explain anything to Miller, but it somehow made him feel better to hear it come out of his mouth and hear it aloud.

"I think the sheriff that saved my grandson's life has already become very suspicious of the rifle, as well as the clip."

"Who is this guy? I thought you said he was just some sheriff in a little Podunk part of the West?"

"I thought so too, but I did some digging and it turns out he used to be a federal agent. He knows something's not right about the gun and now they're running a forensics spectrum on it. It's been booked into evidence and I can't retrieve it. It's now part of a crime."

"Granted, we all knew when we started this little experiment that there was potential for law enforcement involvement and consequences therein, just look at the Dallas incidence, for God's sake!"

"I know, I know, but we made a pact a long time ago that this is something that is deep inside men of action, and I for one am not about to give up a lifetime commitment to this cause because of one lunatic."

"What will we be able to pass down to our children and grandchildren if we dismantle everything we've spent a lifetime honing and fine tuning?"

"Agreed!" Miller answered in a matter-of-factly and knew what had to be done.

"But it's this very same lunatic who's forcing our hands and daring us to try and catch him, probably to blackmail us for some ransom or something."

"I think if he wanted money, he'd have sent a ransom note." At this point, Callahan could only speculate, as there had been no real contact made, no real evidence brought to bear this whole time.

"No, this goes much deeper and shows shades of revenge or some kind of challenge to each of us individually or as a collective."

"Do you think it could it be one of the winners?" Miller posed a question to Callahan that would not be easily answered.

"Look, our recruiters have vetted each and every candidate, then we vetted each and every candidate, and nothing came up!" Callahan announced in an aggressive manner, but he quickly realized he was starting to raise his voice at one of his oldest and dearest friends.

"We've gone over everyone's jacket backwards and forwards and still nothing pops out as it being one of our members. I'm at a total loss."

"Well, we're going to have to go back and re-analyze all the data, because this is hitting too close to home and a shooter with those types of skills would have definitely passed over our desk at some point."

"Yeah, and it looks like he sold out to the highest bidder as well!"

Callahan had spent many a night tossing and turning since the event on the plateau with his grandson.

"Wait, maybe if it's not one of the winners, then maybe it's one of the losers?"

"You mean one of the top three shooters?"

Miller's inquiry would prove to be more telling than the two men would realize.

"No, the top two, not the winner, but perhaps one of the two runner-ups!" Callahan's voice did rise this time, but almost in an excited manner. "What if one of the shooters was holding a grudge, but not for not winning or losing? I mean, after all, our process is certainly subjective. Maybe someone down the line decided they *should've* won, but we didn't agree with them?"

"We're talking photographs, here, not real *kills*! What could be so damn important to a shooter who is trying to take the most difficult photos ever taken? It's a *badge of honor* for Christ sakes, not rocket science!"

"Maybe that's it!" Callahan suddenly had a realization that could answer both their questions. "Maybe one of our shooters never even really wanted to shoot photographs of *kills*. Maybe, perhaps, instead, they had the bloodlust for the real thing?"

"Come on, Callahan, that's why we vet them so damn carefully!" Miller answered, still unable to believe that the assassin could possibly be one of their elite candidates.

"Look, Miller, you were a sniper. Put yourself in his shoes for a moment." Callahan closed his own eyes to envision the scenario for both of them. "You train all those years, become the best shooter you can be—one of the best in the world—and the whole time you're training, you're training for the real thing."

Miller knew exactly what Callahan was talking about. An experience he'd had many times during his own sniper training and what it felt like to achieve your ultimate goal.

"… Not to shoot pretty pictures, or shots that show what an accomplished photographer you are, but to kill! To take a human life and snuff it out like blowing out a candle. You know what I'm talking about, don't you Miller? Admit it."

There was an uncomfortable silence as Miller contemplated the scenario in his head.

"Okay, here's what we're gonna do," Miller quickly interjected as he became excited at the prospect of getting revenge for Stephanie, as well as himself. "We're gonna rally our best cryptos to monitor NSA and satellite coms for any chatter about this guy!"

Callahan didn't have to hear Miller's response; he knew he was nodding his head in agreement at the other end of the line as he could hear his breathing intensifying.

"We need them to seek out any coded references to payments for kills. Any buzzing about loops being closed, all the same references we used to make in the field. We need a trap and trace, satellite surveillance, horizontal and vertical exposure, longitudinal and latitudinal coverage, as well acoustic gunshot detection. Let's tap our pals at STRATCOM and National Reconnaissance. Are you in agreement? Cause this is gonna pull out all the stops."

"Roger that!" Callahan responded.

"And we get our families underground and initiate Protocol Failsafe. Let's contact Khumari ASAP and task him in… good luck old friend!"

CHAPTER 37

ALI KHUMARI LOVED NEW York City. He loved the nightlife, the cars, and the money. But most of all, Ali loved the beautiful women that seemed to be even more beautiful around every corner as he walked out of his five-star hotel across from Central Park.

Ali headed the Advance Team for Falcon Securities that did the groundwork and set up security whenever King Abdullah and the other members of the royal family came to shop or see a Broadway show here and when his majesty addressed the United Nations to plead for calm, security, or compassion for refugees. Plain and simple, Ali just loved New York City.

Like his father, Nassar, Ali was a global child, which meant he grew up around the world, but unlike his father, he was spoiled and therefore grew to gain expensive tastes in cars, real estate, top-shelf liquor, gourmet food, and above all, women. It was unclear if Ali had a great deal of compassion or thoughtfulness, or even love, for that matter, but what he had, he had in excess and that was just fine as far as Ali was concerned.

Although Nassar was a moderate Muslim, like most Jordanians, Ali took that term to a new level. He was excessive, drank too much, caroused, purchased expensive gifts for his friends, and partied on his yacht, but Ali

Khumari was a good man whether or not his actions showed otherwise. He really couldn't consider himself a Muslim, at least by any standards: strict, orthodox, or otherwise, and he knew it would be hypocritical to even consider himself more than a mere *pilgrim.*

"Good morning, Mr. Khumari," the doorman said as he tipped his hat.

"Good morning to you, Clyde," Ali responded, with the very slightest hint of a Jordanian accent.

He bowed slightly as Clyde held the door open for one of his favorite hotel guests as he exited the hotel.

Ali glanced up the side of the tall building as he hit the sidewalk. He preferred the Trump Tower to the other hoity-toity hotels around Central Park. Ali felt at home in what he considered one of the homes of the great Donald Trump. He was sure that if Mr. Trump was to visit Jordan, Ali would gladly extend an invitation to the man and his family for them to join the Khumari family at one of their many lavish mansions or compounds in Aqaba or manor houses on the Red Sea. How could such a like-minded entrepreneur such as Mr. Trump not see the similarities?

Ali was nothing if not a little naïve, but his friends and enemies too knew never to mistake his lightheartedness and lust for life as a sign of weakness.

That would be a grave error, as Ali, spoiled and rich and excessive as he was, was also a 5th-degree black belt in Brazilian Jiu Jitsu, beating opponents across the Middle East and beyond in the ring. He had boxed, wrestled, and fought most of his life and had managed to navigate the streets of the Middle East easily, whether they knew who his father was or not.

This, along with the fact that Ali had done his service for his country as a solider with distinction in the Royal Jordanian Army, and like his king, was educated at the best schools, well-trained, and could hit the broad side of a barn with both a Glock 9 or an AK-47, the latter being far less challenging, but nonetheless effective in Ali's eyes.

Ali was every bit the perfect man to run Nassar's security company, and the fact that he just happened to be Nassar's son didn't necessarily mean that nepotism was alive and kicking, but that Ali may have merely had a slight advantage over his counterparts who may have been vying for the job.

Ali headed right up Central Park West, passing West 63rd, then W. 65th, passed W. 66th, but then decided to double-back and check his six as he tended to do. All military and ex-military personnel knew that straight ahead was your 12 o'clock, to your right was 3 o'clock, your left 9, and behind you, 6!

And, just to make things interesting and to shake any possible tails he might have dogging his every move, he made a quick left turn to traverse through Central Park so he could get a good view of any potential bogies that might be thinking of catching him off guard.

Ali grew up with American television and movies and saw himself as some kind of hero/spy, so he would play these games, mostly for himself, but it was also very good practice for his job.

This day Ali was heading out alone sans his team to do a bit of recon before King Abdullah's visit. He was tasked with the royal family's security issues and, since he knew the family so intricately, they would be vulnerable if anything were to ever happen to him.

Ali crossed West Drive heading toward Center Drive when he decided to engage in an old spy trick. He walked around the corner of a small restroom and rounded it to take up a temporary post behind it to see if anyone was following him. He positioned himself in such a way that he had nearly a 200-degree view and all he'd have to worry about was anything leaping over the small retaining wall behind him. He felt confident that no one would be stealthy enough to sneak up on an old pro like him.

Ali waited a few moments. He turned to watch the Frisbee golfers playing through cyclists and roller-bladers... *do people still roller blade?* he thought. He watched old couples canoodling, young couples arguing, and children running around with seemingly endless energy. He envied those children, especially as he had a soft spot in his heart for children and often dreamt of his own progeny.

Uh, nothing. Ali had many thoughts swirling around in his brain, but when he began to concentrate on what he was there to do, he began to feel relieved. There was a small part of him that wanted to be stalked, and perhaps that someone would be up to no good and wish him harm... little did he realize that his wish was about to come true.

After a few more minutes of this unexpected leisure time, as Ali considered it, he continued deeper into Central Park to check out the different routes and footpaths someone might choose if they were so inclined to do something, well, unspeakable.

The Ramble, as it was known, was originally planned and developed in 1857 as a wild garden that would be the perfect setting for horse-drawn carriage rides and bridle paths and could be viewed in its natural landscape from nearly every angle, especially at the Bethesda Terrace.

Ali was no history buff, but he did enjoy the light fare of the History Channel et al. and would be surprised whenever his information retention would suddenly rear its pretty head and recall fun facts about cities, structures, and people he had taken an interest in while watching a show that revolved around them. As he walked up the slight rise out of the wooded area and upon the lake, he reminisced about how his father would take him fishing there, or sailing or rowing for the day and make it complete with hot dogs from a park vendor and Coca Cola with ice in large Styrofoam cups.

As much of a playboy as Ali was, he also longed for the day when he would have children of his own he could take to Central Park and lavish with every manner of indulgence New York City had to offer a child who was being spoiled for the day by his adoring father. Ali quickly snapped out of his nostalgia and regained his composure. He straightened his head out to get back to the task at hand. Security! It was all about security now. It was always about security. This is a workday and it is all about security and security-issues. That is, of course, when he wasn't at the nightclubs, discos, or corner café smoking a hookah or drinking a fresh cup of tea.

A cool breeze had just kicked up in Central Park, a rather strong breeze that could send a hat or an umbrella flying to New Jersey if one wasn't careful. Ali could feel his clothes flapping and waving in the gale that seemed to come out of nowhere, so he smoothed out his shirt and trousers with a seemingly effortless maneuver of his hands, then looked down quickly at his shoes to ensure they were free of mud or scuffs.

Ali blended in well in Manhattan with just the right amount of panache in his dressing style, business causal, but with a playful bent. He didn't take himself too seriously as other Middle Eastern men often did.

Suddenly, Ali heard a buzz and felt his iPhone vibrate in his pocket.

"Hallo?" Ali said, absently, noting a bit of dust on one trouser leg.

"Ali, you are in danger!" the voice on the other end said, while the crosshairs of a sniper scope focused on Ali's head from more than 1,000 yards away.

CHAPTER 38

WILL PIERCE DIDN'T LIKE to wait on things or people and most everyone who knew or worked with him understood that. It was this reality that had Rusty calling every day, sometimes twice, for any updates from the forensics lab in Cheyenne.

He knew he wouldn't ever personally be blamed for any delays that were truly out of his hands, but Rusty was so desperate for his sheriff's approval, that he wanted to make everything he possibly could easier on Will Pierce.

And now the added respect that Will commanded from the way he'd set those federal agents straight was worthy of a pat on the back, but Rusty would never dare to be that informal, no sir, not with Sheriff Pierce.

The office was abuzz with gossip and whisperings, as is human nature when a local event comes to the attention of the federal government. Rusty had become so adrenalized since the night Sheriff Pierce saved that boy from the mountain top only to find out the little fella was a victim of a heinous crime, he had hardly slept a wink since the occurrence.

Rusty thought about how it must have felt when Will was a federal agent on his first manhunt. That must've been something! He must have felt the exact same way as Rusty did now, only the sheriff was in a big city then, a metropolis, not a Podunk outpost at the end of the prairie trail in Nowheresville, Wyoming.

Heck, even Rusty's girlfriend got in on the action, having been bit by the excitement bug. She put special little notes in his brown paper lunch bag that kept him motivated and psyched-up. He felt it was her life's goal to somehow get on *TMZ* or one of those pseudo news shows so a Hollywood reality show producer would instantly discover her and immediately demand she be on their show.

But Rusty was tired of talking to everyone else in the office about how big a case it was becoming or how remarkable the sheriff was. He knew it. He worked directly for the man as his *official* deputy. The others could only *talk* to the sheriff, know him from a distance and ask questions of him, but Rusty knew he was the man's protégé.

Rusty was hard at work trying to finish his TPS reports while he inputted data into the software program to somehow justify his position.

"Stupid TPS reports!" Rusty yelled at his computer screen. "Who the heck cares about these ridiculous things, anyway? I mean…" The phone on his desk rang, shocking him out of his mindset that had been all things mundane and administrative for the past few hours.

"This is Rusty… I mean Deputy Jenkins!" Rusty said in a mundane voice as he picked up his coffee for another sip. "How can I help you?" Rusty had a bad habit of holding the receiver cockeyed near his ear, but not up to it, so anyone in the room could clearly hear whether or not it was a business call or one that was a little more private.

"Yes, is Sheriff Will Pierce in?" asked a voice on the other line.

"No, Sir, sorry. The sheriff is out of the station right now."

"Well that's a shame."

"Who's callin? Maybe I could pass on a message for you if you'd like?"

"Well, it's about the evidence your office sent up here to Cheyenne Labs."

"Forensics? Yeah, we've been waiting on your final report. That and ballistics, too," he said, raising his voice excitedly.

Rusty placed the phone tightly to his ear and began to listen intently as one of his eyebrows furled with each new revelation.

"No, you don't say?" Rusty said, awestruck.

"OMG, email me that report *STAT*! The sheriff's gonna wanna see that today! Send the rest overnight so we have it here by tomorrow if ya could... you just made my day!"

CHAPTER 39

GIUSEPPE TANTI WAS A craftsman of the highest order, who only created for those people he felt were worthy enough to receive the talents of what God had been so generous to bestow upon him.

He was nearly 80 years old, and unlike most men his age, he had kept himself in fine shape by sustaining himself on a Mediterranean diet, long before it was fashionable; he'd spent his entire life in and around the Mediterranean.

His beautiful wife, Sophia, God rest her soul, had left him years before after a particularly virulent strain of influenza and battling bout after bout of a lung infection here and weakness there, she finally gave in. He missed her madly and cherished her memory with each and every day.

He'd spent almost his entire life in a tiny village called Valnontey, near Cogne in the Aosta Valley of Italy. The enchanted land was the kind of mythical place only described in fairy tales and old forgotten European mysteries that people searched for but rarely found.

In the years after World War II, the long-suffering European, Christians, Jews, and everyone else sought out places like Valnontey to assuage the shock of what mankind had wrought upon them.

But, like so many stories, rarely is there a happy ending, except for the fact that Valnontey was real, it was here, and Giuseppe knew it was his home. Though these days, so many years since the collapse and rebuilding of Europe, this postcard of a hamlet had become a favorite for over-privileged European tourists and backpackers the world over for its resemblance to what tiny villages looked like centuries before.

Giuseppe was not only a master craftsman of leather, fine wood, and metals, but he was also the finest in all of Italy, the Alps, and most of Western Europe. He had learned his trade as a boy in World War II when he was in a German slave labor camp. His father, Guido Tanti, was an outspoken anti-fascist and had serious problems with authority, especially when it was dressed in an SS uniform. Though only a child himself, Guido had fought, and nearly died, in WWII. In the slave labor camps he was forced to learn how to clean, maintain, and ultimately, create and modify modern weaponry. It was a skillset that would serve both he and his father well for the rest of their lives.

Giuseppe's father had chosen Cogne after WWII to settle down, raise his family, and perfect his craft. The business had come to Giuseppe young, as his father had succumbed to the injuries sustained under the harsh German camp life.

An avid hiker, like many of his Italian brethren, Giuseppe loved living close to mountains like the Grand Paradis that soared as high as 4,000 meters. To him, it was all a little piece of paradise. It was the perfect location for him to escape the evil that he had seen his fellow man do, and anyone who knew and had the lira could find him and commission his services.

So he decided in his youth that this place at the end of the road, a place that was less than 100 kilometers from the even more beautiful Lake Geneva and the intriguing and growing city of Montreux would be his final home.

Giuseppe's shop was off Rue Grand Paradis, just beyond the local chocolatier. He needed very little signage, because his clients, many whom he'd known for decades, knew his place of business and frequented it as often as they could, if for no other reason than to experience the beauty that Giuseppe saw on a daily basis from his cobbler's window.

He was more businessman than merchant and had resigned himself to not ask questions of what his requested custom designs were used for.

He was, after all, a master gunsmith, so it would follow that his clients would use his specialties to hunt, for sport, and yes, perhaps to kill. He had no problem with this, as he'd seen the worst that man could do to his brother and he no longer cared. All he cared about was making his specialty creations and selling them well above market value.

He did, of course have a small showcase in the window that would draw oohs and aahs from passerby's, usually drunk English and Frenchmen who were lost and wandering the back alleys in search of their hotel. His handcrafted artistry was glorious and beautiful, yet he hardly ever had a customer actually enter his establishment to purchase something they had seen in the display window.

He was well used to tourists pulling out their new camera phones and taking selfies or merely memorializing his work to brag about upon returning to their own countries. But again, Giuseppe didn't care, as he knew deep in their hearts, all men were good. If a digital record was taken of something he had created with his two hands, then he hoped that person would cherish it as much as he did.

This particular day it was cold, not yet quite winter, but being at such high elevation, this part of the world rarely got into the comfortable temperature range for most people. Tourism had slowed to nearly nothing and he rarely saw footprints in the snow outside his shop, except for his own when he entered in the early morning and left just after the sun went down.

His shop was open for all to see as he crafted the project, yet he had an even larger area in the back behind two long black veils where the real magic happened. If someone did perchance enter, a loud bell at the end of a small circular metal spring would announce their arrival and force him to stop what he was doing and address potential clients. He had not stopped work in weeks.

Giuseppe had been tasked many years before by three good friends to make a custom-designed magazine for a rifle that was rather counterintuitive. It was small, could be made of wood, metal, or porcelain and could only handle up to three rounds of .762 ammunition.

Giuseppe fashioned the wooden clips by first cutting a small block of wood, then digging out a large groove in the center. Sanding, polishing it to a smooth finish, and then soaking it in oil to make sure it stayed smooth.

Finally, coating it inside and out with a moisture-proof sealant that would guarantee the clip would not warp, splinter, or damage from the heat and stress that would be put on it.

When he created the metal or porcelain magazines, he followed the same basic premises, yet each clip would end up being unique to the gun it was being created for and would ultimately have a life of its own.

At the end of his workbench a small fan kept the air moving around the old shop. The fine sawdust and wood scrapings were sucked up by an old Craftsman Shopvac that Giuseppe had received from one of his sons in the late 1970s and had been a workhorse ever since.

On the other side of the workbench closer to him was an old black rotary phone. Today the young would call it *vintage*, but it had worked perfectly since he installed it in the 1950s and he had no reason to change it for a computer-like iPhone or some other cellular device.

He liked the weight of the receiver and holding it in his hand; it was as familiar as an old friend. But his old friend never rang. It didn't bother him too much. He enjoyed working in silence.

He was putting the finishing touches on a set of three-round magazines when suddenly his old friend came to life.

"Pronto!" Giuseppe said after the initial startling of the phones loud ring rattled his ears.

"Si, si, pisano," Giuseppe responded as he listened to detailed instructions. "Okay, ciao il mio vecchio amico!"

Giuseppe slowly returned the receiver back to its cradle on the old phone. He glanced at the rotary dial face and thought for a moment whether he should pick it up and make a call, then slowly settled back onto his comfy working stool and continued measuring and drafting.

In the background, Giuseppe listened to recordings of old Italian operas. Barely perceptible, it always seemed to permeate his entire shop and was a welcome treat for any visitor.

A glance up at his old cuckoo clock told him it was almost time to wind it down for the day, but he felt he could perhaps finish this last step before calling it a day.

He knew it was only a five-minute walk back to his chalet, but he had to be extra cautious these days, as he'd had a terrible tumble a few years before. After the death of his wife, he had been returning from the cemetery and her gravesite, where he still took flowers to her every week, the same as when she had been alive.

That day he had returned to work after lunch and a cold front had moved in, freezing the moisture on the cobblestones into a thin layer of ice. He wasn't prepared with the proper footwear and because of that serious lapse in judgment, he'd taken a spill that landed him in the hospital and forced him into the 21st century with a new titanium hip, complete with ball joint and rods down his femur.

In over 50 years, Giuseppe had never missed a day of work, nor would anyone have believed it if they had been told he would. The local population would be up in arms if someone ever questioned this maestro, regarding his commitment to his craft and clientele.

He was considered a local treasure and whenever a foreigner or tourist would inquire about ancient relics or purveyors of the old ways, they would mention Giuseppe Tanti, telling their tales of his master craftsmanship and dedication to a dying art and how this old Italian would forever be a cornerstone in the tiny hamlet they had been honored to visit.

He was better prepared these days and he kept duplicate pairs of both shoes and boots at his chalet and in his shop in case of inclement weather.

"Coo coo! Coo coo!" the animatronic bird sang as it popped out of its gilded cage to announce the top of the hour.

Giuseppe nodded, placed his tools on the table, and put the nearly finished rifle clip down in the exact spot he had put it the night before and the night before that. He glanced across the room at the tall coat rack that had stood in the corner near the rear door that exited to the alleyway for over 50 years. He saw three jackets: a long dressy camel hair, a thick North Face parka-like jacket for snowstorms and deep winter, and a hybrid of both, a thick black jacket meant to keep out the cold, which was strangely fashionable at the same time.

As he slowly rose from his stool and let the blood circulate back into his legs, he unexpectedly heard the tinkle of the bell over his shop entry.

Who could that be at this hour? Giuseppe wondered.

Instead of heading toward the coat rack, he turned and passed one hand over one side of the black veil to enter the front of his shop. There he saw a very handsome, Italian-looking man whose hands were flat on his counter. It was Gaius.

"Signore Tanti?" Gaius said with a kind smile as if to disarm the old man.

"Si!" Giuseppe answered.

"I need you to make me something very special," Gaius continued, an evil grin crossing his lips.

CHAPTER 40

WILL PIERCE DECIDED HE didn't want the feds around his office. It not only made his employees nervous, it created fodder for gossip. And the very last thing he needed in this small town was everyone gossiping even more than they had been of late.

So Will made a decision to schedule his meetings with the special agents at Cora's Diner. Little did he know this action would create more gossip than he could've ever predicted in his wildest dreams.

Will setting the meeting at Cora's was certainly a violation of evidentiary protocol, and he was very aware of that, but he didn't care and he knew that protecting his people and being able to see the evidence and examining it first, before the feds stomped all over it or screwed it up, was certainly one of his biggest priorities.

Rusty sat next to Will in a large booth, padded with American classic red vinyl, as it was easier to mop up any spills and never left a stain. His palms were sweating from obsessively gripping the large bag. Stenciled on the side of the thick black canvas was EVIDENCE in large white letters that someone about 40 feet away could probably read without really trying. He shifted nervously from side to side.

"Relax, Rus," Will said, with the calm of a sage. "We're simply gonna pass these guys our evidence and explain what it all means to us and them, that's it. No reason to be nervous."

Rusty nodded, a little too many times, tipping his hand that he was even now more nervous, as his boss, mentor, and idol could so easily see through him. He shifted again in the large bench seat, but this time he tried to relax his shoulders and sank into the cushion a little deeper... *ah.*

Rusty had always loved Cora's Diner, even when he was a boy, when he would get excited about coming to Saturday night dinner there with his parents and siblings.

The booths were the same as they were now, with the exception that Rusty and his sister and brother would bounce on them mercilessly, almost daring the fabric to tear. He and his sister were spitfires and on any given day would have been classified as trouble with a capital T.

Rusty smiled at the memory and had a quick OCD moment to micro-bounce up and down just to feel the sponginess of the vinyl-wrapped foam padding that was seemingly indestructible. He bounced again, faking a shift, so Will wouldn't perceive what he was really doing, but unbeknownst to him, since Will had been sitting right next to him on the same side, every move Rusty made would be duplicated and replicated, so every vibration, every shifting movement was a dead giveaway. Will wanted to give him the *look*, but he figured Rusty needed to release some nervous energy.

Rusty scanned the café as suddenly all the heads in the room began to look upwards and the patrons began to stand slightly to see what was happening outside. First Joe, then Sara, then Cora, everyone saw something that Rusty had not yet seen, and Will being the only one in the entire establishment who didn't even bother to look up, continued to sip his coffee, unfazed.

"What the...?" Rusty whispered under his breath, but loud enough for Will to hear.

Looking out the café windows, Rusty and the others watched as four large black SUVs raced down the road and skidded to a stop on the dirt outside Cora's Diner. It was all very dramatic as man after man in either a dark blue or black suit poured out of the trucks, the next one even larger and meaner looking than the previous one.

Special Agent Cordoba was one of the last men to jump out, and he was quickly flanked by a number of other federal agents. Two other important-looking men were flanked and protected by the others. Rusty knew these men must be pretty important to have such a large and ominous security detail protecting them.

Once again he shifted in his seat, this time he became as excited as when he was a boy. He had a fleeting thought: *I hope I don't wet my pants.*

Cling. Cling. The glass double doors of Cora's Diner swung open and in three-by-three formation, the federal agents walked in ahead of their assigned superior and took up a position in and around the diner. Rusty's eyes widened as he wondered if even ISIS or Al Qaeda could penetrate these lines.

Cordoba walked in, nodded and smiled to Cora and the other stunned diners and headed directly toward Will and Rusty at the table. The other two men followed just behind Cordoba in unison with the precision of those who had spent their entire lives in the military.

Cordoba marched right up to Will's table and stopped as the other men blocked any exit Will might be thinking of utilizing. Will was not intimidated in the least. He hardly gave Cordoba a glance as he continued to sip his coffee.

Finally, Will lowered his bifocals, as he had been particularly interested in the blueberry pancakes that morning.

"Sheriff William Pierce!" Cordoba began his sermon just a tad bit louder than someone trying to have a normal conversation. "Would you please stand up?"

Rusty's face turned pale. He was very worried about his boss and had thoughts of him being thrown into a dungeon or at best, a dirty, unhygienic prison cell at Guantanamo Bay or God forbid, Alcatraz.

Will smacked his lips, slowly removed his specs and laid them down on top of the menu he had been reading. He maneuvered out of the deep vinyl seat, stood up, and then scanned the room that now seemed filled with the entire cast from the movie *Men in Black.*

"Sheriff William Pierce, please raise your right hand," Cordoba said bluntly.

Will complied.

"Do you solemnly swear to uphold the Constitution of the United States of America as well as both the federal and state laws that are put forth to maintain sovereignty?"

"I think you forgot about 100 paragraphs, Oscar," Will whispered. Will decided to go ahead and play along with the charade, although he was completely unimpressed with the manner in which Cordoba was presenting it.

"Okay, yeah, I do if it'll speed things along."

Cordoba shot him a look that only Will could see as his face began to turn red. "Then, under the authority, supervision, and administration of the Attorney General of the United States, the U.S. Marshall's Service, and the Special Deputation program, as well as all articles contained in 28 USC 566(c), 561(a), 561(f), 509, 510, 28 CFR, 0.111, 0.112, and 0.113 and under 49 U.S. Code § 44922, and I suppose the great State of Wyoming…" Oscar said as hastily as possible while the other men stood stoically behind him.

"… etcetera, etcetera, etcetera," Will interjected as he whirled his index finger in the air as if to tell Cordoba to move it along.

"… I hereby deputize you for the federal task force, and for the mission from here on out to be known as *Operation Black Jack* for the purposes of tracking and capturing the assassin known from his alias as 'Gaius'."

Will smacked his lips again as he knew the routine but was getting hungry. "Okay, thanks, Oscar, now let's get some breakfast, cause I'm starving!"

Cordoba shot Will another look and nearly grabbed his arm before he could sit back down. Cordoba's eyes narrowed as if to beg an answer from Will.

"Oh yeah, I guess I do, so help me God, and all that other malarkey." Will sat back down at his table, but decided not to scoot in farther. This action was not to avoid being closer to Rusty, but in order to be able to hold court his way and make the other guys face him.

Cordoba sat opposite Rusty and Will and scooted one cheek at a time in toward the window. The other two men in suits followed until all three men were uncomfortably and hilariously squished together in front of Will, who wanted it that way.

"Okay, now for your FYIs," Oscar said. He scrunched his shoulders in so the other men could get comfortable. "You're covered across the board: DEA, DOJ, Tactical, Homeland, and a couple of new ones," Oscar said, hoping Will wouldn't notice his last comment.

"Who are your pals, Oscar?" Will looked both men dead in their eyes as he waved to Cora to come over.

"This is Thomas Quartermaster with the U.S. Marshall's Office."

"Sheriff!" Quartermaster said as he respectfully nodded his head.

"Marshall!" Will nodded his reply. "Where's your Stetson? I thought you guys always wore Stetson cowboy hats?"

"Yes, Sir, we do, thought I'd leave it in the truck so as not to cause too much commotion," Quartermaster said with a Mona Lisa smile.

"This is Lieutenant General Samuel Kincaid, with the Department of Defense," Cordoba said sheepishly.

Rusty gulped as he tried to swallow, but his mouth and throat were already too dry. Again he squirmed in his seat as he turned to look at Will and mouthed *General?*

"General!" Will acknowledged.

"Sheriff!" Kincaid replied in kind salutation as his sculpted jawline barely moved.

Cora made her way through the wall of muscle and meat to arrive at the table with her pen already out and ready to take their orders.

"I'm honored that a One Star would fly all this way just to have breakfast, but Cora is known for making the best dang blueberry pancakes in the county, aren't you, Cora?"

Cora smiled nervously, still fairly intimidated by the size and number of the men who had filled her little establishment to capacity.

"These boys were gonna join me in ordering a whole bunch of flapjacks, weren't cha, boys?" Will said with a wide smile, as he subtly peed on their legs.

"The United States Government has decided to buy everyone's breakfast here this morning. Isn't that true, Special Agent Cordoba?"

Cordoba shot Will yet another glare, this time as his internal core temperature was beginning to spike. He was tiring of Will's games.

"It'd be awful rude to come in and practically take over her entire establishment, her little café, without ordering a whole mess of food and coffee, wouldn't it Cora?" Will said, looking to Cora for her reaction.

Cora didn't know how to respond, so she just nodded her head. "Anything for our boys in blue and green, Sir. Anything in particular you gentlemen would like? We'll whip up something nice and quick for ya'll."

"And since Uncle Sam is treating us all to a nice breakfast, I want you to put a hefty 35% tip on our bill! And that's just gonna be for you, Cora. I know you need to get over to Grand Island and see your grandkids one of these days, right?" Will said, practically ready to burst into laughter.

Cordoba just bit his lip and nodded. "Yes, Ma'am, we'll all have a stack of your blueberry pancakes and a cup of your best coffee!"

The other special agents slowly began to correct the Special Agent, as each one was now all in for a decent café breakfast. Each man began adding to and correcting the order as Cora fought to keep up, writing as fast as she could. She ended up filling over a dozen pages of orders.

"Ma'am, I'd like an Earl Grey tea, if you wouldn't mind?" one Deputy U.S. Marshall sounded out.

"I don't much care for coffee, it does my stomach in, you know, all that acid."

"Yes, Ma'am, and I'd like a stack of your strawberry pancakes," another Special Agent said from the back of the crowd.

"… And could I get a side of crispy bacon, Ma'am?" another man said. "I could smell that goodness a mile outside of town and been think'n 'bout it since."

Cordoba turned and sneered at the men behind him as if to stop them, then slowly turned back around as he knew Will was going to get as much traction out of this morning, as well as the U.S. government, as he could.

"Alright! Alright!" Cordoba shouted, then slowly lowered his voice. "We'll all have bacon, well done, and if anyone else wants something different, tell the nice lady as she walks back to the kitchen one at a time, but for God's sake, can we get on with our investigation?"

"Yes Sir!" A chorus of manly voices rose from all angles of the café as each man under their respected banners realized the situation was getting out of hand and after all, they were all there to help catch a serial killer.

"As I was saying, you're covered under the Attorney General, as well as the SecDef under Directive 5210.56. As you probably already figured, the DOD has a unique interest in catching this guy." As Cordoba spoke, the entire room quieted as the lawman got back to business and the residual customers were completely captivated.

"What about OCDETF?" Will asked.

Rusty shot Will a sharp look in an attempt to try and decipher what that particular acronym was and what it could possibly mean.

"It's nice you still remember, Will." Cordoba shifted on the bench, as it seemed he was just beginning to relax. "Yes, you're covered under Organized Crime, too."

Rusty bit his bottom lip now, beginning to realize why Will wanted to keep this under wraps and how large scale this was becoming.

"FBI currently has the authority, under 21 U.S.C. Section 878, to bestow special federal officer status to state and local law enforcement officers assisting and we'll provide you with Title 18 since you're participating in fugitive apprehension activities and other non-drug task force activities."

"… And what about my deputy, Rusty, here?" Will dropped a quick bomb on Cordoba, as he took a swig of ice water. And just to drive his point home, Will began to crunch down on an ice cube hard and loud, as he continued. "Look, I know you know this, Cordoba, but special deputy status is important to task force members because it enables them to act as federal law enforcement officers while under the supervision of the FBI," Will continued, unabated, even though Cordoba attempted to interrupt him. He reeled off the legalese, as though he were reading one of Cora's menus.

"Special deputy status is more extensive than special federal officer status, as it extends beyond drug investigations. Prior to my deputation, we were both functioning as federal officers without the proper authority. That could have, and most certainly would have, placed us in a position where any civil liability incurred would be without the backing of the federal government, and therefore left it up to this county and this state…"

Cordoba smiled at this and decided to add his own twist on things. "Yeah, and then I'd have had to bail your asses out of jail, so *NO*, your deputy here is *NOT* going to be deputized into our federal task force."

"Deputize him, Oscar!" Will said, as he placed his water glass hard on the table. "We wouldn't be as far along in this investigation without his tireless assistance, and since this is now a matter of national security, you had better do the right thing by this young man or my cooperation may dwindle."

Rusty's eyes bulged and he gulped at the mere mention of these $3 words that he had only heard while watching television crime dramas or reading action-packed political thrillers.

"Goddamn it, Will!" Cordoba shouted. "You are one stubborn son of a bitch!"

Will merely smiled.

Cordoba suddenly smashed his open palms onto the table and pushed himself up. He stood up, towered over the other men and waved Rusty up.

Rusty struggled, then realized Will wasn't going to budge, so he stood up as best he could as he leaned over, buckling his knees on the table and held his right hand up but his left down, palm pressed to the table, in order to balance himself.

"Raise your right hand!" Cordoba barked.

Rusty looked at his already raised right hand, shrugged and pushed it a little higher. Will snorted his amusement and Cordoba fairly hissed, "Do you Deputy Perkins solemnly swear to do and not do all those things I said earlier when I was swearing in your boss, Sheriff Pierce?"

"I do, so help me God, I do!" Rusty said as his mouth suddenly dried and he tried to gulp out another sentence before Cordoba put his hand up to stop him.

"Alright! You're hereby deputized to the federal task force, now sit back down!" Cordoba ordered.

"Okay, enough games. Will, where is the evidence? I want a detailed debrief for these men."

Will nodded toward Rusty who was still in a state of shock. Will softly punched Rusty in the side of the leg to get his head back in the game.

"Deputy Perkins, or should I say Special Agent Perkins, could you please brief our colleagues on the evidence that has been collected and the reports filed?" Will said with the pride of a new father.

"Yes, Sir, Sheriff, I mean, Special Agent Pierce, I have the evidence right here." Rusty scrambled to grab the thick EVIDENCE bag at his side. He hoisted it up and with a loud grunt plopped it down hard on the table with an audible thud. It was only then that he sighed with renewed confidence.

"Y'all aren't gonna believe what we found!" Rusty grinned widely. Just then, Cora appeared at the table with a tray of plates filled to the sky with blueberry pancakes.

CHAPTER 41

CALLAHAN SAT BACK IN his high-backed leather chair and spun around 180 degrees to face the large floor-to-ceiling windows that separated him from a 120-story fall onto the pristine sidewalks of Manhattan.

He had spent a great deal of time these last days away from New York City, and as such had begun to fall back in love with the United States. Each and every trip he'd taken with his grandson, Michael, or his daughter, Claire, or alone when he wanted to get away for a massage in Utah or some fishing on the Russian River brought him closer to his homeland and the place of his birth.

But Callahan seemed troubled. Claire had barely forgiven him since the sniper nearly killed her son while he was in his care, and the fact that now Miller's wife and an innocent civilian had also been killed kept Callahan up at night.

Miller had already called and screamed and vented his frustrations, yet neither of them had been able to get a hold of the third musketeer, Nassar, to warn him and his son, Ali Khumari. This added insult to injury and kept Callahan from relaxing at all.

Callahan felt personally responsible. He felt heavy and that something terrible was about to happen and that somehow he, or the secret society of snipers, no that's not right, his secret society of adrenaline-junkie photographers, had some responsibility for this whole mess, or God forbid, actually created the monster that was terrorizing his friends and family.

His palms sweated as he held the remote to the multi-display LED televisions filling an entire wall in his office. He scrolled through and across the NASDAQ, NIKKEI, and Wall Street Indexes like a tickertape parade from here to the moon and back.

Changes in the market would flash, bar graphs rose and fell, while talking heads and pundits did their best to analyze and attempt to predict what the volatile stock market would do in the coming years. All this under the hopes that the fed wouldn't announce an increase in interest rates.

These distractions used to be enjoyable to Callahan; he thrived on the complexity of the market and would often lose hours of his workday just gambling like an old blackjack player at a Las Vegas casino.

He wondered for a moment if in fact his gambling on the wrong person at some point had put everyone in the danger they now faced.

There was a faint rap on Callahan's office door. His office was so large that everyone knew they'd have to knock hard and loud for the old man to hear it, but it was the size of the room and the insulation that truly kept any noises in abeyance.

"Yes, come in!" Callahan shouted. He hoped this latest distraction would take him out of his mind for a little while.

"Dad, I've got to get your signature on the Advance Team's Prep List for the United Nations' event next week," Claire said as she entered without hesitation.

She was used to doing things her way, Callahan thought as he still saw her from time to time as his stubborn little girl who only had eyes for him.

"Oh yeah, right," Callahan jumped out of his foreboding headspace. "I guess I just forgot to sign those. Here, give them to me and I'll sign them now."

"Don't you want to look them over thoroughly first, like you always do?" Callahan looked up at his daughter who seemed to be towering over him as he aged.

"That's why you're the president of Callahan Security, Claire!" He gave her a reassuring smile, but she was in no mood for his charm.

"I won't be around here much longer, that's why you've been taking on more and more responsibility."

"I know, Dad." Claire smiled, seemingly the first time in a long time, Callahan thought.

"I just know you always take the United Nations security details more serious than some of our other clients, as it's such a high-priority security issue."

"Are you saying that I am prejudiced to one of our clients over others?" Callahan smirked in jest.

"Yes, Dad, that is what I'm saying or you wouldn't still be going over my work on the project."

"How are things looking, anyway?"

"Good." Claire sidled up and sat on the corner of his desk as she had done since she was a child. "Everything's in order. All the guards have their assignments; all weapons have been signed for, translators, dignitaries, and their entourages have been vetted, and it's pretty much by the numbers now."

"Right," Callahan said, with some trepidation. "I've just got a weird feeling about this particular one, you know?"

"Why would this event be any different from the thousands of UN events we've done in the past?" Claire asked, a bit patronizingly for her father's taste.

"It's the first time that all three security teams will be here in New York protecting each of our respective clients," Callahan said, leaning in closer to his daughter.

"Okay, so Miller Strategic has a number of high-ranking dignitaries from Europe as well as all the military and Washington folks, Falcon Securities has King Abdullah as well as the Jordanian Royal family, the House of Saud, and basically all the moderates from the Middle East. I think we're covered pretty well," she said, playing with an expensive Mont Blanc pen she'd had since she was a little girl.

"Something just isn't adding up. I don't know what, but it's something."

"What do you mean?"

"It just seems odd that this crazed sniper is trying to pick off members of all three of our families and no one is seeing a red flag in all of this."

"Dad, you have to relax," Claire said, rounding the desk and putting a loving hand on his shoulder. "Look, I know you're blaming yourself, but I don't blame you anymore. How could you have possibly known anything about this psycho?"

"I'm not too sure I didn't help create him," Callahan said, lowering his head.

"Listen, stop blaming yourself. What you, Miller, and Nassar have created gives a lot of people a creative and challenging outlet for superior marksmen that might otherwise go down the wrong path without that kind of serious skill building you've allowed them to exercise."

"It's quite the adrenaline rush as well, don't forget!" Callahan said as he smiled, which seemed like the first time since the incident on the plateau with his grandson; he was beginning to feel better about his role in the accident.

"I'm worried about Ali Khumari, too," Callahan said as he suddenly lost his smile, remembering his friend's son, whom he now felt was extremely vulnerable.

"Ali? Why Ali? What makes you think, let alone worry, about Ali Khumari, Dad?" Claire stood up with a look of frustration on her face and walked back to the edge of the desk.

"It stands to reason that Ali would be next on the sniper's hit list, as he's already hurt me, killed Miller's wife, and with the exception of you, dear Claire, Nassar's son Ali is most likely his next target."

"I, I don't see why that's any concern of yours, Dad. Nassar runs one of the top security companies in the world, let alone has a stranglehold on the Middle East."

"You know Uncle Nassar is like family to me and Uncle Robert."

Claire nodded, reluctantly agreeing with her father.

"Well, I would want Nassar to be very worried about you in the event that something happens to me!"

"What's gonna happen to you, Dad? I've stationed more clothed and undercover units around you and your home than most small countries have at their disposal."

Callahan smiled as he looked into his elder child's beautiful green, slightly tearing eyes. "I know you have, Claire, and I appreciate everything you're doing for me. But you and Michael are my priority and I will stop at nothing to find out who this man is and stop him. And right now, we have to worry about Ali and pray that he has found out about the threat and is taking appropriate measures and counter-measures to stave off this nut job."

"Well, Ali's a big boy!"

Callahan shot her a disgruntled look at the callousness and lack of concern in her attitude.

"Correction, he's not so much a big boy as he is a playboy! But nonetheless, he's a professional and he'll be just fine, Dad. I certainly believe that."

"We still have to keep vigil to ensure Ali, as well as everyone else is protected."

"Look, Dad, together with our security detail, Miller's detail and Falcon's, Manhattan's probably about to be the safest place on Earth, for sure safer than the White House lawn during a presidential picnic."

Claire picked up his Mont Blanc pen and handed it to him to sign the documents she had brought him. "Sign these papers and go home, Dad!" she said as though she was giving him an order.

"Okay, Scary Clairy!" Callahan called his daughter by the pet name he used when she got too bossy for comfort.

"You haven't seen scary, but ya will if you don't sign those papers, and I mean right now, Mister!"

Callahan and Claire shared a laugh as he opened up the file and began scribbling his John Doe on the series of requisition orders, overtime approvals, and birthday cards for the employees.

Callahan was just finishing up signing his last signature when he looked into his daughter's eyes.

"I mean it! You take care of yourself and Michael," the old man said with a tear forming in his eye.

Claire sneered at him like a contrary little girl refusing to appease an old man.

"I would have no reason to continue on this Earth if anything were, God forbid, ever to happen to you or my grandson. You have my word on that."

"You're getting pretty sentimental in your old age, Dad." Claire moved back and forth around the room, contemplating her father's words. "Stop worrying so much, I've got things covered. You know I'm placing some of the best shooters that we have from the Weapons Into Plowshares program at all points in and around the UN for half a mile in all directions."

"That just covers things around here. What about once you get outside the perimeter?"

"Please, Dad, you taught me everything I know. My house, your house, everywhere you and I can think of, as well as around this building."

Callahan sighed in momentary relief, realizing he may be acting foolishly since after all, New York City wasn't as easy a target as the vast open prairies of Wyoming for an experienced killer.

"Just remember, we still don't know if it's one of our own shooters doing this. We can't be too careful and I know you've vetted everyone thoroughly, but I can't help thinking there is something we're overlooking."

"Overlooking? Really Dad? Overlooking? I don't think the President of the United States has more coverage on his family than you do on yours, not to mention our visiting dignitaries and clients."

"I suppose you're right, but I've seen too many bad things happen in my day and I just wouldn't be myself if I didn't worry about every base being covered."

Callahan, now seemingly satisfied that his daughter's efforts as president of Callahan Security had secured everything without question, finished signing the last form.

Just as he closed the file and was about to hand it back to Claire, he heard a disturbance in the hallway outside his office. Suddenly, Callahan's office door burst open without any warning and a tall, formidable silhouette filled the doorway and stepped inside.

It was Will Pierce, bursting in with Callahan's personal secretary fast behind him.

"I'm sorry Sir, this man just barged in and I couldn't stop him," she said, huffing and puffing as she tried in vain to manhandle Will as he kept walking toward Claire and Callahan.

"It's alright, Norma, this is our hero, Sheriff Will Pierce. And he's always welcome to barge into my office!"

CHAPTER 42

"**W**HO IS THIS?" ALI yelled into the receiver.

He had just purchased a newly updated Smartphone, and although he'd had an earlier version, this one seemed a tad bit more complicated. He pulled the phone away from his ear to check the number to try and figure out who was calling him. *Unknown* is all it read.

Suddenly, the line went dead at the other end and Ali wanted to slam the phone into the ground and smash it into a thousand pieces, but he realized whomever was on the other end was sending him a warning and he couldn't take a chance and ignore what might be a message that would save his life.

Ali's primal survival techniques kicked in. It was fight or flight, and Ali never ran from a fight! He quickly ended the call and took a reading on his position. He was out in the open, standing there like a fool, exposed to every high-rise building and skyscraper the most well-known city in the world had.

Could I be a target? Could it be an ambush? He quickly retraced his footsteps and headed back the way he'd come into the thick overgrowth and brush-lined trail that swerved through this part of the park.

He was on high alert now and placed his right hand into his jacket, gripping his porcelain-handled Glock while simultaneously dialing his troops with the other. He swung his head backwards and forwards, checking the trees and waterways, trail and turf, watching any advancement of joggers, walkers, or the odd athlete out of his playing area. Experience seemed to be telling him he was alone and in no danger. Taking his attention away from his surroundings for just a second, he thumbed the screen of the phone.

"Yeah, this is Ali," he snarled at the voice that answered from the other end of the line. "I don't care about the valet who is not moving fast enough for your taste. Listen to me!" Ali shouted into the phone.

Ali could see the opening to the park where he first came in and headed straight for it. He had already passed endless numbers of ash and ginkgos, witch hazels and elms and had never given them a thought, as study of botany or the love of nature wasn't really his thing. He could see traffic coming to a standstill and immigrant cab drivers screaming at other cab drivers to let them in or for cutting them off, and he began to feel at ease again.

He had just taken his last step next to a large sweet gum, normally seen in the north woods, just before the concrete and bustle outside the park, when he detected the slightest sound.

Fffftttt! He knew it was the sound of a bullet: a bullet with his name on it! Before his muscles could flinch or he could jump or lunge or drop to the ground, he felt the pressure of something against the side of his head and face.

CHAPTER 43

"I WANT SOME ANSWERS!" WILL stormed in with Rusty in tow and marched across the dense wall-to-wall carpet of Callahan's enormous office as though he were a large predator about to capture and kill his prey he had been stalking.

"It's nice to see you again, Sheriff, and you too, Deputy Perkins," Callahan answered in a sarcastic, yet feeble attempt to lighten Will's mood, which looked like he was about to cloud up and rain all over him.

Callahan turned toward Claire and gave her that look she knew all too well from when she was growing up. He wanted her to leave the room so the adults could talk. "Claire, give us a minute, won't you?"

"Certainly, Dad!"

Claire turned to walk out of the office as she passed Will, who was still coming forward. "Good to see you, Sheriff, and thank you again for saving my son. I'll be sending you something special for your efforts one of these days."

Rusty couldn't get over the view of the New York skyline from Callahan's office.

"The pleasure's all mine, Ma'am, and give that boy a big how do ya do for me, won't cha?!"

"I most definitely will, Sheriff."

"… Nice to see you too, Deputy."

"Ma'am!" Rusty said, tipping his hat.

Claire never missed a beat and sauntered out, careful to close the door quietly behind her. She had a sneaking suspicion that things were about to get loud and ugly in there and she had much better things to do with her day than to get into some kind of argument with the brave law enforcement officer that risked his own life to save her only child.

Will turned his head slightly to ensure that Claire was gone and the door was shut behind her before unloading on Callahan.

"Rusty take a seat over there and don't interrupt. This might get a little messy."

"Copy that, Sheriff, Uh, I mean…"

"Never mind." Rusty took a seat closer to the door as Will continued to advance deeper into the office.

"What the hell kind of gun is that you were shooting up on the plateau, and why do you have one like that?"

Callahan had been preparing for this kind of challenge, as he knew someone, somewhere, given the right series of opportunities to inspect his rifle, and especially if that someone knew firearms as well as he did, would be certain to find something amiss. And if that particular, albeit nosy, someone were to look deeper, he or she would began to suspect shenanigans were afoot.

"Okay, there's no reason to keep this a secret, especially from you, Sheriff."

"That was last week, today I'm Special Agent Pierce with the FBI and that's Special Agent Perkins. We've been tasked in to a multi-agency task force in order to catch this lunatic before he kills anybody else, no thanks to you, I suspect."

Somehow that didn't sit well with Callahan as he ran his vulnerability through his head quickly so as not to miss a beat or give the sheriff à la special agent any more reasons to suspect him of wrongdoing.

"Please, have a seat." Callahan bade Will sit in one of his handcrafted leather high-back chairs that were just a tad smaller than his own in order to, much like the North Koreans, intimidate whomever might be sitting across from him. It was childish and manipulative, he knew, but still effective. That is, for nearly any other man, but Will Pierce was not your average man.

Will ignored the chair, marched up to the front of Callahan's desk and slammed his hands down on the finely manicured wood. Callahan could see Rusty flinch in the background.

Callahan, knowing he had some explaining to do, took the beta position, allowing Will the alpha status out of sheer respect or exhaustion from keeping such an old secret that seemed to be transmogrifying into a beast that was now out of control.

Will pulled out a large manila envelope he had been carrying under his jacket and wedged between his belt and shirt above his ass and across his back. He quickly opened the clip and dumped the contents onto Callahan's desk, fanning them out to reveal dozens of slicks.

Microscopic photos had been blown up to 8 x 10s to reveal not only the damage the sniper's bullet caused to the rifle Michael was holding when he got shot, but tiny microchips, motherboards, a video camera, and other electronic circuitry that even Will was uncertain of its function.

"I saw a rifle just like this decades ago, when I was first at the academy studying snipers and other mass murderers. That rifle had all the same weird markings and additions on it too, and, just like this one, the scope was actually a kinda camera. I knew when I first looked at your rifle that it reminded me of something. Well, I finally remembered. Now, I know this one of yours is a heck of a lot more complicated. After all, that one was made back in the 60s when the idea of cellular communications was still just a dream..."

Will thrust his finger downward and hit hard an old photo of a similar-looking rifle. Although it was in black and white, the resolution was incredible and Callahan could see every detail in the picture.

"Do you know whose rifle that was?" Will demanded. "Lee Harvey Oswald's!"

"Yes. I do know that," Callahan said, nodding calmly, meeting Will's eyes.

Realizing the jig was up, Callahan felt no need to keep any more secrets from this man. After all, he'd come this far when no other man had and he knew that this lawman possessed certain skills that the layperson did not. He was actually quite envious at the moment.

Will stood back, rather shocked at Callahan's response. He took a moment to let it all sink in and compose himself as he had had the advantage but was in dire straits to keep it at this point in the conversation.

Snapping out of his momentary hesitation, Will went to bear down again, meaning to redirect his line of questioning.

"Let me stop you there, Sheriff... I mean Special Agent Pierce. Please sit down. If you don't want to sit there, we can move over to the conference table. In fact, that will probably be more convenient anyway."

Standing, Callahan reached to gather up the photos Will had poured onto his desk, but Will's hand stopped him and he shrugged, gesturing to the ebony conference table off to one side of the enormous room.

Tipping his head at Rusty to join them, Will took one of the thick leather chairs lined up along the table. Instead of taking the psychologically stronger seat at the head of the table, Callahan chose to sit across from Will.

Placing his hands on the table, he took a deep breath. "Many years ago, my colleagues and I decided to create a sportsmen's club, a hunting club, if you like. We named it Weapons Into Plowshares to reflect our beliefs in what we'd hoped would be a peaceful future for this world."

"Yeah, I've heard of it. I think someone put me up for membership once upon a time. I turned them down. Not much of a joiner. ... you started WPS?"

"That's too bad; you would have made a wonderful asset to our organization.... Yes, I started it with two other childhood friends of mine as a reaction to the gun violence and fascination we grew up with and witnessed around the world in our youth."

"Well, sorry to break the news to you, Chief, but after that speech and the fact that you started a hunting club where the members use guns and rifles on a regular basis is a bit oxymoronic, wouldn't you say?"

"Yes, I see your point. It wouldn't be the first time, so let me clarify. What we realized as young men, more accurately, as young boys, was that man's obsession with guns isn't a result of the gun itself, but of man's own nature. A nature that drives a man not only to create, but destroy, and a gun, whatever shape or form it comes in, is an easy way to destroy and that is a sexy, seductive feeling to a human."

"Okay, I see your point, no matter how skewed that logic is, but I'm still not following your justification for creating a rifle like that." Will pointed to the photo of Callahan's rifle next to the photo of Lee Harvey Oswald's. Callahan was about to speak when this time it was Will who held up his hand as if to say to Callahan, *don't bother!*

"And I'm sure you've guessed by now that I've figured out the magazine that goes on that rifle can only hold three shells… three *blank* shells!" Will leaned in, his forefinger pressed hard on the table to underline his point. "Any amateur shooter can tell the difference between smokeless powder, cordite, and that cheap Chinese crap they try to pass off as gun powder they use in blank cartridges. Come on, did you really think you could keep that kind of a thing secret for all this time?"

"Yes, I really must hand it to you, Will, if I may call you Will? You really are not earning enough money for your level of talent."

"Ah, praise from Caesar! Let's cut the sweet talk and tell me *exactly* what this gun is for and why you have it, before I turn it over to someone above my pay grade."

"Certainly. I won't insult your intelligence again. The Weapons Into Plowshares Association is one of the greatest outlets for skilled men and women to fulfill their primal needs of hunting prey, killing it, and possessing it, however you want to put it. It is an organization that has dedicated, skilled, and disciplined members who take firearms very seriously and are probably the most responsible people in the world, of course, they are also some of the most heavily armed."

Will sneered and looked down at his watch in boredom. He knew Callahan was giving him the standard recruitment speech and was anxious for him to move on.

"Yes, right," Callahan acknowledged he was taking the long way around to answer. "Our hunters are some of the most accurate shooters on Earth and take great pride in raising the bar in terms of their shooting prowess. Many are ex-military, dead-eye marksmen, weekend warriors, gun enthusiasts that come from all walks of life and from all around the globe merely to compete on the same level with their only known rivals."

"Blah, blah, blah! You know I've already figured this out, so let's get to the good stuff. The stuff I don't know about but will find out whether you're behind bars or not. The stuff that is creating havoc around you and the other families connected to you and your company."

"Yes, we recruit from gun ranges, shooting competitions, events, annual hunting competitions. We only invite those shooters we feel are like-minded and have a drive to not only win, but be the best. The WPS has recruiters throughout the organization and we screen only the top shooters in the world to join..." Callahan gritted his teeth and soldiered on.

"This is starting to sound like a commercial for the NRA. I thought you were going to tell me what's really going on?"

"I am. I have to give you ALL the information, or what I tell you won't make sense." Wiping one hand across his forehead, Callahan went on. "What we are recruiting for within the ranks of the WPS is for another club: a club within the club. Yet, this second club is not on the books and is vastly different from the WPS. We keep it hidden and out of the public eye for very specific reasons and purposes."

"I'm listening, but you've only got about 10 more seconds before I have my deputy slap the cuffs on you—we'll figure out what the charges are later," Will said, mimicking boredom when he was really beginning to get interested.

"These top shooters, highly trained and highly experienced snipers are invited to join our *secret* club, if you will, to compete against each other. We hold a dinner, not unlike our WPS Foundation dinner, but this one is more of an award ceremony. And there's big money at stake."

"Why did I know that money was going to have something to do with this?" Will asked Rusty in a sarcastic aside.

"Once a year, our shooters get a specially made, handmade magazine with three blank shells. I have a gunsmith in Italy that custom designs each and every one of them. Then those shooters have a certain amount of time to carefully choose their targets, track them, look for vulnerabilities in their security, wait for the perfect opportunity, and then take their shot... the one shot that will make them famous. The winner each year is awarded a cash prize worth one million dollars."

"Callahan, if you're somehow trying to tell me that you have created a secret society of snipers, a cadre of killers that you reward with cash and prizes to kill people, then I'm going to put a bullet in you where you stand, because you and I both know if I don't, your stadium full of attorneys will get you off on a technicality and that would leave me to hunt you down... I really don't want to work that hard. I've been trying to retire for years."

Callahan smiled and pushed himself up from the table. Suddenly Will sensed a problem. He whipped out his service revolver faster than you could blink. Callahan did not see that coming and since he wasn't expecting that kind of reaction, this stopped his body from rising another inch from his chair.

He raised one hand carefully and gestured toward his desk. "Top drawer, left side. Press combination buttons, 85677."

Will signaled Rusty to go get whatever it was in the desk drawer. "That better not blow up in my deputy's face," he warned Callahan.

Rusty returned, having said not a word and passed a small-framed photograph to the sheriff before retaking his seat.

"What am I looking at?" Will couldn't see anything special about this particular photo.

"That's a photo of one of our third awards dinners in 1962. Not the WPS dinner, but the second club I've been talking about, the secret shooting club. Look closely, can you make out the winner standing behind the podium?"

Will holstered his gun, his jaw dropping. "Jesus Christ, is that Lee Harvey Oswald?"

"Yes, and what I am about to tell you may be hard to believe, but I assure you on my grandson's life, it is the absolute truth. Lee Harvey Oswald didn't kill President John F. Kennedy!"

Will was stunned by this revelation, but quickly became skeptical as anyone would. "What the hell are you talking…?"

Callahan stopped him in his tracks. "… And I have the photos to prove it!"

Will gave Callahan an indescribable look as he slowly placed the frame down in front of him.

"You see, in our other little club, our members aren't photographers. It's more accurate to think of them as historical biographers! Yes, they do carry rifles, they do have scopes mounted on them, and yes, the clips only carry three shells. Shells loaded with blank cartridges in them, because you see, the object of our club is not to actually kill, it is to take the most difficult shot in the world."

Will tilted his head like a hound who was trying to figure out what a particular sound meant.

"Our shooters have to use their primal instincts to complete their "kill" by getting closer to taking the life of that one special person: be it a queen, prime minister, celebrity, even the president. The climax of their training, their skills, their pursuit, and ultimately their capture is a single shot, a shot that will hurt no one, a shot without actually killing."

Will sat back a little deeper into the high-backed leather chair as he contemplated what he was hearing.

Callahan knew Will now understood what he was saying, although there were still many unanswered questions that he would be pressed for. So he decided to intrigue Will further by tantalizing him with the emotions these shooters feel after completing their mission.

"You would not believe the rush that you get when you know you are about to take the life of someone so important it could literally change the course of history. And for that split second, you have them in your sights, dead to rites. Maybe you chose a shot behind the ear, or in the liver, or even center-mass, it doesn't matter. You've tracked your prey, held your position, drawn down on them and lined up the perfect shot. Then, when all is still and you can hear the sound of your own breathing, your own heart beating, the world stops for that instant. You take a single, shallow breath, then slowly exhale as you draw in your finger… *Bang!*" Callahan smacked his hand down hard on the desk, causing Will and Rusty to nearly jump out of their respective seats. This is not something you do to a man who has suffered from years of PTSD. Will had been listening intently and was following the story in detail, even visualizing it as Callahan spoke, when he was wrenched out of his zone.

"Once you pull that trigger and hear the report of the bullet, nothing else in the world can make you feel that good and that satisfied at the same time."

"This is nuts! Are you kidding me? Even if you get your rocks off shooting blanks at some dignitary from a rooftop, once the sound of that shot reverberates and people hear it, your number's up! No matter how you try and spin it, in this day and age, everyone's going to be coming after you full force, and there are no exceptions to that rule!"

"Precisely! Taking the ultimate shot is only half the challenge; the other half is getting away with it! Oswald is the perfect example of how difficult that part of the process can be, wouldn't you agree?"

Will shook his head trying to contemplate it. "You're telling me that Lee Harvey Oswald only took pictures of Kennedy and didn't actually shoot him?"

"What I'm telling you is far scarier and far more dangerous than that! Oswald wasn't taking pictures of Kennedy. He had tracked him, knew where his motorcade would be that morning in Dallas, had prepared his vantage point weeks in advance, chosen the right perch, the right distance, the perfect angle. But he never shot Kennedy, not even a snapshot. You see, he was all ready to take his shot when something odd caught his eye and he redirected his rifle sights to another part of the grassy knoll that day. He ended up taking pictures of the real men who actually killed President Kennedy!"

Will could only shake his head as he took all this information in. He knew that there was a better than good chance he was telling the truth, and if, in fact, Callahan did have the real photos of the men who killed Kennedy, it could have consequences and reverberations for years to come.

"I know it's a lot to process, but I assure you, I have the original photos; they're safe in a secure location and I've instructed my attorneys to hand-deliver those photos to you in the case of my untimely departure from this world."

"Well that's all nice and dandy, but let's get back to the real issue and that is there is a crazy-assed sniper out there killing people and I have a strong sense that it is one of your country club members that decided he wanted to get that *feeling* of killing to a whole new level!"

"Yes, you're right once again! My colleagues and I have come to the same conclusion. This has to be the work of a disgruntled sniper from our organization."

"Petty as it sounds, you must've seen some poor sports after losing the Photo of the Year contest."

"Yes, but we think it's a little more dire than that. We think it may be this man. No one else has a photo of him. At least that we know of." Callahan rose now with no objection from Will and opened a cabinet door. Another combination let him into a file cabinet and he pulled out a dossier and tossed it on the table in front of Will.

Will opened it quickly to reveal a passport photo of a dashing young man.

"The passport is Sardinian, but we think he is originally from Lithuania."

"Hannibal Lecter was from Lithuania," Will commented, as he buried his nose in the file, trying to take in as much information as possible.

"We think his real name is Vitas Vladimiras. He is a Lithuanian national, but we believe he carries several different identities and passports to allow him access into probably every friendly and unfriendly country on the planet. He hires himself out to the mafia, warlords, drug cartels, you name it, he is now one of the foremost contract killers in the world."

"No one has ever been able to get a picture of this prick, how did you do it?"

"Please, Will, I do own one of the largest privately held security companies, and besides, I knew there was a good chance we'd eventually recruit a shooter who may have ulterior motives, and I wasn't going to let that happen on my watch."

"Ah, too late! I have to get this information to the Bureau right away. I'm supposed to be one of the lead investigators, so don't try and stop me from taking this file."

"I wouldn't dream of it. That is yours to keep, as I'm sure you've already figured out we have copies of all types of things about all types of people."

"Including me, I suppose?" Callahan smiled as Will sprang to his feet. He knew this was just the break he and the Bureau needed to catch their man and he was already running his workaround in his head as to how to trap and catch this psycho-killer.

"Rusty, come on over here. It looks like we're gonna be unofficially tasking in Mr. Callahan into this manhunt, as he seems to have more answers than we do. So you're gonna stay on Mr. Callahan here like a tic on an old hound dog the entire time we're here, understand?"

"Copy that, Sher… Special Agent Pierce. I'll be right beside him the whole time. I won't let him out of my sight for a New York minute!"

Rusty had been looking for just the right time to use that phrase. Will sighed and closed his eyes for a second.

Suddenly, the phone on Callahan's desk began to ring furiously. Callahan liked old technology and kept an old low-tech dial telephone that had a loud and obnoxious ring to remind him of his past.

Callahan quickly answered. "Yes? What?" Callahan held his hand over the receiver and shot Will a fearful glance. "Ali Khumari has been shot!"

"Let's roll!" Will shouted.

As they made their way out of the office, Will had one more question.

"By the way, what ever happened to those two men on the grassy knoll?"

"We were able to track them down, we never told them how, though," Callahan said with a smirk. "We told them their bosses gave them up, which apparently they believed since the last we heard of them was when their boss turned up in the *Obituary column.*"

"It looks like justice was served after all," Will said quietly.

CHAPTER 44

THE PARAMEDICS HAD ALREADY stabilized Ali and brought him to Mount Sinai Hospital on East 98th for surgery by the time his security team arrived.

"Who is this guy?" One of the surgical nurses kept commenting to the other staff members as the enormous phalanx of security guards, undercover police, fire, and personal visitors began filling up two floors of the hospital.

Ali had just been released from surgery and a bevy of nurses, both male and female, wheeled him back into a semi-private room that was about to become permanently private, secured, and locked-down for his protection.

Will, Callahan, and Rusty thought they would be the first to arrive, but when they had to push their way through the crowd of Falcon Securities, they realized they were already late for this party.

Will knew it would take Cordoba at least 90 minutes to get through traffic in order to question Ali, unless he took a helicopter, in which case it could take him less than 15 minutes. That is, he reckoned, if Ali could even talk or hold a thought or was not already dead. Those were all crucial questions floating through his head.

"What do you think the chances are that he's alive, Special Agent?"

Callahan was nearly out of breath when he queried Will for an answer. Rusty, being as young as he was, hadn't even broken a sweat and was beginning to be an annoyance due to the fact that he looked like he actually enjoyed running up and down the streets of Manhattan.

"I don't know. I really don't. Why didn't he kill the boy? Then did kill not only Mrs. Miller, but also the poor man who tried to save her? There just doesn't seem to be any rhyme or reason to this man. The Bureau's mobilizing our task force and then they'll be here pretty soon to try and glean whatever they can from Ali, if he's in any position to talk… or remember for that matter."

Will scooted past a number of large, bearded men in the finest suits he'd ever seen, as Callahan had to fight to keep up with him.

"All these guys in one place is just going to cause problems. I'm going to have to nip this in the bud. Rusty, you follow my lead and don't let anyone intimidate you or keep you from following us into the room."

"Roger that, Special Agent. These Hadjis ain't gonna scare me."

Will could see a number of Ali's men posted outside a dimly lit room at the end of the hall. He also watched as the head nurse on the floor was in the face of one of Ali's security guards trying to get him to move out of the way so she could do her job and either draw blood or give him an injection.

"Move ya big oaf! If I don't get him this painkiller soon, he's gonna wake up in an awful mood."

Ali's lead security guard, and one of his oldest friends, Kassim, was taking his role a tad too seriously when it came to his boss, mentor, and friend.

"I don't know what's in that syringe," Kassim said in a thick Jordanian accent. "For all I know that shot is filled with poison or you're going to inject him with a massive air bubble that will rip through his system until it gets to his heart where it will explode like a roadside bomb."

"You've been watching way too many episodes of *CSI*, now move!" the middle-aged woman snapped. Before the nurse could kick, punch, or intimidate Kassim, a deeper, more powerful voice came from inside the bedroom.

"Kassim, 'innah bikhayr, alssamah laha min khilal, habib, hsna?!" A tall lean man with golden skin and light hair slightly balding appeared in the doorway of the hospital room. Kassim did as his boss instructed and allowed the nurse to enter.

"Fahal tabdu waka'annaha 'iirhabi?"

This made Kassim chuckle as he tried to envision this small, white suburban pampered woman, probably a mother of four children, carrying out an assassination attempt in the midst of one of the greatest security forces on Earth.

The old man placed a kind hand on Kassim's shoulder as he turned to walk back in the room.

It was then Will appeared with Callahan and Rusty in tow through the crowd.

"Nassar, is that you? Oh my good friend, I'm so glad you're here!" Callahan rushed in front of Will before Rusty could stop him to race toward his old friend Nassar. It was then some of the security guards decided to quickly close in their ranks to protect their patriarch.

Nassar, hearing his old friend's voice in the crowd, turned to greet him.

"Callahan, *habibi* how are you my friend?" The two men embraced and Nassar kissed his friend's cheek twice, as was custom in his world. Will stepped up and brought his hands up slightly as though he were going to start spinning around like Wonder Woman. Rusty backed his play with a look of seriousness that Will had never seen on his young protégé, but he liked it.

"Okay, gentlemen, I am Special Agent Will Pierce and this is Special Agent Rusty Perkins, and we are ordering you to stand down! The Federal Bureau of Investigations will be taking over the security of this case from now on, so if you would all kindly disperse in a calm and organized fashion, we can all get back to doing our respective jobs."

Will knew he had to vocalize as loudly as possible as even he didn't know who or how many people on that floor spoke English, so he hoped the forcefulness of his words would be enough to get them to take notice and begin to disperse.

Nothing. Nobody moved. Not out of fear or intimidation, but due to the fact that they were there to protect Ali Khumari. Come hell or high water, they wouldn't be moving anytime soon as far as they were concerned.

"I think y'all heard Special Agent Pierce, y'all need to disperse… now!"

The nurses and other staff members on the ward looked as though they were going to sigh in relief when Will and Rusty spoke up, but soon they realized this was going to be a tougher prospect than they thought.

"Khudh rajalik aleawdat 'iilaa mawaqieiha fi alfunduq w nantazir linasmae min li!" Nassar ordered Kassim in Arabic to take his men back to the hotel and reestablish their positions elsewhere. Kassim bowed to Nassar but was careful never to take his eyes off Will as he knew the only person in that corridor, or perhaps in the entire hospital, maybe even in all of New York City to worry about would be the FBI agent in front of him at that moment.

"Wasawf ytm dhlk, aintaqal mae alllah," Kassim answered.

He acknowledged the order, but gave Will and Rusty a tough look before leaving. It was starting to get tribal in the hallway, Will thought.

"Daena nadhhab alrrijal!" Kassim shouted to his men as he waved his arm in the air like a helicopter propeller to rally them together. Each man fell in line, one after another as Kassim passed each one who had staggered their post every 10 to 12 feet for maximum coverage and exposure.

"Okay, nurse, if you could spread the word that this man will be isolated and only pre-approved necessary personnel will be allowed in his room."

"Yes, Special Agent, I can do that." The head nurse had come out of Ali's room and walked right up to Will as the hallway was beginning to clear of Ali and Nassar's men, but he knew it was only a matter of time before the feds would be darkening the doorway.

"May I ask who he is and what happened to him? And may I ask where the heck you boys got those gorgeous cowboy boots?"

"There's a very bad guy running amok out there and he is now in New York City. This poor bastard was on his hit list, so we gotta find out if he saw anything 'cause this crazy bastard is planning on killing again."

The nurse stood dumbfounded, both at the idea of a crazed lunatic or at least another crazed lunatic on the streets of New York, and also that an FBI Special Agent would actually tell her the truth. She was both honored and humbled at the same time, but had to spread the word.

Rusty gave Will a strange look. Will always broke protocol. He said if you gave people the respect they deserved, they'd work a lot harder and a lot faster than you need them to. It was like taking out an extra insurance policy.

Callahan and Nassar had already gone into Ali's room to see how he was doing. Will entered slowly as he approached his bedside. Nassar had a hold of a strong hand that was connected to Ali, who had various tubes going in and out of him and a bandaged left side of his face.

"'Ana walid bikhayr, w hadha hu kull shay' la lizum laha dhlk!" Ali said.

"In English, my son, we are in America now," Nassar corrected him.

"Come on, Pop, this is unnecessary, I'm okay, it's just a scratch!" Ali reached across his face and began to pull the bandages away to reveal a deep gash in the side of his cheek and a number of smaller cuts and scrapes across the left side of his head and neck.

The dozens of stitches and the combination of yellow-seeping sera and iodine that covered the interior of the bandages made it look more uncomfortable than it really was.

"Dang!" Rusty said, not realizing what he said had come out of his mouth.

"Ali, don't touch that! My son just came out of surgery to remove the wood splinters that shot into his face from the ricocheted bullet."

"Thank God it was Skip Shot!" Callahan said to the other men who nodded in agreement.

"Yes, Ali was very lucky. It looks like the sniper positioned himself at the end of the path my son had taken already twice in and out of the park."

"Poppa, I didn't break protocol, I had to come out the same way because I couldn't get a cell signal so deep inside Central Park, so I had to get to the street."

"… Where he was waiting to blow your head off! *Allah* has blessed you!" Will and Rusty stood next to Callahan and Nassar as they looked at the sniper's latest victim.

"Are we sure it's our shooter?" Will asked.

Callahan shifted back and forth on his heels, a distressed look on his face.

"I'm sorry, old friend, we tried getting through to you and Ali to warn you about this guy… it looks like we were just a little too late."

Nassar put his hand on his old friend's shoulder and smiled, as he looked him in the eyes.

"It is not your fault in the least, *habibi*! Ali knows the risk in the business we are in. Thankfully, he is all alright."

"Yeah, he sure was lucky. Luckier than the others from what we can see."

Callahan realized he had not yet formally introduced Will or Rusty to Nassar and that was something that their generation was very strict about.

"Nassar Khumari, this is Sheriff, I mean Special Agent Will Pierce and Special Agent Perkins with the FBI. They have been following this case closely since that bastard tried to kill my grandson."

"Special agents." Nassar bowed slightly and reached out to shake Will's hand as Will reciprocated. He then turned to Rusty.

"Special Agent."

"As-Salaam-Alaikum!" Rusty answered. Rusty bowed slightly, placing his right hand over his heart.

Will, Callahan, Nassar, and even Ali were taken aback, surprised that this young man was worldly or savvy enough to greet a Muslim in his own language with the words, *Peace be unto you*.

"Wa-Alaikum-Salaam," Nassar responded in kind, also pleasantly surprised.

Will knew he had to get down to business and not lose sight of their objective.

"Mr. Khumari, it's a pleasure. I'm just sorry to be meeting you under these circumstances."

"Thank you for the kind words, Special Agent Pierce. I should let you get back to your important duties to find this maniacal killer as soon as possible before he has the opportunity to kill anyone else."

"Yes, Nassar, take care of Ali and I'll be back as soon as possible. I just have a few more things to wrap up with Special Agent Pierce first," Callahan said.

"Please, gentlemen, do not worry for my son. Ali will be released tomorrow morning. Although, sadly, he will just miss our client, the King's arrival to these beautiful shores. My son was very lucky, after all, it is only a flesh wound, alhamd lillah!"

As Will led Callahan and Rusty out of the hospital room, he looked to his right and suddenly heard a loud commotion at the other end of the hallway. It was Cordoba leading a large group of federal agents to lock down the facility and protect the latest victim.

He hadn't yet caught sight of Will or the others, and that's just how Will liked it. Will grabbed Callahan's shoulder by the shirt as all three men headed toward the other end of the hall that had been darkened due to budget cuts as the hospital would shut off every other light to save money.

"Come on, there's a service elevator."

"Where are we going?" Callahan had no choice but to question Will's logic as they raced to make the elevator.

"I'll explain it when we get there!"

Cordoba popped up at the nurse's station just as Will and Callahan entered the large service elevator dedicated to carrying multiple gurneys and larger pieces of medical and X-ray equipment.

As Cordoba pointed to set up his men throughout the hallway, Nassar stepped out of his son's room to greet the other federal agents who were obviously taking over security for not only his son, but seemingly the entire hospital.

In the midst of the crowd, a beautiful redheaded woman came walking up through the dense mass of men and guns, holding the hand of a young boy. It was Claire Callahan and her son Michael.

She seemed to easily slip past the other agents setting up to take their positions nearly completely ignoring her as one of the nurses was just coming out of Ali's room as Claire and Michael were going in.

"I'm sorry Ma'am, this man is under tight security, unless you're family you can't go in."

Claire softened her usually sharp and professional eyes and the nurse knew she couldn't stop her.

"It's okay," Claire answered. She pushed the door open and led Michael to Ali's bedside.

Ali, who was still drifting slightly from the anesthesia, tossed and turned in his hospital bed. It didn't have anything to do with the pain he was in, but because he couldn't get comfortable between the sheets that had no more thread count than a camel's blanket.

Claire winced when she saw Ali, perhaps due to how bad his injury appeared to be or maybe for another reason. Then the tears began to flow.

"Claire, it that you? Oh Claire, I have missed you so. Am I dreaming?" Ali tried to focus on Claire when Michael came into view.

"Ali, meet your son, Michael."

CHAPTER 45

KING ABDULLAH AND HIS entourage took up more room than the Sultan of Brunei when they came to town.

They had already flown into JFK Airport in their own Jordanian-designed, American-made 757s, and with the police escort, the line of vehicles numbered well into the thirties before they arrived at their destination in Middle Upper Manhattan.

Falcon Securities' Away Team, led by Ali, had already secured the hotel, had eyelines on the rooftops for miles, and was fully prepared to do their job with or without their fearless leader.

Kassim now took point and was in the lead bulletproofed car that had picked up King Abdullah and his advisors from JFK after their flight had landed.

The Falcon Securities detail was present in each vehicle and all the personnel where outfitted with state-of-the-art body armor, as well as the latest assault rifles, snub-nosed firearms, mini assault machine guns and pistols, any counter-insurgent weapon one could think of was at the ready of each man.

Kassim was being especially cautious, as his friend and mentor Ali was planning to be when his king arrived on American soil to give a speech at the United Nations.

Kassim, like Ali, and every other Jordanian and perhaps even Middle Easterner, adored King Abdullah. He was tough but fair, generous and kind and was the type of moderate Muslim that not only Jordan, but the world needed as well.

When the NYPD motorcycle units pulled up in front of the lavish hotel, Kassim had his driver pull behind them and wait for the officers to give the all clear signal. Then he and his men would open their vehicle doors, do another check, note and observe their surroundings for anyone dumb enough to get too close to the king or the royal family, and then bid his royal highness out of the car, not before.

Kassim took point and jumped out before the vehicle had come to a stop. He looked up, especially as he couldn't imagine having a maniac sniper taking a shot of his king like he had done to Ali.

After a moment, Kassim realized the coast was clear and cleared King Abdullah to step out. Four other security officers that were clearly a head taller than the king boxed him in and began the march into the hotel. The king couldn't have been safer as no one could even see him in the mass of muscle and Oakley wrap-around sunglasses that preceded him.

Kassim breathed a sigh of relief as his men led the rest of the royal family inside and secured them in their rooms.

CHAPTER 46

GAIUS LIKED TO TREAT himself well, very well, all the time. He felt he deserved every bit of luxury the world could offer since he provided a service to those who had the ability to pay top dollar.

He especially liked to treat himself just before a big hit, and today was no different. He pulled the thin drapes back from the window of his 42nd story corporate apartment with the perfect view of the Manhattan skyline.

Gaius' rifle was disassembled on the floor of the suite as he had taken it apart to oil, rub, and prepare his working tool for one of his finest pieces of work, at least he thought it would be.

Each piece of the gun, from the spring loads, to the slide, to the barrel, even the scope, was carefully, almost obsessively, inspected, cleaned, and then placed next to its neighbor prior to re-assemblage.

A full tray was strewn on the kitchen counter as Gaius had ordered a full breakfast, complete with the most expensive items on the Concierge Level dining list. He had the tray brought to his room, instructed the waiter to leave it in front of the door, knock three times, stop, then knock another three times.

His instructions then were for the waiter to leave and he would retrieve his meal when no one was in the hall.

Gaius, as worldly and impressed with himself as he was, never, ever wanted anyone to see him during business hours or when he was travelling for a job. It was simply too dangerous. Any ridiculous bystander or snooping doorman could open his mouth and draw unwanted attention to him.

Gaius didn't like attention, at least not the type that could get him thrown into prison, or worse. He finished the last of his Chai coffee and set the porcelain cup on the coffee table. He carefully sprayed the rim of the cup with an alcohol-based clear mist, then took an absorbent paper towel to remove any traces of his saliva or DNA.

He had already scrubbed the bathroom, the shower, the kitchen, and everywhere he had touched or could have left his genetic marks. He had stripped the linen off the bed and sent it down the laundry chute to ensure no one would be able to link his sheets with anyone else's, that is after he gave them a good soaking of liquid bleach in the bathtub as well as his hand towels, bathing, and swimming towels.

For fun, Gaius would challenge himself to see if he could beat his time of reassembling his rifle. He'd always been well under a minute, but today he was especially impressed with himself, as he had gotten his time below 20 seconds.

He reached into his thick canvas bag to extract the last piece of his puzzle. It was the three-cartridge magazine that he had custom-made from the Italian gunsmith, who, he had found out, hand made all three-cartridge clips for Callahan and the WPS shooters.

Gaius chuckled to himself at the irony, as he had planned on leaving this one piece at the scene of his next crime. He was vigilant about *never* leaving anything behind, but this time he was instructed to do so by his employer, for what particular reason, he wasn't yet sure.

Gaius looked at his watch and realized he was cutting it pretty close, so he packed up his rifle in a long black tube that was similar to what artists used to transport their works and stood to look around his temporary digs.

He thought for a moment if it would be more economical to just set a fire in the kitchen and burn the place down in order to be absolutely sure his DNA wouldn't be traced. But then he thought this might be an important place his employers would bring their mistresses or whomever, so he decided he'd just leave well enough alone.

He took a handkerchief out of his vest pocket and opened the door to the hallway. He was careful to check and see if anyone else was curious or perhaps walking back to their own apartment. Nope. He was alone.

He closed the door quietly and quickly wiped down the outside. He pulled his tweed cap over the top of his face and looked down as he headed for the elevators that would take him to street level.

As the elevator doors opened, Gaius opened a copy of the *Wall Street Journal* as he headed past the attendant at the Concierge desk.

"Have a good day, Sir," the concierge said.

Gaius just kept walking without acknowledging the man and entered the busy streets of New York. After a moment, he was lost in the crowd.

CHAPTER 47

"I HAVE A BAD FEELING whatever's going to happen is going to happen today."

Will had sort of a second sight for crime and he was hardly ever wrong. It was almost like what women claim to have in terms of intuition, but in Will's case, it was decades of good detective work on investigations that would go down in history as some of the most important.

"How can you be sure?" Callahan asked.

"Oh the Sheriff, uh, you know what I mean, once he gets a notion in his head, he can track it til the cows come home. He always gets his man!" Rusty was prouder than ever of his mentor and didn't care who knew it.

Callahan struggled to keep up with Will and Rusty as they headed down First Avenue.

"Why are you in such a hurry?" Callahan continued.

"Something doesn't add up! Okay, he shoots your grandson to make it look like an accident, but thankfully, Michael doesn't die in the fall off the plateau."

"Okay."

"Next he kills Miller's wife and an innocent combat veteran who was merely trying to protect her. But that vet was also an employee of Miller's at Miller Strategic Management, so that could be a link as well."

"Yeah, I'm with you."

"Then finally, he has a clear shot at Ali Khumari, and remember, this guy's one of the best snipers in the world, but somehow misses and hits the tree next to him and Ali ends up with a few stitches and a new appreciation for wood bark in trees."

"Now that you put it that way, it does seem a bit out of character for him to miss."

"So this shooter tracks you all the way to the middle of isolated Wyoming. He takes his shot there, then makes a side trip to Colorado to shoot Stephanie Miller and our veteran, who, by the way, should be getting a medal for his heroic actions, then exposes himself for the very first time in his illustrious career by coming to one of the biggest, most modern cities with the top security in the world?"

"Hum, it does sound a bit fishy. What is your gut telling you?"

"It's telling me that New York City was always his final destination and the other shootings were just decoys to keep us chasing our tails. Whatever he's going to do, he's going to do here. And if I'm right, he's going to do it sometime today."

Just then, Will, Callahan, and Rusty approached the corner at East 42nd Street and 1st Avenue, but were stopped by an NYPD officer in a blue uniform.

"Sorry, gentlemen, you'll have to go around, we got a secure motorcade coming through in a moment," the officer said.

"It's okay, we're on the job," Will said, pulling out his dark leather bifold and flashing it at the officer. Rusty followed Will's lead and duplicated his actions. The officer nodded and seemed momentarily impressed by Will and Rusty's credentials.

"Yes, Sir, Special Agent, come on through, you boys have the E-ticket."

"This man is with me too, officer," Will dragged Callahan along past the barricade.

"Yeah, yeah, go ahead." Will, Callahan, and Rusty crossed the street and could see the motorcade in the distance and flags waving on the dignitaries' lead vehicle. Will turned his head toward the officer who had let them through, but was keeping the other nosy bystanders from entering the area. He suddenly had a strange look on his face.

"Officer, what's going on here? It seems like a lot of activity, even for this part of New York City."

"Ah, just another big to-do at the United Nations Headquarters. I think the King of Jordan is speaking today in front of the General Assembly. Something about tightening the reins on terrorism in the Middle East, you know, and the need for more security in the region and some such."

Will nodded in thanks as he and the other two men kept going across the boulevard. Suddenly, Will stopped dead in his tracks.

"What do you think the outcome would be if the King of Jordan were to be assassinated on American soil?" Will asked aloud.

"The damage in the region would be devastating!" Callahan said, as Rusty took particular interest in his explanation.

"King Abdullah is a moderate Muslim and one of our allies, so if someone were to take him out and assassinate him, the other factions in the area would fight endlessly for control of little Jordan, who, by the way, has been keeping its country free of radicals in the midst of crazies like ISIS and Al Qaeda."

"Not to mention the Russian invasion," Rusty added. "Putin would seize the opportunity if there was a power vacuum like he's doing in Syria and take advantage of the situation by sending troops in while really his plan would be to control the western ports for more of his oil reserves to flow through, and of course, there's the whole Israel issue as well."

This seemingly innocent country bumpkin who kept surprising them with profound wisdom and insight once again dumbfounded Will and Callahan.

Will hesitated for a split instant as Rusty and Callahan watched him process this latest piece of the puzzle. "That's it! He's gonna try and hit King Abdullah sometime today before his speech at the U.N."

Will ran back across the street as both Rusty and Callahan could see him making broad gestures with his hands and pointing toward the United Nations Headquarters building merely a few blocks ahead.

The officer quickly grabbed his radio that was Velcroed to the epaulet on his shoulder and began yelling into it and pointing to Will as he called in backup and running it up the chain of command.

Callahan watched as Will hoofed it back across the busy Manhattan street toward him. Rusty's adrenaline began to kick into high gear. If he could, he would've shouted *hot damn*! But he knew that wasn't professional.

"Come on, there's no time to lose! We've gotta figure out where this psycho's nest is."

"Shouldn't we split up?" Rusty asked.

"Absolutely not! Callahan, you're not armed and even if you were, you'd get in serious trouble, because now the NYPD, the feds, and all the security teams are being notified. And Rusty, you're barely a Special Agent, so we're all sticking together until we find this killer."

"Roger that, Boss!"

"Right, give me a second." Callahan reached deep into his pocket and pulled out his Smartphone. "Yeah, this is Callahan, this is a Code Red! There's going to be an assassination attempt today on the King of Jordan. Coordinate with Miller Strategic and Falcon Securities and find this guy before it's too late!"

Callahan finished his call as he, Rusty, and Will began to race toward the U.N. building. Will stopped Callahan from going any further. "There's no use going into the United Nations. We've got to figure out where the best place for someone to take the perfect shot at a king is."

Will and Callahan looked up and began to scan the New York skyline for possibilities as Rusty followed suit.

"He won't be on a roof this time; he'll take his shot from a window somewhere… but where?"

CHAPTER 48

GAIUS HAD PICKED HIS venue far in advance of this day. He had checked and rechecked every conceivable angle from street level, above and across the Manhattan skyline, and from other buildings even taller than the one he finally chose.

He checked the timeline between 911 emergency calls and the police response time with a stopwatch, and he had triple-checked his escape route. Gaius never left anything to chance.

He would draw down on average New Yorkers going about their day as they headed to work, those who would run to catch the subway train for their daily commute, tourists—he wasn't overly picky. He'd set his sights, dialed in on the top of the scope. He'd range his targets, moving or stable, and decide what would be the best kill shot: head, neck, gut, center mass; Gaius liked to toy with his prey.

He had decided to take a large trifold flyer from outside the United Methodists' bookstore to cover his face as he always did and headed toward the restrooms like all the other visitors to the Church Center of the United Nations that just happened to be within eyeshot of the United Nations Headquarters and International Organization buildings.

Gaius thought it somehow ironic that he was about to put a bullet, as well as a very large hole, into the skull of a devout Muslim, as he liked to call the bell tower in a Christian church. Let's see how that plays out on Al Jazeera, he thought.

Gaius made his way toward the back area where the service elevators were, reached into his trousers and produced a keycard from his left pocket. He waved it quickly in front of the keypad. *Bling.* Gaius smiled as the light on the keypad turned from red to green and activated the elevator that shuttled men and machines to and from the upper floors.

Once the elevator stopped and opened, he cautiously entered. Once again he was careful to keep his head down so as not to show his face to the camera in the upper-right corner of the elevator and swiped the card once again.

The elevator rose quickly and smoothly and eventually stopped at the 12th floor. When the doors opened, Gaius quickly exited. He looked right to see a sign that directed maintenance crews toward the rooftop access, but decided to go left toward a suite of offices under remodel.

He passed under some scaffolding, as he didn't believe in superstition and had to reach out with his arms to separate a thick plastic liner that was draped over the covering of the entrance to a long office. When he cleared all the debris, he entered the office and smiled; it had windows from floor to ceiling.

"Ah, still perfect!" he said.

He walked to the edge of one of the windows and pulled out a pair of surgical gloves and quickly snapped them on over his hands and wrists. He then carefully knelt down, taking care not to leave an imprint anywhere, then pushed the bottom half of the window open as it was secured with a strong metal hinge to ensure it never gaped farther than a few inches.

Gaius flung the black tube up and over his back and quickly opened it. He slid out three pieces of the rifle first: the barrel, the stock, and the muzzle-suppressing silencer.

He pulled a second rifle, this one longer and leaner with less wood and appointments and also with a silencer. It looked homemade. A long spring and what looked like a round caster mount followed. Then a tightly rounded roll of monofilament wire, then finally a long chain of bullets connected one after another. This was a machine gun.

Gaius quickly set out to assemble his sniper gun. He took off his jacket and laid it down on the bare concrete before carefully extracting then mounting the scope to the top of the rifle.

He would keep both eyes open, at first, and peered through the scope to range the distance and calculate wind direction with his digital readout. He, like most contract-killing snipers, didn't have a spotter or partner to range his quarry. Those types of luxuries were strictly kept within the military.

He quietly began humming low as if he had just come to work and it was just another day at the office.

He took his time to set up for his prey, prey that would be entering his kill box. Technically, it wasn't an integrated three-dimensional target area with coordinated joint weapons firing and air coverage, but Gaius did like his movies and he liked to think himself smarter than anyone else... well, really, everyone else.

Gaius drew down again and peered through his scope to find a suitable first target. He followed a young mother as she pushed a pram across Ralph Bunche Park on their way to Robert Moses playground. He lined up an older couple holding hands as they walked their granddaughter, lifting her up, letting her down, then lifting her up again as she laughed.

Then Gaius decided to train his attention on the long line of limousines dropping off dignitaries at the United Nations Headquarters where his prey was due very soon.

He'd given himself more than enough time. He'd allotted for the miserable New York traffic, and he'd found walking better than taking a cab or Uber in Manhattan.

He focused on the Nigerian Ambassador and his entourage that had just arrived from their consulate on 2nd Avenue and East 44th. They had come from their Consulate General, nearly passing under Gaius as they made their way to the U.N. for their daily schedules and briefings. This day was exciting for many foreign dignitaries, who were looking forward to what King Abdullah had to say.

He zeroed in on the Nigerian Ambassador's head, then dropped his view to the brightly colored *dashiki* and moved the scope to follow the other men and women in traditional tunics and dresses.

"Very colorful," he said patronizingly. Gaius made a few turns on the top of his scope, then rolled his right hand over the front to turn it one click, then two clicks before settling on the correct range for the distance.

He laughed as he remembered movies of the shooter wetting his finger to judge the wind. The wind up here was going to be the same as the wind at street level. Modern technology gave him a lot of advantages as he input the latest readings from his Smartphone into the scope on his rifle.

After sighting in his rifle and preparing for every eventuality, Gaius retrieved the three-bullet magazine from the tube.

"Grazie, Signore Tanti. You do exquisite work!" Gaius took a moment to admire the craftsmanship of the old Italian gunsmith, one of the few people on Earth who he would allow to see his face and live to tell about it.

Gaius would think it rude to kill a man who was so gifted at his craft, even if he did still make the specialized magazines for the WPS hunting clubs.

"Oh well, there's certainly no accounting for taste."

Gaius loaded three shells into the clip, but before inserting it into the rifle, he decided to give it a quick tap tap on the ground to ensure the projectiles were packed in tightly.

"Alright, let the games begin," he said as he began to laugh hysterically.

CHAPTER 49

ROBERT MILLER'S SECURITY DETAIL team leader skidded the large black SUV to a stop right before the staging area where Will, Rusty, Callahan, Cordoba, and dozens of federal agents had collected. Suddenly, the car doors opened and large bodyguards jumped out and surrounded the others. Miller stepped through the wall of linebackers.

"I've got everyone posted and on high alert. We'll find this son of a bitch!" Miller yelled, approaching the two men.

"Do you remember what this guy looks like?" Callahan spoke with urgency when he pressed Miller to reflect.

"No need!" Miller produced a stack of BOLOs and held them up so his men, the feds, and everyone else could see the photos. It was a "Be On The Lookout" color flyer with a single grainy photo of the man who called himself Gaius.

"I had a dozen people back in Colorado pulling security footage and dossiers from 10 years ago just to build a full composite of this guy. He always seemed to keep his head down around the cameras, even in our facilities, but he didn't know we had them in the bathrooms as well!"

"The bathrooms, isn't that illegal? I mean, yeah, I can see public areas, but…" Rusty was having trouble wrapping his mind around the concept of cameras in any bathroom when Will interrupted him quickly.

"Let's let Mr. Miller finish his brief, shall we, Special Agent Perkins?" Miller handed Will a small stack of flyers, as there were plenty to be distributed before it was too late.

"I'm sorry about your wife, Sir," Will said in a moment of compassion.

"She was the best thing that's ever happened to an old jarhead like me. And I hope to hell I'm the one that finds him first, cause I'm gonna make sure he remembers Stephanie Miller's name for the few seconds he has left on this Earth!"

Cordoba was about to interject and set Miller straight by reciting state and federal laws about killing another human being in New York City, when Will stopped him.

"We understand your pain and frustration, and I think we feel the same way about finding this guy and doing our jobs as well."

Will knew it was futile to argue with anyone who had been touched by Gaius' black hand of death, so he lifted his hand to stop Cordoba before he sounded like a fool yet again and pissed off the wrong victim.

Cordoba realized this, perhaps a moment too late, but realized it nonetheless. Will once again had been right, so he governed his tongue.

"All right, gentlemen, you have your grids and assignments and you know your target. Here's his photo with all the details: height, weight, eye color, hair color, etc., but as we know, this guy is a chameleon and probably won't look anything like his photo. You will, however, build alternative views in your head. Let's get this perpetrator before he kills again and really causes some international problems."

Cordoba looked around at the hundreds of men from more agencies than he could count as he whirled his hand in the air to start them off.

"As you know, we believe King Abdullah of Jordan is the target and his motorcade is set to arrive in less than 15 minutes, so you better be bringing your A game on this mission, ladies and gentlemen!"

"Now let's move out! Haul ass!" Before everyone started to move, Callahan yelled something loudly that could've got him instantly thrown into federal prison.

"First man to bag this shooter gets a $500,000 bonus from Callahan

Security. You all know he tried to kill my 10-year-old grandson. Think about your own children and what kind of college they'd be able to go to!"

The NYPD officers, feds, and U.S Marshalls stopped in their tracks at the mention of money for bagging the suspect. "Callahan, you can't put a bounty on this man! I should throw you in a hole for yelling something like that to my men and starting a riot."

"Make it a cool one million!" Robert Miller shouted above the din of the other man talking. "Miller Strategic will come through with the other half—a million dollars in memory of my wife! Which one of you wants this bastard taken down as bad as I do?"

Cordoba began to pull his hair out while the men scattered to their assigned positions.

"What in the hell is going on here? Are your men f---ing crazy?" Will quickly grabbed Callahan and Rusty and pulled them into the crowd of law enforcement officers and federal agents scrambling to get to their grids.

"Perhaps we will get lucky today and something might help us in our mission to bag this bad guy, Special Agent."

Will gave Callahan a weird look of curiosity as he suspected Callahan was hiding something from him.

"Firstly, you've earned the right to call me Will. Secondly, what do you mean, 'we might get lucky today'? Are you holding out on us, Callahan?" Callahan had a smirk on his face, but didn't answer, instead he decided to keep his cards close to his vest.

"I'm just saying, today could be the day we all get lucky and end this nut job's reign of terror."

Will looked at him strangely, but shook off any divergent thoughts as they only had minutes.

"Where do we start?"

Just then the men heard the chimes from the bells above their heads as Will, Callahan, and Rusty looked up and across to see they were right in front of the Church Center of the United Nations.

"What is the one thing that would unite terrorist groups like ISIS, Al Qaeda, or Boko Haram, even if they hate each other?"

"I don't know, a common enemy maybe?" Callahan responded.

"Of course, and America is always going to be their common enemy,"

Rusty interjected with surprising confidence in his knowledge of world politics.

"Well, that goes without saying."

"But what if the leader of a major Middle Eastern country and a devout Muslim were killed in America… from inside a Christian church?"

"Holy cow! Muslims in every nation would rally together. Heck, even other non-Christian radical factions would use that as an excuse and claim *Jihad*!"

"Absolutely! Come on, I think I know where he's gonna try and shoot King Abdullah from."

"Where, Boss?" Rusty asked, almost bursting with excitement watching his mentor work.

Will looked up and pointed to the top of the Church Center for the United Nations. The other men followed Will's finger as it rose with the size of the building.

"I hope my heart can take all this cardio! You know I'm not as young as I used to be," Callahan sighed.

"Look, that's the least of your worries if we find him! I think having a heart attack is low on the list compared to a bullet. Come on guys, we've only got a few minutes, so you better start praying your old ticker can keep up!"

With that, Will, Callahan, and Rusty turned and raced up the stairs into the Church Center.

CHAPTER 50

GAIUS TURNED HIS RIFLE barrel toward 1st Avenue and into the tunnel. He knew the king's motorcade would have to emerge from the long tunnel and enter the circular drive before his armed guards would open the door and let him exit in front of the United Nations Headquarters.

He kept a close eye as limousine after armored vehicle passed through the tunnel and entered the area where dignitaries were brought.

Suddenly he caught a glimpse of a large motorcade with Jordanian flags mounted atop the hoods of each vehicle. He made a calculated guess that King Abdullah would be in the third vehicle, so he set his target and followed the entourage until it entered the large circular drive.

As the vehicles slowed, one after another and pulled up into position, dozens of men jumped out and headed toward the third vehicle in a line of seven. Shooting fish in a barrel, Gaius snickered.

As the men flanked the car, a short, well-dressed man with perfectly coifed hair emerged. Gaius closed his left eye and stroked the trigger lightly as he readied himself for the singular shot.

"Drop it, Gaius!" Will shouted at the top of his lungs, even shocking

Callahan who was now huffing and puffing from more exercise than he'd seen since he was a young man.

Will had his .357 Magnum long barrel out and ready to discharge at a moment's notice.

"Can't you see I'm working!" Gaius laughed, allowing himself a short glimpse of the invaders.

Lunging forward, Will felt the tip of his boot catch on something and desperately tried to throw himself to the side, calling out to the others in a futile attempt to warn them.

RATTA-TAT-TAT! Gaius' machine gun lit up and began firing, strafing the men as it cut a swath across the doorway. Gaius had set the ultimate death trap for anyone deciding to try and stop him.

Will caught three or four rounds center mass in his chest and was knocked hard backwards. Rusty, who had followed behind him, keeping Callahan at his 6 o'clock, took the next few rounds. Rusty had just enough time to react and push Callahan backwards into the hallway.

Will momentarily lost consciousness and realized he was now on the ground. He turned back to see Rusty laid out on the ground, bleeding, but had no idea how badly hurt he was. This enraged Will. Rusty was like a son to him.

Will looked over in the corner of the room to see a custom-made machine gun, almost like a British Sten, but with an automatic chain feeding it bullets. It was mounted atop a caster made of ball bearings and a spring at the end that would force the gun in the opposite direction after strafing 180 degrees, then bouncing back to fire an arc of bullets back and forth in a rainbow pattern.

He saw the trigger of the machine gun was tied with a long length of monofilament wire that was taut and led from the trigger down the mount through an eyehole screw, across the room and ran the length of the floor at about one foot off the ground. No one, not even an experienced Special Forces soldier, could've seen that trap coming.

Will knew he had to stop this man, no matter how badly he was hurt. He mumbled to himself something motivational and put his hands on the ground to push upwards.

He looked down and saw his leg and arm were badly bleeding, but his boots were intact. Somehow that made him smile inside, but his adrenaline was pumping so hard, it masked the pain and injury and gave Will the precious few seconds he needed to stop Gaius... or at least try.

"How rude! You don't see me coming to your place of business and bothering you while you're working. So please be a dear and try and die quietly—you must realize I have to concentrate!" Gaius shouted at Will without flinching or moving a muscle from his sniper's position. He continued to steady himself and then Will saw his chest heave as he drew a long breath into his lungs.

Will knew what this meant. Gaius' next move was to inhale, then exhale slowly as he pulled the trigger on his target. Will knew he couldn't move easily, but he had to move fast.

BAM! Will fired a single round into Gaius' leg from his position on the ground. The force of the blast hit him so hard it actually shifted Gaius' whole body two feet over.

Gaius screamed, all humor lost. This moron had actually shot him! Gaius quickly tried to scoot back into position, but his leg wouldn't move and kept him from centering his body. Gaius didn't waste any time. He lined up his shot as best as he could, knowing he'd probably only get one.

"Too late!" Gaius shouted back at the other men. He tried once more to regain his position and resight his target, but pulled the trigger too quickly before he could get a clear shot. He peered through the eyepiece of the scope and saw the king in his sights.

As Gaius did this, Will began to scramble fast. He dragged his legs with his upper body strength as best as he could to try and get into a better position.

Suddenly Callahan appeared out of nowhere. Somehow he had crawled back into the room, dropping low enough to avoid the automatic fire of the machine gun. He had to crawl around Rusty's body; he had no time to check on his well being, even though the young man had saved his life.

Gaius' trap was still firing, but by now was nearly out of rounds to shoot. Callahan knew he had barely a split second to react and try to help Will.

He grabbed Will and helped him to his feet. By wrapping his arm around his shoulder, he pulled Will up and over so he could get a better shot at Gaius from a different vantage point and perhaps finally end him.

BAM! Will had managed to maneuver around to Gaius' right side with the help of Callahan and shot another round at him, this time into Gaius' hand, in the hopes that it would stop him from firing again, but unfortunately, Will was too late. Will had taken his shot, but not before Gaius pulled the trigger.

BOOM! The unexpected explosion in such a small space stunned the men into staggering for their balance.

Will almost looked at his gun in wonder. Did he hit the magazine and explode the ordinance? Will wondered. Did someone else take a shot from outside with an exploding tipped round? For a quick second, Will had all sorts of thoughts running through his head.

"What happened?!" Will demanded. Callahan continued his hold on Will, though who was supporting whom could be called into question at this point.

"His gun exploded when he pulled the trigger the second time," Callahan put into words what he and Will had both seen.

The instant Gaius fired, and even before Will could shoot at his trigger hand, the gun suddenly, and without warning, blew up. When it exploded in Gaius' hands, it sent shrapnel deep into Gaius' face and head, blowing his appendages to Kingdom Come.

Will used what strength he had and dove toward Gaius. He saw the walkie-talkie on the ground and slid it to Callahan as he crawled over to secure Gaius, or at least what was left of him. As much as he hated the idea, he knew he'd have to render aid, if that was even possible.

Will pushed the burning hulk of metal and wood that used to be his sniper rifle away from Gaius as rivers of blood began to pour out of him. It was obvious that something on the rifle, or perhaps in it, had exploded and the force from the blowback sent the entire explosion and the ammunition into Gaius.

As Will looked closer for a way to help Gaius, he could see the detonation had originated from where the magazine would have been. Could the bullets have exploded from his shot? He thought again. No, he shot a split second after the explosion. What on Earth could've caused it to blow up like that?

Will saw that both Gaius' hands and his arms at the elbow were practically blown off and his entire face was barely recognizable. The only thing Will could make out in the bloody mess was a gaping hole sucking a mixture of blood and air in and out in a last-ditch effort to live another instant or two. Will saw one of Gaius' eyes was still intact as he watched Will's valiant effort to save him.

"Who hired you to kill King Abdullah?"

A deep gulping came as Gaius respired and tried to gasp in more air than fluid, but it was an exercise in futility. Will was unclear if he would be able to speak, but knew one thing—this man was dying quickly and there was nothing he could, or perhaps would, be able to do.

Gaius struggled to inhale enough air to try and exhale to form words. He coughed and spat the blood out faster than he could breathe.

"Who else would gain from the destabilization of the Middle East?" he wheezed.

Will looked at Gaius oddly as though receiving a clue to a mystery. "What does that mean? Do something good at the end of your life. We both know you're not going to make it, so just tell me who hired you to kill the king and the others, like Callahan's grandson."

Gaius struggled to turn his head slightly with all the strength he had left to see Callahan standing above him with hateful pity in his eyes. The words were slurred and misshaped, but Will could understand him well enough. "It was nothing personal, you know, only business. Your grandson looks like a fine boy!"

Callahan raised his foot as if to stomp Gaius' head like a melon, when Will stopped him.

"Why, damn you? Why would you try and kill my grandson, Miller's wife, and all those other innocent people? Who the hell put you up to this, you bastard?"

Gaius began to laugh, or what they thought was laughing, but was really a mixture of coughing, gagging, and huffing.

"You don't even realize you have a Judas among you, do you?" Gaius coughed once more, but this time a puncture in his carotid artery that wasn't apparent until he turned his head burst forth and arterial spray shot to the ceiling with every beat of his heart.

Will and Callahan had to jump back quickly in order to avoid being drowned by another man's blood. And then the killer was gone.

Will stepped back, barely holding his balance, before taking a breath and pulling at Callahan. "Come on, we have to help Rusty!"

Will and Callahan rushed over to Rusty. The silence was incredible as between the stuttered shots from the machine gun and the exploding rifle, their ears felt like they had been stuffed with cotton wool.

As Will checked Rusty's vitals and looked to plug any holes, Callahan looked at Will strangely.

"What do you think he meant by a Judas?"

CHAPTER 51

CORDOBA SAT ON THE edge of Will's hospital bed that was in the same trauma unit on the same floor and merely a few doors down from where Ali Khumari was recuperating.

"Do you just live to show me up, Pierce?"

"I'd happily let you take my place right now and all the credit too."

"I bet you would. Okay, I'm off to do the paperwork and bury as much of this story as we can before the conspiracy theorists blow up the Internet."

"Well, ya know what they say, 'it's not paranoia if they really are after you!'"

"Okay, Mr. Sunshine, I think those painkillers are finally kicking in. I'll come by tomorrow and check on you and Rusty over there. You know, it's against my better judgment, but I have to put you up for the FBI medal for Meritorious Achievement as well as the medal for Bravery and Valor, don't you?"

"Give it to the kid, he deserves it, not me!"

"Well, at least we agree on something. Just be glad it's not the Memorial Star."

Cordoba looked across to the other bed where Rusty was sleeping quietly. "I suppose we're gonna fly you guys out to Washington for the ceremony… and don't hold your breath for first-class tickets, either! Uncle Sam's been tightening the purse strings lately."

Just then Callahan entered the room with a bouquet of flowers.

"Well, that's my cue. It looks like you two love birds have a lot to talk about. See ya in D.C., Special Agent Pierce!"

"Don't let the door hit you in the ass, Special Agent Cordoba!"

Callahan and Cordoba marched past each other, exchanging odd looks.

"Don't think for a minute I bought you these, Will! It was Claire. I'd be happy to buy you a new car, or a horse, hell, even a ranch for what you've done for me, but I draw the line at bouquets of pretty flowers."

"Yeah, that might send the wrong signal."

"How's Rusty? You know he saved my life! He saw the gun and pushed me into the hallway… I didn't have a scratch on me. He's one tough kid and I'm gonna make sure he knows it when he's feeling better. I'm also gonna have Cordoba put him up for a medal."

"I think you missed the boat on that one," Will laughed.

"Thank God we were wearing our Kevlar vests! None of us would be here if we weren't."

"What was the final count, anyway?"

"Well, I took three ricochet rounds off my flak jacket: one through my quadriceps, one through my bicep, and one grazed my shoulder. That one just missed shooting up through my jaw. Least ways, that's what the doctor told me after surgery. The one in the leg caused the most damage cause it had already bounced off the wall, so the bullet was torn up."

"Skip shots! They were all skip shots!" Callahan seemed unable to get over that.

"Yeah, seems like they were."

"How about Rus?"

"Well, he took the brunt of it: four shots bounced off his jacket, one cut through his forearm, one through his foot, one nicked his ear, and one caught him under the jacket and bounced off his rib, puncturing his lung. Looks like he took your bullets as well."

"Jesus!"

"Doc says the lung will be okay as it just missed tearing it apart. He's gonna need a lot of therapy and he'll be sore for a while, but he should be okay. What a way to cut your teeth working as a federal agent, huh?"

"I'll make sure you both have the best care money can buy, you'll never need to worry about that."

"Did you do that thing we talked about?"

"Yep!"

Robert Miller entered the room just then with Nassar Khumari at his side. With the room filled with just the men, Miller shut the large hospital door for privacy. Nassar approached Will and softly took his hand.

"May the blessing of *Allah* be upon you for stopping that menace. You truly are a credit to law enforcement!"

"Shakar." Will decided to thank him in Arabic.

"And you, my old friend, thank the heavens that you were not hurt in this mess."

"Yes, Nassar, my old friend. If it wasn't for Will here and his deputy Rusty, over there fighting for his life, I wouldn't be standing here with you now."

"Praise be Allah!"

"Yeah, I'd like to talk to you about Allah!" Nassar turned to face Will, but had a strange look on his face as Will's statement of interest seemed insincere.

"We had a chance to talk to your most recently hired security employee just before he died and he told us a very interesting story."

Nassar's face suddenly paled as he searched his mind for an answer. "I really do not know what you could possibly mean."

"We know you hired Gaius to kill King Abdullah."

"This is ludicrous. I will not stand for such lies and accusations." As Nassar attempted to turn and leave the room, Miller blocked the door as Callahan closed in.

"How could you, Nassar? We've been best friends for nearly 50 years. My grandson is just a boy. You've ruined Miller's life by taking the only woman he ever loved."

Nassar's face suddenly changed from a look of concern to a look of calm and contentment. "My old friend, it was just business!"

"What!?" Miller and Callahan shouted simultaneously.

"With King Abdullah gone, the region would destabilize and the

Middle Eastern countries, Saudi Arabia, Iran, Syria, and Jordan, would pay Falcon Securities handsomely to come in and stabilize the region again. We're talking billions of dollars in government and private contracts!"

"Why you…!" Miller lunged at Nassar, who quickly drew a weapon from his jacket.

"Please, Robert, my dear friend. I've offered you a new life. Now that that woman is out of your life, you can get a younger, prettier one. You should be thanking me."

Nassar swung the pistol around the room to ensure that everyone knew he was in control. He pulled out his cell phone and began texting.

"You'll never get away with this, you son of a bitch!"

"But of course I will, my old friends. Not only do I have diplomatic immunity when I'm on these shores, but I have this gun, and… suddenly the hospital door burst opened and five of Nassar's security guards poured into the room.

"Well, gentlemen, it's been a pleasure catching up, and my goodness, what an exciting day. Please, all of you, get better and I'm sorry it appears we won't be meeting together as friends again. I did so cherish these years together and will remember you all fondly. *Wadaeaan*, old friends."

With that, Nassar's men encircled him and led him out of the room and eventually the hospital. Miller, Callahan, and Will could only look at each other, dumbfounded.

"Call Cordoba! Don't let him get to the airport!"

"It's no use, Callahan. He's right. We can't do anything while he's on American soil. Looks like he beat us at our own security game."

"I'll be damned if I let him get away with this!"

"I know how you feel, Miller, but if you interfere with him now, either his men would kill you or the feds would arrest you, so it's not worth it."

"Tell that to my wife! Tell that to Callahan or to his daughter who almost lost her only child. Tell that to that young man lying in the other bed who may never completely recover from his injuries."

"Don't worry, Miller, things have a way of working out in these situations," Will answered calmly, letting his weight fall back against the bed.

CHAPTER 52

"**W**HADDA YA THINK OF my truck, Sheriff?" Rusty slapped his hand on the side of the brand new pickup truck. The fresh paint looked as though it were still dripping from the factory as Rusty proudly paraded it through the streets of the small town.

"Callahan says he gonna pay for our wedding, too. Can you believe that?!"

"Yeah, he sure is a good man."

Will slowly crossed his right leg over his left as he propped his boots up on the railing of the stoop in front of the sheriff's station. His arm still in a sling, he tried to place his cup of coffee back down on the table next to him.

"That's a right beautiful truck, Deputy Perkins! You two are gonna raise a family with a truck like that."

Molly leaned over Will's lap as she took the coffee cup from Will and set it down.

"Thanks, Molly, you take care of our sheriff, now, hear!"

"Oh you can bet on that, Rusty! He's not going anywhere for quite a while." Will gave Rusty a grimace as Rusty began to laugh, his trademark braying cough.

"I don't think I've ever seen him so happy, Molly. So whatever you're doing, keep it up."

With that, Rusty floored the accelerator and peeled out of the parking lot.

"He's right. I've never seen you so happy before in your life. Must be all that good livin' you're doing now that you're retiring."

"Don't bet on it. As soon as my arm heals and my legs are feeling better, I'll be back to work bright and early."

Molly's demeanor suddenly changed. "What did you say, Will Pierce? You promised me you were gonna retire and we could start travelling. Dang, you promised, Will!"

Suddenly a big grin appeared on Will's face. *Gothcha*. He didn't have to say the words. He pulled Molly closer and she laid her head on his chest.

"Well, maybe I'll slow down just a little bit."

EPILOGUE

THE SUN WAS HIGH in the eastern sky as the morning lit up the desert mountains and created a red and blue hue in the shadowed areas.

Nassar Khumari had already taken his morning swim and was sitting down to have his poached eggs and tea. Not a traditional Middle Eastern breakfast, but one he had learned to enjoy during his days in England.

The flat screen television near him scrolled the daily stock reports on one channel and gave the Al Jazeera news on the split-screen.

Nassar had always enjoyed the soothing sound of a silver spoon tinkling the sides of a good china teacup as he stirred, once again a small earthly pleasure he had developed in his youth spent studying in the British Empire. It was at that moment, a moment when he was most relaxed, in his head experiencing the nostalgia of his youth when he suddenly became aware of the tiniest of sounds that was unlike the spoon tickling against the fine china.

Tink. He knew that sound. He had heard it before many times. He didn't have time to look up, as he knew that would be futile. He merely looked down at his thick cotton robe to inspect the strange feeling now in his chest as it quickly began to turn claret through the cotton fibers. He would have laughed at the irony or realized that he had been bested if not for the fact that his heart had already stopped.

In the distance, the crosshairs of a sniper's scope slowly lowered, then darkened, as the shadowy man retrieved the single brass shell from the rocks under his feet and placidly uncoupled the muzzle blast suppressor.

He carefully closed the two rubber flaps down at either end and unclipped the scope from the rifle. He then buried it deep in his *thawb*, perhaps in a secret pocket and straightened his black cord *agal* over his *ghutra*. Like many Arabs, he had pulled the white fabric across his cheeks and under his eyes to cover his face and locked it down so it would not come undone easily when he rode through the desert.

He then placed the rifle back into a long canvas sheath and tossed it over his back for the short walk back down from the top of the mountain. Pushing himself up, he rose slowly so as not to make much movement in case anyone below might have caught sight of him. It only took a few steps to put him below the crest of the hill and he moved with more confidence after that.

It was a quiet stroll in the dawn air as he walked back to the snowy white Arabian horse that had been waiting patiently for him. He approached the magnificent animal and ran his hand affectionately down its silken neck, stroking the elegantly sculpted head.

Laughing as the horse bumped his nose around in his robe seeking his treat as though saying, "Yeah, yeah, I'm beautiful. We all know. Now where are the treats?"

Having rewarded the beautiful animal, he thrust the now-covered weapon into the leather sheath firmly tied to the high back of the saddle, tugging the straps to make sure they were secure. Wouldn't do to lose this weapon, he noted, amused. Tightening the cinch, he tossed the rolled blanket that contained his minimalist cooking gear and other camping necessities behind the saddle and snugged them down, effectively hiding most of the rifle case from view.

Swinging up on the traditional saddle, he gave the horse a direction and left it to his natural sure-footedness to carry them safely down the rock-covered mountain to the ancient trading route now no more than a goat trail.

In the distance, he saw a nomadic Bedouin tribe whose caravan was made up, even in this day and age, of dozens of camels, mules, and of course, other Arabian mountain horses. He thought he might follow them out of the valley.

THE END

ACKNOWLEDGEMENTS

A writer may author a book, but it takes a lot of people, friends, family, and sometimes even a community to help him write it. I'd like to thank the following people who had a hand in helping create this novel, whether they knew it or not: Áine, Pat, and Ken Fitzharris, Kim Hart, Michael and Ursula Hansen (who've helped me immensely), John Notter Sr., John Notter Jr., Joel Luna, Wine-Meisters Austin and Amanda Grant, Charlie and Lauren Hirsh, Paul Flynn and all the top-shelf wine at Stonehaus, Mary and Andrew Pallant, Don Kittleson, Richard Wohl and Timi Vaughn, Dan and Brenda Herron, Boaz Milgalter, Stephen Campanelli, Steve Maturo and Nancy Jacobsen, Todd Bathke, Marc and Nikki Madnick, Jayne and Bryce Betts, John, Tyler, and Jesse Posey, Johnny Horvath, Missouri Darren Foster, Vitas Narutis, Zaid Khurma, David and Kelly Moran Brown, Steve Lambert, Jamie and Dennis King, Sean Doyle and Harry Koslowski, Jazz and Gene, Christin Sporny, Jacob Shearer, Michelle Karamooz, Alex, Abbey, Josh, and everyone at Stonefire Grill, Mark Wagner and Sophie Gorton, Des Carey, Jason O'Mara, Caroline Bean and Company, Bob Hamer, Gary Hanson-Marine Corps: Wounded Warrior Regiment Head Cycling Coach and his W.I.R.E.D. (Warrior: Integrated Reconditioning Educating Developing) Non-Profit Organization-www.wiredathletes.org, Prosthetist & HiFi Inventor Randall Alley & Julie Alley at BioDesigns for their cutting-edge work in prosthetics, limb replacement, Osseointegration, and amputee rehabilitation-www.biodesigns.com, The Writer's Guild Foundation and any and every one that helped me who I forgot to mention… Thank you all!

- Kyle C. Fitzharris

***

My collaborator on this project asked me to give a shout out to anyone who may have helped me get this story told. I am approaching 75 years of age and in thinking back over the years that I've survived, many people come to mind that I have not thanked for the support and encouragement over the more than seven past decades. The first to come to mind are my siblings: eight brothers and three sisters, Mom and Dad, and in particular Marian, Vernika, R. J., Jerry, Guy, and K and Pearl. The names in my family could make up a book. I would like to mention the people that I interacted with during the years of breeding, training, and promoting the Peruvian Paso Horse. This includes people in Canada, Europe, Australia, Peru, and of course, the U.S. of A. Also, I would like to thank, Lisa Pujals. I have known Lisa for years and admired her talents. So, when it came time to ask someone to do cover art for this novel, her name was the first that came to my mind. Thanks, Lisa, for the enthusiasm and for the great art. Most importantly, the current person is Colleen Reid. She has listened to this story evolve over the past 40 years and she did the first edit. She deserves much more thanks than I can verbalize. Thanks Colleen.

— Harry Stedman

KYLE C. FITZHARRIS is an American novelist, screenwriter, and the best-selling author of political thrillers, *The Eighth Plague* and *The New Americans.* Fitzharris worked intelligence under Non-Official Cover (NOC) in Central America and Mexico and led a task force of eight federal agencies. His efforts helped indict international conspirators responsible for drug smuggling, money laundering, murder-for-hire, and terrorist funding.

In 2012, Fitzharris was handpicked by the U.S. Secretary of Defense Leon Panetta and nominated by the Joint Chiefs of Staff as well as the Department of Defense to the prestigious JCOC & DOCA. At the Pentagon, Fitzharris was assigned liaisons, briefed, and then flown by C-17 to Army, Navy, Air Force, Marine Corps, U.S. Coast Guard, Homeland Security, and ICE bases up and down the Eastern Seaboard. He was honored further by being tasked with the mission of bringing greater attention to Wounded Warriors, as well as creating awareness of the struggles and needs of the families of deployed and post-deployed men and women of the U.S. Armed Services. His upcoming thriller, *Scorched,* centers on a Wounded Warrior amputee fighting the effects of PTSD while racing to stop cyber terrorists bent on starting World War III. Fitzharris resides in Southern California.

For More Information About Best-Selling Author Kyle C. Fitzharris, SKIP SHOT, his other novels, or his Ghostwriting Services, please visit WWW.KYLEFITZHARRIS.COM

In **HARRY STEDMAN**'s first 10 years, his dad was a farmer, but he gave up farming in 1951, after three years of very wet conditions in northeast Kansas. He has always thought that was too bad, because he felt the youngest five of his nine sons, of which Harry was the fourth youngest, would have been a great asset to him on the farm; still, they all turned out to have great work ethics.

Harry spent four years in the Air Force and then eight years in Mechanical and Electrical Training and servicing equipment, most of which was at Vandenberg AFB, in the early days of missile development for the space program. He then had the opportunity to get into the horse business and he never looked back.

Work ethic is a must if you make a living farming and raising livestock and it's also important in the breeding and training of Bloodstock horses, which Harry did for over 30 years. His most enjoyable part of working with horses was training the young horses. Although he became bored with most of them once they were fully trained to the bit.

While a trainer is putting miles, which translate to hours, on a horse for the purpose of conditioning and then later to create muscle memory, one has a lot of time to think… which is when the ideas for the characters and story in this novel came to Harry.

Printed in the United States
By Bookmasters